*PRAISE FOR SI CLARKE*

'This book is tailor-made for armchair scientists who enjoy the process of world building. *Devon's Island* is a surprisingly topical book for our moment, and I look forward to seeing where Clarke takes the story next.'

– MIRANDA, THE LESBIAN REVIEW

*PRAISE FOR LIVID SKIES*

'This beautifully queer civilisation on Mars was absolutely delightful to read.'

– LADY AMANDA, GOODREADS USER

'An engrossing and enjoyable read.'

– MELINDA FIERRO, GOODREADS USER

'A wonderful blend of characters, cultures, and beliefs give a modern take to the classic scientific dream – colonising Mars.'

– MAX WATSON, AUTHOR OF *CHAINS OF NURTURE*

# LIVID SKIES

## A WHITE HART NOVEL

### SI CLARKE

Livid Skies

Print edition ISBN 978-1-9162878-2-2

E-book edition ISBN 978-1-9162878-3-9

www.whitehartfiction.co.uk



Editing by:

- Michelle Meade of Michelle Meade Reads
- Lucy York of Lucy Rose York
- Hannah McCall of Black Cat Editorial Services

Cover design by: Rejenne Pavon

Map and building illustrations by: Sasha Fedorova

❀ Created with Vellum

We can have fully automated luxury gay space communism when we find a supply of unlimited resources – until then, we'll have to make do with partially automated queer social liberalism.

*For **Sarah**, because what the hell do I know about babies?*
*For **Dave**, because who else would put up with my nonsense?*
*For **you**, because you cared enough to read this far.*

AUTHOR'S NOTE

This book is written in British English. If you're used to reading American English, some of the spelling and punctuation may seem unusual. I promise, it's totally safe.

This story also features a number of Martianisms. Well, it would do, wouldn't it? I've tried to ensure the concepts are explained clearly in the text, but there's a glossary at the back if you're curious.

This work contains the following:

- Domestic violence and emotional manipulation
- Suicide
- Injury by fire
- Conversations and arguments about contentious topics, including: religion, politics, capital punishment
- Pregnancy, miscarriage, and babies

Also, please note that trans women are women. Trans men are men. Non-binary people are who they tell you they are. This book is not for TERFs.

There are a lot of characters in this story. Below, I've named the ones who play a key role in one way or another. If you encounter a character and they're not listed here, their role is only incidental.



DEVON: Advance mission crew member. 3D printing specialist. Autistic. British.
BRIAN: Advance mission crew member. Botanist. Texan.
LISA: Commander of advance mission. Part of provisional government. Former Canadian Special Forces. Electrical engineer. First Nations-Chinese-Canadian.
NORA: Nursing team leader. Former Médecins Sans Frontières worker. Trauma nurse. Dutch-Scottish.
JUPITER: Daughter of the head of the company that facilitated the mission. Former spoiled brat. British.
DAVY: Part of provisional government. Former economics

lecturer and theorist. Former Member of Parliament in Canada. Canadian.

GABRIEL: Mission commander. Head of provisional government. Trauma surgeon. Former French Foreign Legion. American.

GEORGIE: Part of provisional government. Food scientist. Multi-faith chaplain. Married to Gurdeep. Romanian.

GURDEEP: Previous head of mission planning. Part of provisional government. Mechanical engineer. Former captain in the Royal Engineers. Amateur baker. Married to Georgie. British-Indian.

DESMOND: Botanist. Married to Mike. South African.

KATYA: Software engineer. Roboticist. Ukrainian-British.


*ELSEWHERE*


The MENaCE: An American military unit.

JAMIE: Seaman (lowest rank) in the coast guard.

Pearce (aka 'LONE STARR'): Lieutenant in the navy.

Cobb (aka 'JAYNE'): Sergeant First Class in the army. Mission chief.

# DEVON'S ISLAND COLONY MAP

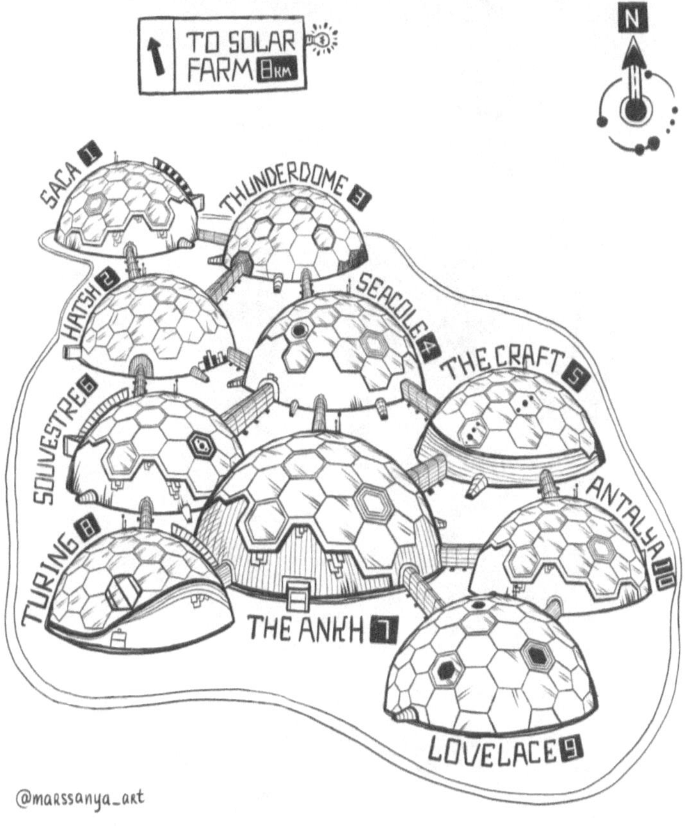


Note: At the beginning of the book, domes one through four (Saca, Hatsh, Thunberg, and Seacole) have been built. The others are added over the course of the story, beginning with number five (the Craft).

# LAYOUT OF A TYPICAL BUILDING COMPLEX

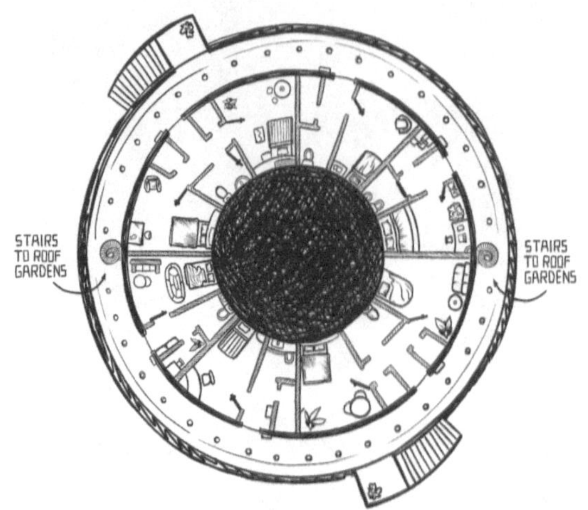


UPPER
FLOOR
UNITS

GROUND
FLOOR
UNITS

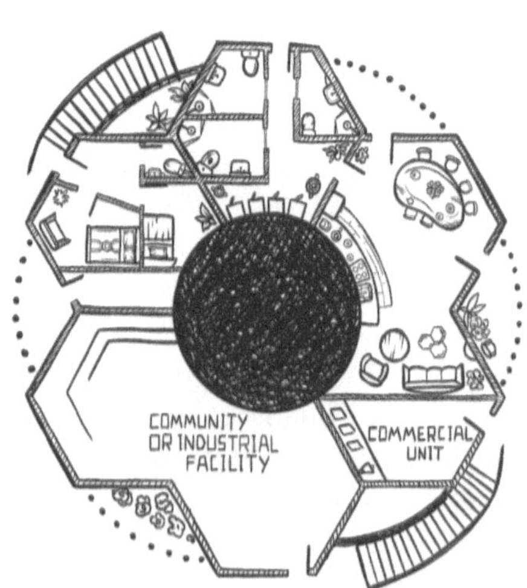

Although this novel follows on from the events of *Devon's Island*, it has been designed to be read as a standalone. If you enjoyed *Devon's Island* and want to read more, all your favourites are back. But if you've not read it, don't sweat it.

As for the fact we've got a character sharing a name with the colony… I'll let Devon explain that in her own words.

---

This was my home. Devon Island. *Devon's Island*.

Yes, yes. I know they named the colony for the home of the Mars analogue facility on Earth; it wasn't actually named after me. But it was my home in a way no place on Earth had ever been. I hoped the others considered it theirs as much as I felt like it was mine. Lisa's Island. Brian's Island. Soon it would be Gabriel's Island and Davy's Island and everyone else's. It was ours. And I wanted us all to feel like we owned it.

*- DEVON'S ISLAND*

---

*ACT ONE*

MEAR -1, DAY 299

*THUNBERG DOME, DEVON ISLAND COLONY, MARS*

Leaning over the balcony railing, I breathed in the scents of life on Mars: delicate apple blossoms, grassy bamboo, loam, and compost.

The buildings were clustered together at the centre of the dome. From here, I could see clear across the open space. Thunberg was the third of our four domes. We'd opened it a few months ago – and it was already awash with green. The seeds and saplings we'd brought from Earth had flourished.

We should have been building the fifth dome now – but our plans had been thrown into disarray three weeks ago.

Somehow I missed the sound of Brian's door. 'Hey, kiddo.' *Kiddo*... He was two years younger than I was – but he seemed older than his twenty-seven years. Earth years. 'Bet you're grateful I ain't the one cooking tonight, hey?' He didn't touch my arm as he spoke, though I could see he wanted to. Brian was a huggy kind of person.

It wasn't so much that I didn't want to be touched at all –

more that I wanted to decide who could touch me and when. Most people didn't understand that.

I turned to face him. Best (and only) botanist on Mars – like our very own Mark Watney. We were about the same height, though he was a stockier build. His skin had an olivey complexion to my fair, freckled tones. 'You're a good cook, Brian.'

'And you're a terrible liar,' he said with a shrug. He headed down the stairs.

*It wasn't a lie*, I thought but didn't say. At the bottom, we turned onto the pathway leading west towards Sacagawea, the first dome we'd built. The centre of the path had turned a muddy brown from months of being trod on, but the edges – where they met the rich reddish-black soil – retained their crisp whiteness.

All eight members of the advance crew ate our meals together in Saca's lounge: an open-plan community kitchen-living-dining space. The corresponding areas in the other three domes wouldn't be opened until the rest of the colonists arrived twelve months from now. Social living was a feature of our life on Mars – now and later. I'd been surprised to find I enjoyed it – I could have privacy when I needed it, but our set-up encouraged me to be more social than I otherwise would.

Brian touched some leaves as we passed. I tried to remember the plant's name – I was sure he'd told me. Big variegated leaves. *Diefenbaker?*

At the airlock, I cranked the handle to open the door. Once we were inside, Brian pulled it shut behind us. Because the pressure in both domes was the same, we didn't have to wait for it to equalise. I opened the door to Saca dome as soon as the other one was closed.

As we stepped outside, I inhaled the different smells and

felt the reduction in humidity. The plants had changed, too – hence the slightly altered odours. Brian had been teaching me about which plants liked which conditions, although he'd laughed when I'd pointed out they lacked the mental capacity to like or dislike anything.

Three minutes after we left home, Brian pushed open the door to Saca's lounge. He called out, 'Hey, Lis, is that your loogie-shookem I smell? Love that stuff!'

'Luskinikn, Bri. And yes, it is,' our team leader replied. She was sitting on the floor where the awful sofa had been, her phone held up in front of her. Her grey T-shirt was neat – almost as if she had ironed it. I looked down at my own clothes: a well-worn long-sleeved top over dinosaur-printed leggings. The quick breads she made – her grandfather's recipe – were delicious. 'And Sun's making soup – mushroom and corn.'

'C'mon, Devon, let's get the table set,' Brian said, nudging my side.

----

After we'd finished eating we stayed at the table. 'Today's meeting will be brief,' Lisa said, her hands wrapped around her mug of herbal tea. 'Thornback, you're— Sorry! Devon, you're with me in the morning.' Sixteen months after leaving Earth – including more than six on Mars – we'd finally persuaded her to call us by our first names, but her years of military training made it hard for her to adapt.

'The two of us will clean the solar array. Ife and Paxton, you'll be outside-outside doing the weekly inspection. Everyone else will be in the gardens. We've got to start producing as much food as—' She ran a hand over her long black plait. 'Sorry, you all know that. I shouldn't keep repeating it.'

A few years ago, scientists had calculated a high risk of an extinction-level event on Earth. In response, a group of countries, businesses, and ultra-wealthy individuals – not that we had any idea who they were – created plans for a colony on Mars.

The ships carrying the other 152 colonists and all the supplies from Earth we were ever going to get had launched five days earlier – six months ahead of schedule amidst a deadly pandemic. Lisa took a deep breath. 'I do have some good news: it looks like Chris Ngata is going to pull through.'

The haste meant that some people arrived at the launch site in Cornwall just hours before takeoff. Those who couldn't quarantine ahead of time had been isolated in space-suits – the reasons for which had become obvious when two people began experiencing symptoms.

Chris survived. The other woman hadn't. None of us knew Chris – a reserve colonist – but with at least half the people on Earth gone, anyone who survived felt like a win.

Once the four ships arrived, our little colony would be independent and self-sufficient – alone against the universe. So to speak.

———

The daily meeting lasted only a few minutes. We had work to be getting on with – although tonight's project was a break from the monotony. And the benefits would be almost immediate.

While two of the team cleaned up, Lisa, Brian, and I popped out to my workshop next to the community space.

'Hey,' said Leah when we returned to the lounge, our arms laden with big cushions. 'What do you folks think?'

Lisa set her bundle down. 'About what?'

Paxton and Sun walked in, carrying stacks of plastic and wood.

'We need a new word for outside,' Ife said.

Brian carefully balanced all the cushions on the dining table. 'What's wrong with outside?'

Ife pressed the button to start the dishwasher. 'I mean an option beyond inside and outside. When you leave a building, you're outside – but you're still in the dome. We need something that means outside the buildings *and* outside the dome.'

Lisa moved to the living room area and gave the upended coffee table and stacked armchairs a shove, maximising the open space. A rolled up rug stood in the corner. 'Yes! I keep saying outside-outside, but that's not really sustainable, is it?' She took a few slabs of wood from Paxton's arms and began arranging them on the floor.

Brian and I gathered all the pot plants and moved them to the kitchen counter to protect them.

Leah joined Lisa on the floor and helped sort through the pieces. 'Hmm... What about al fresco?'

Habi arrived just then. 'Hope you haven't got the party started without me.' She raised her bag of tools high before setting it on the ground. 'Though, I'm not sure how you could've.'

Lisa held up a hand. 'Oh, good, you're back. Could you pass me the cordless screwdriver, please?' She balanced a screw between her lips and turned back to Leah. 'Choo obvush,' she said.

'I like the idea of looking to another language, though,' said Ife. 'It should reflect the multicultural nature of the colony. Who's got the remote? Can someone call up the video with the assembly instructions, please?'

Setting the last of the plants down, I said, 'I'm on it.' I found the remote and clicked a few buttons. A person appeared on the screen on the room's exterior wall. We paused our conversation as we worked on assembling the pieces according to his instructions. The video was one we'd found on the internet archive we'd brought with us.

The man talked us through the process of assembling the sofa's frame from the pieces we'd created.

'What kind of bastard,' I demanded for the whatevereth time, 'sent us up here with ten of the most godawful, literal-pain-in-the-arse-and-everything-else sofas ever devised?'

Brian and Sun upended the new sofa frame and set about tightening the bolts. Without turning around, Brian said, 'Probably the same sumbitch that decided coffee was a luxury we couldn't afford very much of. Lucky for all y'all, I got a plan up my sleeve.'

Ife scowled. 'Don't forget – we've still got eight more of those bad boys in storage, waiting to be assembled.'

Lisa was sitting cross-legged on the floor, shoving one of the cushions we'd brought into one of the covers Paxton made. 'Nope, no way. Executive decision. Those bastards will be used as salvage. They'll be repurposed into something that will benefit the colony.'

I shook my head as I stretched the fabric cover over the arm of the new sofa. 'Seriously, who designed them? Who approved them?'

Habi grunted as she pulled the cover over the last corner of the frame. 'I don't know – I thought the original sofas were pretty. Very sleek.'

I snorted. 'Sleek, yeah... Just like the ones they had at

my dad's office in Canary Wharf. Designed for appearance. No thought spared for functionality.'

Leah pulled the zip shut on one of the new cushions and tossed it onto the frame. 'I don't get it. Why would they go to all the trouble of ensuring we have everything we need for sur— No, not just survival. They considered every aspect of life and how to make it as good as possible for us – and then they were just like, "Here. Have a sofa that feels like a stack of breeze blocks covered in static electricity." Why?'

Paxton stopped what she was doing, tears streaming down her face. 'The Earth is in turmoil – millions of people dying every day. And all we care about is a sofa and our own comfort. Sitting up here in our carefully controlled, plague-free bubble.' She slammed her fists down onto the striped surface of a sofa cushion. 'We ought to be doing something!'

Habi climbed over a pile of cushions and put her arms around Paxton.

Lisa leaned back, putting her weight onto her hands. 'We are doing something. We came to Mars – we *chose* to come here – because we knew this was a possibility. We can't do anything for the people on Earth. It's just…'

She shook her head. 'But what we can do – what we *are* doing – is preparing *this* world for the ones who made a lucky escape. Those people need us. They need food and water and air – and yes, sofas. And we've got our work cut out for us. They'll be arriving six months ahead of schedule. We're going to have to work harder than any of us have ever done. And for a few minutes at the end of each day, we're going to need somewhere comfortable to sit and relax.'

Lisa reached out a hand and touched Paxton's knee. 'Okay?'

Paxton gave a small nod and looked away.

We all sat in awkward silence.

After a few minutes, Paxton sniffed and began re-arranging cushions around herself. 'So, back to our earlier conversation about outside-outside… How about *ngoài trời*?'

My auditory processing was terrible. Brian's eyes flitted back and forth. Leah held up her phone. 'Sorry, could you repeat that for my hearing aid app?'

Paxton smiled. *'Ngoài trời.'*

Brian opened his mouth, closed it, then tried again. *'Why choi?* Now, I always said Australian was a beautiful language.' Paxton rolled still-glistening eyes at him.

Leah looked down at her phone. She frowned. 'Okay, my app tells me the spelling and that it's Vietnamese. It says it means "open air". I'm still not sure I'm getting the pronunci-ation. *Nway tree?*' Paxton had been raised in Australia, but her family was Vietnamese.

I tried. *'Wah tsee?'*

Lisa chuckled as she arranged the last of the cushions on the new sofa. 'Pax, you're being cruel – trying to get people who didn't grow up speaking tonal languages to leap into the deep end.' Lisa's first language was English, but her father had taught her Cantonese from childhood.

Paxton threw up her hands in defence. 'Not hardly. If I wanted to be mean, I'd try to get them all saying *bà ba béo bán bánh bèo bên bờ*. But, yeah, I'm not sure I want to listen to your garbled attempts to manage two simple words.'

'No, I like it.' Ife shrugged. 'Pax, what time do you want to go—' She was laughing so hard, she had to pause to breathe. 'When do you want to go *wah tree* tomorrow? Can I vote we don't get started until about eight?'

Paxton stuck her tongue out at her. 'Forget I said anything. Who's got another suggestion? Bri, how about Spanish? Got anything good for us?'

'Well now.' Brian pinched his lips together. By this point

everyone had the giggles. '*Bajo las estrellas* does have a certain ring to it.' He wiped tears from his eyes. 'But no, my vote still goes with *wai chee*.'

Paxton let out an exasperated breath. 'I give up. I can't listen to you people butcher the language of my foremothers anymore. I'm going to bed. You coming, Sun?'

Sun looked serious. 'I was thinking I might take a walk *ngah tsu* first.' Our doctor's first language was Cantonese, another tonal language. Surely she should have been capable of pronouncing the words – if she'd wanted to. She cracked a grin.

I couldn't help myself, fanning my face with my hand, desperate to quell the giggles. 'Sun, don't forget we agreed no one is allowed to go *wang chung* alone.'

Paxton clenched her fingers to her thumbs, forming little circles in front of her chest. '*Ngoài trời. Ngoài trời.* What is so diff—' She doubled over laughing. When she finally looked up, tears were streaming down her face. 'I love you losers. But I really am going to bed.' She and Sun walked to the door. She turned back to face us, still chuckling. 'Good night, you dags.'

Everyone wailed with uncontrollable laughter even after they'd departed. One by one, the others left until only Lisa, Brian, and I remained – sitting on the floor, gazing up at our handiwork.

At length, I said, 'Oh, bollocks. We didn't even get a pic of us all piled onto the sofa we made.'

Lisa waved the idea away. 'Meh. It's after midnight. We'll do it in the morning.'

Brian rubbed his hands together. 'Well, come on. We're gonna try it out, ain't we?'

Lisa hauled herself to her feet with grace and ease. 'Definitely.'

I climbed up – with considerably less decorum than Lisa had.

We walked over to our creation and turned our backs on it. 'Right,' Lisa declared. 'Three, two, one.' We all fell backwards into the sofa we'd created together.

I leaned back into its perfect blend of squishiness and support with a sigh. 'This is the comfiest sofa ever.'

Brian chuckled. 'Not that you're one to break your arm patting yourself on the back, naturally.' He had a campy, absurd saying for every occasion.

'What?' *Did he think I was bragging*? 'It was a group project. All I did was…'

Lisa stretched her arm the length of the sofa. 'True, but you made the cushions.' Although she was careful not to touch me, I was aware of her closeness.

Brian pushed his glasses up the bridge of his nose. 'It ain't the beautiful lines you're singing the praises of, now is it, kiddo? Nor the way the colours work together. It ain't even the quality of the craftsmanship.' He moved his hands as he spoke, making big gestures that reinforced each phrase.

'We're only teasing you, Devon,' Lisa said. 'And it is a helluva comfy couch.'

———

*SACA DOME, DEVON ISLAND COLONY, MARS*

The next morning, I looked through the windscreen at the icy light of the sun against a blue sky. A blue sky – how weird was that? It wouldn't last long; it would return to its usual dull salmony colour once the sun was above the horizon.

Once the airlock door was fully open, I slid the gearstick into drive and inched the rover down the ramp.

'I love this time of day – don't you?'

Lisa's voice reminded me I wasn't alone. I didn't mind her; she was a good person and an ideal leader. But for a moment I'd forgotten she was there.

'My favourite part is when we come out a few minutes earlier and we see the Earth rise before the sun does,' I replied.

I heard her take a sip of the tea she had in her travel mug. We'd driven the route between the colony and the solar farm often enough that the way was relatively smooth. 'Mmm, yeah. That is good. Would you like me to rejig the duty roster so we're out in time to see that?'

Good boss. 'Thanks, I'd appreciate that. I didn't want to ask, because people don't like getting up early.'

'Not a prob. I'm an early bird, too. I'll switch it so when the two of us are on solar duty, we leave base ten minutes before dawn.'

I turned the vehicle northwards, away from the rising sun and the crater wall.

'Where we're going, we don't need roads.' *Crap, I didn't mean to say that out loud.* Sometimes I couldn't help myself. Certain words and phrases just popped out of my mouth before I could stop them. A bit of autistic echolalia.

I hoped Lisa didn't think I was losing my grip on reality. I glanced over, but she just chuckled. I'd gone off the rails on the trip to Mars and I didn't want anyone to ever look at me the way they did when I wasn't okay.

'Livid,' I said.

Lisa sniffed. 'What?'

I lifted one hand off the steering wheel and pointed

outwards. 'The colour, I mean. The sky. It comes from the Latin word *lividus*, meaning a dull leaden-blue colour.'

Lisa clicked her tongue. 'Really? I didn't know livid could refer to a colour, but if you told me it did, I'd have guessed it was a sort of angry purple. Like a livid bruise.'

She leaned forwards in the passenger seat to get a better look at the sky. 'On Earth, the sky appears blue because blue light bounces off air molecules. At sunrise and sunset, the light has further to travel within the atmosphere, so it scatters more. Volcanic ash, dust from fires, and contaminants make for those fiery sunsets we used to take for granted.'

Small talk scared the pants off me. I normally hated these two-person drives – much as I adored spending the day doing manual labour under the open sky. People felt compelled to fill the silence with meaningless jibber-jabber. But this was the kind of chat I could get behind. Even though she was cool by conventional standards, Lisa was still a proper geek.

'Here, it's the other way around,' I replied, stating the obvious. *But isn't that all small talk ever is – just repeating things everyone already knows?* 'The way sunlight scatters depends on what's in the atmosphere. Some particles only interact with specific wavelengths, which determine the colours we see.'

Twenty minutes after we left, I stopped the rover at the edge of the solar farm. The sky had melted back to its usual colour as we drove. I turned the engine off. Time to get to work.

'Go fish.'

After eight months on the ship, my mind was always wandering. We all took a share of the general duties – cleaning, inventory management, handing out rations. Like bairns doing chores to earn pocket money. There was nae to focus on.

Those of us with certain skills had extra responsibilities. Botanists looked after their plants; engineers did repairs and maintenance; pilots kept us on course. And, of course, as the only nurse on board, I helped deal with scrapes, bruises, and sniffles. There was no end to the minor injuries. Take a metal tube filled with heavy machinery and supplies, add in thirty-eight people and crates full of stuff, and subtract gravity. It got messy.

And the illnesses were even more prevalent than the injuries. If one person sneezed, a few days later, the whole ship would be a chorus of coughing, sneezing, snorting, and hacking. And that time the norovirus went around... I shuddered just thinking about it. It had taken weeks of cleaning to remove all the— Nope. I fought the urge to boak. Two months later, we still occasionally found unknown globules hiding in nooks and crannies throughout the ship.

Still, the monotony was enough to drive you into madness. When you threw in the fact that live signals from Earth were fewer and further between... Well, people needed more of a distraction than our ships could offer. A couple days ago we'd seen what looked like a rocket launch from Earth, but we were too far away for it to be aimed at us. The gossip had already died down.

Fingers brushed my hair from my eyes and grazed my forehead, drawing my attention back to the present. I looked up into Jupiter's brown eyes. On Earth they'd been clear and open. Here, they were puffy and red – just like everyone else's.

'You asked me if I had any sevens. I said, "Go fish". Then you were away in outer space,' Jupiter said. When I raised an eyebrow at that, she rolled her eyes. 'Fine, whatever, you were on a planet somewhere. Wherever you were, it wasn't here.' She stroked my hair again. 'We need to stay here – we can't let ourselves dwell on what's happening on Earth. Not yet. There will be time to grieve, but if we start now, we'll never be able to dig ourselves out again.'

I looked at Jupiter as I considered her words. She'd buzzed her dense brown curls down to almost non-existence. It enhanced rather than diminished her beauty. She had gorgeous skin that looked only slightly sallow in the artificial light. When did she get so smart? No, not smart; she'd always been that. When did she get so wise?

We were sitting in her bunk; the card game she referred to was on our tablets. Beyond the thin plastic door, I could hear people moving around. I'd been lost in thought long enough that my screen had gone dark.

'I'm sorry. You're right – we cannae afford to get stuck inside our own heads. That's not a safe place to be. We all joined this mission knowing we'd never be able to hug our friends and families again, that we'd never have a real-time conversation with anyone we left behind. But we didnae expect to lose contact almost completely. We didnae sign up kenning it was either this or an immediate death sentence. My mum, my uncles, my friends, my ex-boyfriends.' I heaved a sigh as I forced myself to stop.

She shushed me gently and gathered me in her arms. 'We can't let it consume us – we can't. If we stop to think about things now, they'll destroy us. We have to stay focused on the present. Stay here with me.'

Being friends with Jupiter was funny. Not funny-ha-ha, just unexpected. When I'd met her four years ago, she'd been a spoiled sixteen-year-old. She'd been thrust onto this mission at the behest of her father, the man who owned the company that managed the logistics of our mission. It had been a surprise condition he'd added once the planning was well underway.

I'd resented her presence right up until that day she held my hand as I called the Danish-Korean sperm donor who was my biological father – two nights before we launched. I saw her in a new light in that moment. Maybe it was nae only politics that made for strange bedfellows. The end of the world did, too. *The start of the world? An interplanetary road trip?*

Without stopping to think about it, I leaned forwards and kissed her. I wasn't even attracted to her, not really. Just randy – randy and bored.

She pulled away, eyes wide and mouth hanging open.

*Bollocks!* 'Oh man, I'm sorry, Jupiter. I've no idea what I was thinking. I mean, I was nae thinking. I just, I dinnae ken, I guess I was wondering what it would be like. Shagging a woman, I mean.'

She blinked saucer eyes. 'I'm straight.' Blinked again.

*Ugh, Nora, you eejit.* 'Me too. I'm so sorry.'

She smiled. 'No, I meant I've been asking myself the same thing.' Her eyes twinkled like the stars on the other side of the opaque wall – except stars didnae twinkle in space. She reached for the handle on the bunk wall and used it to pull herself closer to me. As she touched my face tentatively, she began to float away from me. I reached out and drew her back. Our faces were almost touching.

'With a hundred and fifty women and ten men, I suppose we'll have to. Sooner or later.' In order to achieve the best outcome for humanity, including likelihood of survivability and maximum genetic variation, the colonists were almost all women. Unless we wanted to become nuns, this was the future.

'Nine,' she whispered, her mouth so close I could feel her breath in my ear.

'What?' I was having trouble focusing.

'Gurdeep changed the balance, remember?'

Gurdeep had been in charge of the mission until three years ago, when a test revealed she had a faulty gene, ruling her out from coming to Mars. She'd continued to serve as our leader up to launch day, but Gabriel was in charge from the moment we took off. Except somehow we were short a mechanical engineer – meaning Gurdeep had to join us after all.

'Oh, aye. Sure.' I kissed her again. 'Just our luck the only man on our ship is taken, anyway.'

Jupiter shifted her body gracefully in the small space.

'We need a distraction.' To my surprise, she wrapped her legs around my waist.

I nodded. 'Something to keep our minds off everything.' I kissed her harder, letting my hand trace the line of her arm. Up and over her shoulder and then back down, following her collarbone.

With her legs still around me, she arched her back and pulled her top over her head. Her breasts were restrained only by a purple sports bra. I watched as my hand slowly reached out to touch her smooth brown skin. 'Just to pass the time, you understand,' she said. Her top floated towards me, so I shoved it into a drawer without looking. I pulled her closer again.

'Just two straight women adapting to what life throws at them,' I added.

'Making do.'

As I pulled my own shirt up over my head, I tried not to panic. I was nae wearing anything underneath. It wasn't as if Jupiter had never seen me naked – after a few weeks of trying to maintain a sense of decency, we'd all given up. Decency. Dignity. Propriety. They'd all gone out the windows we didn't have. Still, we usually managed to avoid looking at one another – but in that moment I *wanted* Jupiter to see me.

I struggled to find words in my head to describe how I felt.

My breath caught as I reached behind her to unhook her sports bra. She ran her tongue along my neck.

The ship-wide tannoy kicked into action. *Seriously? Now?* Three quick tones and flashes of light. Three meant a full-blown emergency.

'Attention: Nora Sanna to medlab. Nora to medlab now,

please.' Caoimhe's voice. Our ship's doctor would nae call me unless it was something big.

I groaned – but not in a good way. Pulling my shirt back on, I whispered, 'I'm sorry. Still totally straight, though.'

'Me too. We'll continue this experiment when you get back.'

'I'll hurry.' I drew myself back into the bunk and kissed her once more.

She bit my lower lip teasingly. 'No rush.'

I used the ship's handholds to propel myself through three different sections, the taste of Jupiter still on my tongue. In the medlab, I spun around and discovered Davy right behind me. Anxious face and short mousy brown hair. Of course, it made sense that the ship's leader would respond to the alarm as well. I squeezed a glob of sanitiser onto my hands and rubbed it in. I handed the bottle to Davy, who did the same.

Caoimhe had her hands full. Sam was dancing – there was no other word for it – around the room maniacally, opening cupboards and drawers and gleefully flinging the contents as Caoimhe struggled to catch things and re-stow them safely.

'Have you ever thought about how beautiful it is? Motion, I mean…' Sam's voice sounded raw, pained. 'Watch as all the little plasters start out in such neatly ordered stacks, but without gravity to hold them in place, entropy works its beautiful magic as soon as the drawer is open.' She opened medicine bottles, sending pills and liquids everywhere.

'Sam, Sam, Sam.' Caoimhe put on her best soothing voice and reached for the woman's hand. 'I need you to stop that now. It's going to take us a long time to put everything away again.'

Sam's brown eyes were wide and bloodshot. The light

caught her fine ash-brown hair, giving the appearance of a halo. 'Why? Why bother? There's no point to any of it. Just let the beauty be true to itself.'

I processed the sores on Sam's lips as Davy spoke. 'What have you taken, Sam?'

'Nothing,' Sam and I said in unison, as the meaning of what was going on sucker-punched me.

Caoimhe turned to me and I saw understanding dawn in her eyes as she raised a hand to her mouth. Sam continued to speak as she manoeuvred herself towards me. 'You are so beautiful – you move with a grace that resembles entropy, but it belies a tightly controlled order. It's wonderful! Kiran was beautiful, too, but now he's gone.'

Kiran was the mechanical engineer who could nae be located when we left Earth. He was the reason Gurdeep had unexpectedly joined the colony. I'd heard a rumour that he and Sam had been in a relationship.

Davy was getting impatient. 'Would one of you please explain?'

I pulled myself closer to Sam as Caoimhe applied light restraints to stop her wilful destruction of the infirmary. 'Sam, you've not taken anything, have you?' She shook her head sluggishly, her shoulder-length hair drifting in response to her motion. 'Nothing at all for what – about five or six days? Am I right?'

She turned her head languidly, looking at the restraint Caoimhe had placed on her right arm, then her left. Her head swam and bobbed. 'Nothing.'

I bit my lip as I checked her gums and her skin. Her lips and gums were burnt. Closing my eyes for a moment, I turned to Davy. 'She's dehydrated. Severely.'

Davy looked cross. 'So hook her up to an IV.'

Caoimhe stroked Sam's hair gently before coming over to

where Davy and I were floating. Sam's eyes drifted closed as she lost consciousness. 'It's not that simple. What Nora's saying is that she's taking her own life.'

Davy whisper-shouted at Caoimhe, harsh words slapping me in the face. 'You're her doctor. Stop her!'

I grimaced; this was a touchy issue. Suicide prevention was one thing – but we'd already missed the boat on this one. Sam had made her decision and taken action. To force treatment on her now would be assault.

Caoimhe shook her head slowly, a raw reminder of Sam's response mere moments before. 'We need to get the ship's counsellor to assess her. If she's fit to make this decision, it's hers to make. If that's the case, I won't treat her.'

Davy took a deep breath and held it for what felt like a long time. 'I believe in death with dignity. Terminally ill patients who are of sound mind should be allowed to make their own choices. I accept that – I don't like it, but I accept it. But Sam isn't terminally ill. She's a healthy young woman with a bright future ahead of her.'

I touched Davy's arm. 'There's never been a situation like this before. Three-quarters of the human race are dead.'

Davy clenched and unclenched pale fists. 'You think I forgot? Surely that's all the more reason we can't afford another death.'

We glanced at Sam, who groaned. The wave of euphoria had passed; muscles along her jawline trembled.

'Make her comfortable while I discuss this with the leadership team,' Davy instructed Caoimhe. The colony leaders were spread across four ships, plus Lisa on Mars. They'd have to talk this through by video link.

Caoimhe nodded. Davy pushed off in the direction of the privacy room – a telephone-booth-sized space two levels down. 'I'll be back as quick as I can. And tell that counsellor to get her ass in here on the double. I want to know why this wasn't uncovered in her weekly session.'

Caoimhe and I returned to Sam. I took her hand and spoke softly. 'Sam, can you tell us, are you refusing food and water?' Sam grunted in reply.

I asked *the* question. 'You're choosing to end your life, is that right?'

Sam squinted. 'Life is beautiful, but its story is ending.' She removed her phone from a pocket, unlocked it, and passed it to me. Large, unmistakeable letters confronted me. It was a suicide note dated almost a week prior.

I smiled as I bit back tears. 'Would you like me to get you some ice chips?' She struggled against the restraints. 'No, shh, shh. I dinnae mean to rehydrate you, hen. Just to stop the pain in your mouth. I bet it burns, eh?'

'Mmm. Like fire.'

We kept her as comfortable as we could. Despite the insulation around the privacy booth, the leadership team's impassioned argument was audible throughout the ship. Davy never returned to us, but she could be heard crying in her bunk late into the night.

Sam died four hours later, as dehydration took its toll. I wish I could say she looked peaceful in death, but like most of the dead bodies I'd seen... Ugh, what a tragic waste.

It had been nine months since we'd last had a message from our liaison on Earth. The odd email from friends and family made it through and we still got stray satellite and radio signals. None of what we read or saw painted a rosy picture.

Billions dead. Actual frakking plague! As in, scourge-of-mediaeval-Europe plague. Fever, chills, massive swollen lymph nodes. Bleeding into the skin and other organs. Dead, blackened extremities. One of our colonists on the *Aderin-Pocock* survived infection; another didn't.

Few people on Earth avoided catching it and of those who were infected, only about half lived. And then there were the secondary deaths.

Here I was, hurtling through space aboard transport ship *Chawla*. The ship's oblong social room was divided into zones. A series of fancy, high-tech baffles bisected the space. Through the leaf-shaped cut-outs, I saw people gathered around the large dining table, their feet looped under the footholds. Several of them leaned back against the bench encompassing the table.

Above them – at least from my perspective – Desmond, one of our botanists, hung from the ceiling. He'd hooked his knees around a bar, anchoring him where he was. His tablet was open and he was deep in conversation with someone. Mike, no doubt. I'd heard rumours that the accountant had been assigned to us due to a familial relationship with someone important.

Desmond and Mike had grown close over the course of the voyage – but a few hundred metres or so of empty space between them made theirs a long-distance relationship. Mike was on the *Aderin-Pocock* – colloquially known as the *Poke* – one of our other three ships, travelling alongside us in the vast emptiness of space.

Kitchen facilities lined the far wall. A few people floated along the edge of the work surfaces, prepping snacks or drinks – taking care not to let them float away.

I caught snippets of a whispered conversation. 'But how do we even calculate sunup and sundown in outer space? The sun is always just there.'

'I'm not sure,' came the reply. 'I've been trying to figure it out.' I looked across the lounge to where two women were sitting. I didn't know Robin or Rizwana well.

'I've been planning to use AST,' I said aloud. Both women turned to look at me. 'Arabia Standard Time? You know, as in Mecca?'

Rizwana's mouth opened and closed repeatedly. Robin looked like she was desperately trying to form words.

'You guys are talking about Ramadan, right?'

They both nodded. Robin eventually grunted a single syllable that may or may not have been 'What?'

People were watching us. Anything out of the mundane was followed with eager interest.

I grinned. 'It surprises you to learn I'm Muslim?'

They both nodded again.

'What? You don't think a black American lesbian can be Muslim?' I chuckled – it was a bit mean.

Robin held up a single finger. 'Black. Sure, I've known plenty of black Muslims. There's nothing unusual about that.' She added a second finger. 'American? Dude, seriously? I am American, so yes, I know there are American Muslims. Though most of the ones I knew got out before it got too bad.'

I cut her off before she could move to the third point. 'You're American? No way! I thought you were Canadian.'

'My family was part of the Muslim Exodus.' For at least ten years, Muslims had been fleeing persecution in the US. Many had gone to Canada, where society was a bit more accepting. 'I was born in Michigan, but we were among the first to move north … so to speak. We moved from Flint, Michigan, to Windsor, so it was actually south. Anyway, from there I went a few kilometres up the four-oh-two to London for university. I'm ethnically Persian. My family is – that is, they were – from Iran. But I am – or was – American.'

'Get outta town,' I replied – a bit too loudly, judging by the looks I got. 'Gimme five, girl.'

'For reals,' she said, reaching to bump my proffered fist.

'Though you lose American points for saying kilometres instead of miles,' I added.

'Went to school in Canada, eh? Anyways, yes, I do know Americans can be Muslim.'

Things had never exactly been easy for us, but life had grown more difficult over the last decade. My parents had gone into hiding several months before we launched. And I wasn't sure where my brother was.

I'd known I'd miss my family – this was always gonna be a one-way trip. But I thought I'd still be able to talk to them. Knowing that we might never speak to anyone on Earth again? That most people I'd ever met were probably dead?

*Nah, man, gotta bring myself out of it.*

'And thirdly, yes, it's true – out lesbian Muslims are uncommon. But you wouldn't be the first and it's not my place to judge. I'm sorry – I shouldn't have made assumptions.'

'Nah, I'm just messing with you,' I said with a wave. 'I know I'm not exactly anybody's idea of the typical Muslim. But I look at it this way: Allah created us all, right?' Both women nodded. 'And we agree He doesn't make mistakes, yeah?' Again, nods. 'So I am who He made me to be and I'm going to be the best me I can be. And that me *loves* the ladies. I mean, seriously, you guys. I love women. I love everything about 'em. And I love sex. Phew, I'm getting hot just thinking about it, know what I mean?'

That got bemused smiles rather than nods.

'And that is who He made me to be, so I'm gonna run with it. What better way to honour Him than by being true to the person He created me to be.'

'Hallelujah! Preach it, sister.' Georgie's head was poking through the hatch to the sleeping quarters above us. From Georgie's perspective, she was coming 'down'. Given how tight we were crammed into the ship, I doubted she'd been deliberately eavesdropping. The *Chawla* had seemed so monstrously big eleven months ago. Now it felt – and smelled – like all thirty-eight of us were all packed into a single outhouse.

Georgie was head of food and agriculture for the colony –

food-ag. Before I took over, her wife, Gurdeep, had been the mission commander.

'But you're not Muslim,' said Rizwana, sounding somewhat puzzled.

'Well, no,' Georgie replied. 'We may call Him by different names, but we're not so different when it comes down to it. And Gabriel has just rather eloquently expressed my own beliefs. Except, of course,' she said, grinning cheekily, 'in place of "the ladies", substitute "my lovely wife". But otherwise, I completely agree. And I'll be forever in Iulia's debt for swapping places with me so I can be on this sardine can with her.'

'Hey, man, I'd love to find what you two have got. It's the goal. But for now…' I shrugged.

Rizwana asked, 'So, how did you come to the faith?'

I couldn't help grinning as I retold my favourite story. 'My mom was a doctor in the Iraq war. This was back when the US still allowed Muslims to serve. She was based in my dad's village. He volunteered at the local mosque. One day there was an explosion. I don't know what it was. Mom always swore it was a propane tank, but Dad was convinced it was an American mortar that had been stolen and hadn't been stored properly or something. Neither of them knew for sure. But there was an explosion and a child was wounded.'

I had everyone's full attention now.

'My dad picked the bleeding girl up and ran to the army base, screaming and crying. My mom was just coming out of the showers when she heard the commotion. She dropped what she was carrying and ran to help. They hauled that girl into the nearest building and operated on her right there in the mess hall. Saved the kid's life. The whole time, my dad was there, playing scrub nurse and anaesthesiologist. No medical training, no clue what he was doing, no care for anything but saving a life.'

More people appeared through the hatches both above and below us.

'Anyway, they saved the girl, who stayed on the base for about a week. Her parents went to visit every day – and so did my dad. He and my mom became friends. When it came time for her to ship out a few months later, well, they confessed their undying love for one another.

'He moved to the US and, what can I say, they've been happy ever since.' Shaking my head, I added, 'I wanted to join the marines like my mom. Of course, by the time I turned eighteen, that was out of the question. I joined the French Foreign Legion instead.' I said a silent prayer for the world we'd left behind. Rizwana lifted out of her seat and pushed over to me. She put her arms around me and pulled herself down to sit beside me.

'Don't worry,' she said with a wink. 'I'm not going to try and snog you. It's against the Ramadan rules.' I leaned into the very welcome hug. 'Do you need a few minutes to grieve or do you want to talk about cheerful things instead?'

I looked up at her gratefully. 'Let's talk about what we're going to do on Mars.'

'I've heard they've got apples,' someone said.

'Maybe, but it's not like they'll hand us each a home-made apple pie as soon as we land,' replied Robin.

'I don't even care,' I said. 'All I want is a proper toilet.' There was laughter all around. 'One without all the' – I screwed up my face and tried to imply the motions with my hands – 'hoses and bits.'

Rizwana sighed. 'Ugh, I just want a shower. That's all I care about. Just push me in the shower, clothes and all. Whatever. Don't care. I need a shower.'

A couple who'd been making out dislodged themselves to join the conversation. 'I want to be able to comb my hair without getting lost in it,' said one woman, pulling the hard-working band that held most of her hair back and running both hands through her wild mane of curly brown locks.

Her companion whispered, 'I would happily get lost in your hair.' She added something I couldn't hear and the two of them disappeared through the hatch.

'I want what they've got,' I said.

Rizwana laughed and wagged a finger at me. 'Not until Ramadan ends.'

'Hey, by my calculations, I've still got a few hours before it starts.'

She laughed and tossed her empty coffee mug at me. I could see in her eyes a decision was being made. I hoped I knew what it was, but I wasn't going to push my luck.

Rizwana whispered the words I'd hoped she was thinking in my ear as she took my hand and pulled me toward the hatch. 'Good, we'll need all the time we've got.'

SACA DOME, DEVON ISLAND COLONY, MARS

Afară, beyond the dome, the dust storm raged. During one of the video meetings with the colony's leadership team, Georgie had suggested the Romanian word for outside and it had stuck.

Within the dome, though, the simulated sunlight was warm on my skin.

When I was a kid, I thought storms could blow our house down – like in the fairy tale about the pigs. If this storm damaged one of our domes, we could die. My breath quickened at the thought.

The domes had two skins with a layer of clear gel in between for exactly that reason. If the gel came in contact with oxygen, it would liquify to seal the breach.

Shaking my head, I stood up and headed for the toilets. Inside the building, the door to the lounge was slightly ajar. Lisa's voice drifted out. I opened my mouth to announce myself when angry swearing erupted. At first I couldn't make out the words, growled or muttered as they were.

Then, suddenly… 'No, don't give me that crap again, Gabriel. We're tired and frustrated. We're ready for this. We *need* this.' The shouting caught me by surprise – and the fury behind it even more so.

An English accent. Maybe Manchester? The voice was familiar. It took me a second to make the connection. Gurdeep, the person in charge of planning the mission.

Multiple voices overlapped. I risked peering around the door. Lisa was sitting on the sofa with her back to me. The TV screen on the wall was divided into five windows. One showed Lisa herself; the other four must be the transport ships. In the largest one, three women were visible: Gabriel, Gurdeep, and a heavyset pretty woman with curly hair. While I wasn't good with faces, I figured she must be Georgie.

On screen, everyone seemed to be shouting at once, so I couldn't parse any of it. I thought I caught the words *safety*, *arrogant*, and *paramount*. Or possibly *tantamount*.

All the jumbled-up voices hurt my brain – and I probably shouldn't have been eavesdropping, anyway. I decided I could wait to go to the toilet, so I crept back outside and returned to work.

———

*SACA DOME, DEVON ISLAND COLONY, MARS*

That evening, we gathered in the same lounge for our daily meeting.

'I reviewed our productivity this morning with Brian,' Lisa said. 'We're doing well. Most things are growing nicely. Unfortunately, it seems we've been, ahem, particularly productive in one regard. We weren't due to empty the composter until later in the week, but it's filling up faster than expected. Leah and Habi, you'll be assisting Brian with it tomorrow first shift.'

Even though most of the dirty work was done in a suit, it was still gross. At least we didn't have to smell the decomposing waste matter. The toilets and garburators voided into the big composting vats in DownBelow. Leah wrinkled her nose. From Lisa's other side, Habi groaned.

'With the dust storm now well into its second month, we're hoping it'll let up soon. I spoke with Commander Mifsud and the rest of the leadership team this afternoon.'

I wasn't exactly the master of body language, but from what I could tell, she seemed perfectly relaxed. Given what I'd seen this afternoon, it had to be a mask. *But isn't masking an autistic thing*, I wondered.

'The transport ships are in their eighth day orbiting Mars,' Lisa said. 'The colonists are, as you can imagine, feeling anxious. It's important we get them down here as soon as we can do so safely – lest they murder one another.'

By the sound of the shouting I'd heard earlier, violence didn't seem as far-fetched as one might hope.

'When they join us, the pressure on our power grid will be enormous. If people want to eat hot food, take warm showers, send messages to one another, watch videos, and what have you, then we need the solar farm working at max capacity. Electrical issues will be a recurrent feature of our lives from now until we find a sustainable solution.'

Because the colonists left Earth earlier than planned, they hadn't been able to obtain as many RTGs – big batteries that produced most of our electricity – as planned. The RTGs had a half-life of around forty-five mears, their output steadily dropping. We'd been on Mars for less than a full mear and already the output had fallen around one per cent.

We could keep making solar panels. They provided plenty of power – when we weren't in the midst of a dust storm. This was something we'd need to resolve for our colony to have a future.

'Not only have they been trapped in those ships for more than a full Earth year, they're also processing the fact that so much of the human race has been lost. Down here, they'd be working through the trauma with physical labour – like we are. Up there, they're just sitting around, with nothing much to do except think about things and get in each other's faces. It's not healthy.'

Even with knowledge systems intact, rebuilding on Earth would take generations. I got emails from my dad – but communications were sporadic. Massive global servers went down for days at a time. It was good we'd copied so much to our intranet. The US had been especially hard hit. Brian had an auntie who'd stayed in touch for a few months, but he'd not heard from her in a while now.

'Still, until the storms let up and it's safe for them to land, we carry on as usual – however frustrating it may be. So, with that in mind, let's move on to tomorrow's duties. Devon, Sun, Paxton, and Ife —' Lisa looked at each of us as she said our names. 'You four will be afară, doing the damage inspection in the morning.' Normally two people spent an hour or so once a week doing a full exterior check of all four domes. With the dust storm, it had been taking four people an entire morning.

---

Afterwards, Brian and Ife surprised us with apple mojitos concocted with spiced rum they'd made.

'There ain't enough to go around, so we may as well get it

down us now – afore we have to share it a hundred and fifty-six ways,' Brian said. In addition to the woman who'd died of plague, three people had taken their own lives on the journey.

'I'm so excited to see people,' squealed Paxton. 'Aren't you all stoked for our community? I mean, it's— How long has it been since we've seen another living human?'

'Not that you don't love us, of course,' Brian said.

'Eight hundred and fifty-one days,' I said. 'We were travelling for two hundred and fifty-nine days and it's been five hundred and ninety-two since we landed.'

Everyone stared at me like I'd said something funny. *What? She asked; I answered. Why is that weird?*

Paxton leapt up out of her seat and ran towards me. 'I love you, Devon.' I braced myself for the incoming hug, but Lisa deftly cut in and redirected Paxton's affection, taking it on my behalf. *Best boss ever.* The mojitos were yummy – but alcohol turned some people into space invaders.

'I honestly don't know how I'll cope with having an extra hundred and forty-eight people in the colony,' I said.

'What? You can't mean that!' Habi was another socialite. She and Paxton were the most extroverted of our team. And Brian, obviously. 'There are only eight of us on the entire planet. Don't you want to see people, go to parties, hang out with your friends?'

*What a strange question.* 'I *am* hanging out with my friends. What do you think we're doing right now? And look at us! We're spread out across four domes, each of which was designed to accommodate up to thirty-two people comfortably – though how anyone decides what constitutes someone else's comfort is beyond me.' I had a flat to myself in Thunberg dome. The dome's only other occupant, Brian, lived next door.

'We're opening up our domes – not to mention our homes – to people we barely know,' I added. 'Squeezed into four domes. Four people per bedroom!'

Sun and Lisa both responded with defensive body language. The divide between the introverts and extroverts was stark.

Leah was sort of a middle ground between the two camps, with one foot in each. 'Yeah, it'll be crowded for a bit – but the fifth dome will be ready soon. It'll give us seven new flats.'

'True,' Brian said, nodding, 'but we do need at least seven domes to be able to grow sufficient food for everyone.'

I tapped my lip six times. *Six is half of twelve. Twelve is a good number. We should have a base twelve numbering system. Base ten is stupid. Ten is divisible by five and two; that's rubbish. Base twelve is more logical. Twelve is what I call a 'whole' number. Six is half of twelve, so if I only tap my lip six times, then it's only a few times, not a whole set. Then I know I'm okay.*

I would continue to worry about it until I had my flat to myself again. *What if I never have my own flat again?*

MEAR 0, DAY 1

*TRANSPORT SHIP CHAWLA, MARS*

I was wet.

*Why am I wet? I don't think I was wet when...*

When what? Why couldn't I remember?

'Georgie?'

Water dripped into my eyes. I tried to brush it away with my hand, but I couldn't move. Searing pain ran the length of my arm and I couldn't feel my legs. Everything was heavy. *Do I have plague?*

'Georgie?'

I reached for the light switch with my left hand. Instead, I found a tangle of wires and ... I didn't know what else. Hot. Much too hot. Even for me.

'Georgie, you a'right, love?'

I blinked rapidly to bring things into focus. There were lights somewhere. Not enough to see anything by – strange orange lights that seemed wrong.

'Georgie?'

The world slipped away from me.

———

It might have been a few hours later or a day or two seconds, but a thunk jerked me awake. Suddenly the life support bay – so that's where I was – was flooded with light.

No, a light shining straight at me. My eyes followed it as it moved away and – *Is someone sleeping in the life support bay? Do we have a stowaway?*

Something didn't seem right.

I smelled meat. *Is someone cooking?* I would be so hacked off when I found out who it was. *Who authorised meat?* Our supplies were limited. Meat was a waste of precious resources. *How dare someone violate one of our most basic rules. It's flagrant disrespect.*

A helmeted head loomed above me.

'Someone is cooking meat,' I bellowed. 'We do not permit meat. Leave me to rest and go find out who it is. The culprits must be brought to justice.'

Everything faded away again.

———

SEACOLE DOME, DEVON ISLAND COLONY, MARS

I opened my eyes and then squeezed them shut. Too bright! I tried again, slower this time, forcing myself to look around at the clean, white, well-lit room.

Georgie was sitting next to my bed, holding my hand. Her face looked pained, but she smiled. 'Hey, sleepyhead.' She brushed my cheek, but even that gentle pressure hurt. I tried to lift my arm to touch her but couldn't. *Why is every-thing so heavy?*

As she stroked my hair, I felt myself beginning to drift. I opened my eyes again. Georgie was still there, but she was sitting on my other side. *How did she get over there?*

'Did they find who—' My voice sounded sticky. How could a voice sound sticky? It hurt to talk; the effort wore me out. Someone was standing next to her. Leah? No, that couldn't be right. Leah was on Mars.

'Shh, shh… Try not to speak. You're safe – in hospital.'

'Is it…' My voice cracked. 'Is it plague?'

Georgie's chin trembled. 'No, babe. There hasn't been any plague since Chris recovered.'

'Welcome to the Ida Scudder Memorial Hospital,' said Leah. 'We had hoped to show you around under happier circumstances. But you had to go and test our facilities on your first day.' It was a joke, but she wasn't laughing.

I opened my mouth to speak, but Georgie shushed me again with a finger against my lips. Something about the weight felt strange. 'I know what you're going to say. You're going to ask about casualties.' I hadn't been. 'Five dead so far, four wounded, but those numbers are likely to change.'

She stretched her back before slumping forwards. 'There was a fire as we tried to land. We're not entirely sure why yet. A few of you got up out of the berths to put it out.'

Georgie tugged her sleeves down over her hands. *She never wears long sleeves.* 'The ship was moving under several Gs by that point, though. Desmond injured himself when he tried to open the hatch leading to the next deck. He was—' She took a jagged breath. 'He was partially crushed by the weight of the door. He never made it to the fire.'

I closed my eyes. 'Was Gabriel able to save him?' My voice was a whispered croak.

Georgie tilted her head and touched her mouth with her fingertips. 'Fr … Frankie saved him. She had to amputate his arm, but she saved his life.'

'Frankie?' Why would a veterinarian operate on a man? Gabriel, the *Chawla*'s doctor and our colony's trauma surgeon, should've been the one to save Desmond.

Oh no – that could only mean one thing. 'Wait, Gabriel was too busy saving my life, wasn't she? Desmond almost died because Gabriel prioritised my life over his.' My breath was coming fast and short. The little blips from the machine I was hooked up to, the machine I hadn't even noticed until now, sped up. 'I need to speak to her. That was a terrible decision. She's got a lot to answer for.' I tried to sit up.

Georgie pressed her hand to my chest. The weight of it crushed me. 'Stop.' She pushed me back down. 'You saved our lives, babe. You, all of you.' She wiped a tear from her cheek. My mind was stuffed with popcorn. *What was I missing?*

'That fire would've engulfed the whole ship. It would have killed all of us and destroyed our supplies.' She squeezed my hand, my left hand. My right was wrapped in bandages.

*Oh*. Her meaning began to permeate my mind.

'Who?'

'By the time Lisa's team arrived, Qiang and four others were dead. Helen's operating on Gabriel now and Sun is working on one of the others. Babe, I'm so sorry. They're doing everything they can, but… Well, they're not in good shape.'

I closed my eyes. It was foggy. I couldn't remember why, but I knew this was all my fault.

As Georgie's lips touched my un-bandaged hand, Leah said, 'Let her sleep.'

When I woke, Georgie was still sitting next to me wearing the same uncharacteristic long-sleeved outfit. A lab coat, I now realised – though that didn't make sense.

On my other side, Leah was taking my blood pressure. She beckoned to someone across the room. As the figure approached, I recognised Helen. She changed places with Leah. Her hair was a mess and she looked like she hadn't slept in a fortnight.

'I'm glad to see you looking so well,' she said – though I was certain I didn't. 'You suffered smoke inhalation, second- and third-degree burns to your face and chest. Your arm was impaled. There was a twelve-centimetre laceration to your scalp which narrowly missed your right eye. You had a crush injury to your left leg that Sun couldn't repair.' When she paused, I followed her eyes to the shape of my body under the blanket. My leg was...

'She removed your leg just above the knee. I'm sorry. You'll recover, but we couldn't save it. Once you're healed, we'll get you fitted for a prosthetic. You gave us quite a scare, but you'll pull through.' She touched my hand before hurrying off.

I began to cry. 'I'm sor—' I coughed and then couldn't stop hacking. Georgie held a cup of water to my lips. I looked at the perfectly ordinary drinking vessel. I'd forgotten about glasses. What a wonderful thing they were.

I leaned back after I had a few sips and promptly fell asleep again.

Later, I felt a bit more human – like a human who'd been run over by a bus. Or, indeed, a spaceship.

Georgie was still by my side. *Still? Again?* She was wearing different clothes – normal clothes. I recognised the lightweight sleeveless cotton dress. Although I couldn't make out the details, I knew the whimsical print by heart. She looked clean but tired. *When had any of us last been clean? Even the air smelled clean.*

For the first time, I noticed the red spots in and around her eyes. *Petechiae*, the word came back to me.

'Hey,' she said.

'Hey,' I croaked back. Before she could shush me again, I managed, 'Tell me everything.'

Her hand trembled as she raised it to her lips. 'I'm not sure what you remember, so I'll pick a point. Don't strain your voice – just squeeze my hand if I'm repeating stuff you remember.' She nodded her head once as she took my good hand. 'And, I guess squeeze twice if you need me to back up.'

She swallowed. 'We'd been orbiting Mars for several days, waiting for the dust storms to die down so we could land.' I clamped her hand like a vice grip. Gabriel and I had argued extensively; I remembered that. I wanted to land as soon as there was a break in the storm; Gabriel wanted us to wait until the weather near our site had been still for at least a full day.

She used her free hand to firmly unclench my fingers from around hers. 'Okay, well, we were filthy, strung out, and desperate. The mood was ugly.'

A scene popped into my head. I had argued that the risks of the storm picking back up during our descent and also impacting our ability to land safely were vanishingly small. Gabriel countered that we had a duty to the human race to put our safety ahead of everything else. I had been … cross. Harsh words had been spoken.

Tears streamed down my face as Georgie spoke. 'Everyone bickered relentlessly but especially you and Gabriel.' She was the commander of the mission; I wasn't. My words should have counted for nothing. 'You arrived at a compromise, eventually. Gabriel agreed that we would land if the winds fell below – I don't remember the speed, sorry.'

She looked so helpless. 'Numbers aren't my thing at the best of times. Anyway, you agreed that if the wind speed fell below that figure for twelve hours, we would land.' Because I had once been the leader of the mission, Gabriel had allowed herself to compromise with me.

Georgie picked my hand up in both of hers and brought it to her lips, kissing it gently. 'The storms returned as our ships landed. There was a fire on board. I don't know, Ife says maybe metallic dust got into something and it over-heated. We'll probably never know for sure what happened. But whatever it was, the fire damaged our braking system. We accelerated as we approached the ground. Under heavy gravitational forces, you ran to put out the fire and repair the damage. You, all nine of you, ran towards danger instead of away from it.'

She closed her eyes. 'Desmond was injured, so he didn't make it to the life support bay. Eight of you battled the fire. I've no idea what you did, but you saved us – you all did.'

Now people were dead. Because of me.

'Our landing was' – she bobbed her head back and forth as if searching for the right word – 'difficult. Remember those classes we had with Ife and Qiang?' She wiped her eyes.

*Was Qiang one of the names she mentioned? Ife couldn't be*

*impacted; she was already on Mars, wasn't she?* I hated not being able to think clearly.

'Do you recall them telling us the human body could take up to something like nine Gs without losing consciousness?' I tried to nod. 'Well, I was lying there, strapped into my bunk and thinking that as long as I was still conscious, we must be below that. But then—'

She withdrew her hand from mine and folded hers in her lap, knuckles white. 'As I came to, I heard an insistent bleeping followed by Lisa's voice barking out of every speaker, instructing us all to stay put. It was only then I realised we were no longer moving. But there was still gravity – which surprised me for some stupid reason. None of you were strapped in, so I guess you bore the full brunt of all that.'

Nora appeared and pumped out a portion of hand sanitiser. She took my vitals again. When she'd finished, Georgie resumed her tale.

'They got to us within minutes of landing and the medical teams from both *Cristoforetti* and *Bondar* arrived not long afterwards. The first people they encountered were the most injured. There was nothing to be done for Qiang or the others, but they rushed Petra, Gabriel, and you back to the colony. Sun operated on you in the back of the rover as you sped towards the domes. On the ship, Frankie and Rizwana did what they could for Desmond.'

A vet and a midwife amputated a man's arm in field conditions.

Because of me.

Georgie blew her nose. She got up to go wash her hands and get a drink. When she returned, she continued.

'Once the rovers transferred you to the colony, they came back for the rest of us. Desmond was stable. He's going to be okay. I came back on the rover with him. You were still in surgery when I got here.'

Sun walked onto the ward and headed in our direction. Never a large woman, she looked even tinier than I remembered. She smiled at me then frowned at Georgie.

'You both need sleep.' Sun commanded Georgie to go 'home' and get some rest. Unexpectedly, Georgie complied. She kissed me on the forehead before leaving.

Lying alone in the hospital bed, I cried.

MEAR 0, DAY 4

*HATSH DOME, DEVON ISLAND COLONY, MARS*

These community meals reminded me of undergrad. They were more regular than the ones in my university days, though, as we kept to a strict schedule. Everyone who lived in a dome shared the community spaces and facilities – and that meant shared mealtimes.

I looked at Lisa and Mehmet, who I knew so well. To my left were Frankie and Caoimhe, two French-Canadian sisters. Adopted, of course, not biologically related – that would interfere with the genetic diversity of the colony. The last person at the table was Caoimhe's husband, Korri, a botanist.

Mehmet pushed his empty porridge bowl away and leaned towards Lisa and me. 'Where are we meeting?'

Lisa swallowed the last of her breakfast. She slid Mehmet's dish back towards him.

Mehmet scowled at the bowl. 'It's rude! My father would be horrified.'

The others stopped what they were doing and watched

the exchange. The relaxed grin disappeared from Lisa's face. She placed both hands flat on the table and looked from person to person to person. 'You're on Mars now. Your parents are not here – will *never* be here. The rules have changed. We do not have resources to spare, so we conserve everything. Every scrap of food must be used. So go on, eat up.'

Leading by example, I lifted my bowl to my face and licked the shallow surface clean. Mehmet followed suit.

Lisa's tone was calm and clear. It seemed to be a military thing – most of the ex-soldiers had that skill. 'I know you're not used to our ways – this still feels strange to you. But you all know how precious our resources are. We have a closed-loop system. In order to sustain ourselves, we do not waste *anything*. Am I understood?'

Ultimately, everything was recycled, but that took power – something else we needed to be conservative with.

Murmurs of assent circumnavigated the table. Lisa wasn't satisfied. 'I asked you a question: am I understood?'

The response was louder this time. 'Yes.' *Man, I envied that skill.* People licked the remnants of porridge from their bowls and drained the dregs of their drinks.

Lisa leaned towards Mehmet. Her voice was softer this time. 'Thunberg dome. I've designated a space for our meetings.'

Mehmet laughed. 'Thunderdome?'

A few seats away, Caoimhe shouted, 'Thunderdome!'

Frankie raised her fist and roared. 'Two men— Nah, two *women* enter; one woman leaves!'

We all broke out into rowdy cheers. Caoimhe's husband Korri thumped his hands on the table. It was the first time I'd seen genuine smiles in… *How long had it been?*

Lisa dropped her head into her hands and whimpered.

'Ah, man. No one is gonna call it Thunberg dome anymore, are they? Devon will *never* forgive us for bastardising the name of her hero.'

———

THUNDERDOME, DEVON ISLAND COLONY, MARS

Lisa, Mehmet, and I walked to the aforementioned dome for our meeting.

With our leader dead, the most logical option would be for Gurdeep to resume the role she'd held until we left Earth – except she was still in hospital. We'd have to play it by ear.

I swept an overhanging palm frond out of my way. 'I talked to Santosh yesterday. He doesn't want to be part of the government.' He'd been Gurdeep's assistant on Earth and I had expected him to carry on that role.

'Huh. Did he say why?' Lisa asked.

I shook my head. 'Wouldn't talk about it.'

Mehmet said, 'Santosh was different during the trip here. I don't know what or why, but something changed.'

Lisa opened the door to the building and held it for me. 'Thanks,' I said as I entered the small outer room. 'Without him to provide admin support – I took a bit of a liberty.'

'Morning!' Jupiter stood up, an earnest smile on her face. I looked back at Lisa; she cocked an eyebrow.

'I asked Jupiter to join us to help take notes and keep us organised,' I said. 'Those intensive admin courses we put her through back on Earth have been paying off. Over the last year, I've come to—'

'Half a mear,' Lisa corrected me. 'Year is an Earth word. We use mears here.'

'I don't get it. We still use days – why not years?'

Lisa sighed. Maybe I wasn't the first person she'd had to explain this to. 'A day doesn't feel different. Our days are only thirty-seven minutes longer. So, who cares? May as well stick with the familiar word and just adjust the definition. But a Martian year is almost two full Earth years. I'm thirty-three years old – so it would feel ridiculous to describe myself as being seventeen. But a mear is a new and different thing.'

My jaw fell slack as I realised. 'Oh God. I was thirty-seven when I left Earth – and now I'm a teenager? No, thank you.' I shook my head. 'Anyways, thank you for joining us, Jupiter.'

Jupiter swallowed. 'No probs. Happy to help.' The front room had a desk and a few chairs; beyond that was a meeting room with a round table. It had a 'window' on the opposite wall – configured to show a scene of an offshore wind farm against a clear blue Earth sky. The dust storm had finally died down, so we could afford this little extravagance.

Over the next few minutes, the remaining members of the colony's leadership team arrived. Georgie, Helen, and Iulia attended in person. Even now, Iulia managed to look smart, her brown hair somehow glossy. Given that she'd lost her husband in the landing, I was amazed. Tom and Faz – our co-heads of mental health – dialled in via video.

Lisa opened the meeting, assuming that same all-business tone she'd used at breakfast. 'Right. This marks the first official meeting of the provisional government. I'd like to welcome Jupiter Hartley-Richards, who'll temporarily take over Santosh's role as assistant. She'll be a non-voting member of this committee until we settle on a permanent replacement.'

Lisa closed her eyes for a moment. 'As you know, I sent messages to the next of kin we had on file for the victims of the fire. For obvious reasons, most of those messages have gone unanswered, but I received a reply this morning from Asha Mifsud – Gabriel's mother. I'd like a volunteer from this team to open a dialogue with her. Someone who knew Gabriel well would be best. Anyone?'

Georgie looked like she was struggling to keep her eyes open – she must be exhausted. 'It should be me.'

Lisa nodded. 'Thank you. Now, we've got about forty-five minutes before our satellite passes out of range and we lose comms with the *Aderin-Pocock*. On today's agenda, Helen will present a health update and we'll discuss the plans for the "missing"' – she made bunny ears with her fingers around the word – 'ship and her crew.' The ship and her crew weren't really missing – they'd just landed elsewhere on the planet. 'And lastly, we'll discuss the colony's electricity demands and ideas for meeting our long-term needs.'

She folded her hands on the table. 'Helen, please go ahead.'

With her brown hair pulled back into an untidy ponytail and dark circles under her eyes, Helen looked like she hadn't slept since we landed three days ago. But then, none of us looked our best. Georgie had bruising and red spots around her eyes. We were all clean and relieved to be on solid ground, but we were still a long way from being well rested.

Helen took a deep breath and leaned forwards, resting her elbows on the conference table. 'I did everything I could – I wish I could've saved her. Them. I'm sorry I couldn't save them all. Sorry.' Helen wasn't one to show emotion. Georgie put her hand on Helen's shoulder, giving her a reassuring squeeze. 'There is some good news, though. We're unlikely to lose anyone else. At least, not because of the crash. Also, I retrieved ovaries from most of the crash victims. A few were burnt. Some were crushed.'

Georgie raised an eyebrow. 'Gabriel's?'

Helen sighed. 'I got one of them. The other was too damaged, but I saved one.' Everyone had signed waivers saying that if they died, any viable organs could be used – including reproductive organs. Helen drew a deep breath. 'Right, um… Next up is our need to train a new surgeon. We've lost the best we had. We need to consider who's best placed to take on the responsibility.'

She took a drink from her water bottle and then pushed her glasses up her nose. 'The most obvious candidates are Nora and Frankie, as both have had a good chunk of the training already. Nora would make a fantastic surgeon, but then we'd need to train a new nurse. As a veterinarian, Frankie has many of the right skills – plus it'll be a while before we have many animals for her to practise on. She did superb work with Desmond's arm. He would've bled out if she hadn't intervened.'

The committee agreed, so Helen said she'd speak to Frankie about the possibility.

Lisa moved us on to the next topic on the agenda: the *Aderin-Pocock*.

'We've determined our position,' said Tom. On screen, he and Faz were seated at a small table. Tom's hand loomed in as he reached out to click a button. Their image shrank as a map popped up next to them. 'We're about a thousand kilometres from you, but there's some complicated terrain between here and there.' A fat yellow line appeared, connecting their landing site and our base.

Iulia nodded. Outwardly at least, she appeared calm and composed. 'I am working with relevant teams, both here and at landing site, to calculate best route to bring you here,' she said. She'd told me once that she'd battled definite and indefinite articles for years – a common complaint from Russian speakers learning English – before concluding they weren't necessary.

'Thanks, Iulia,' Lisa said. 'Right, we need to discuss the best plan to get you folks home. Let's talk options. The original plan was to split the group: some people drive to the colony while the rest wait for the rovers to return.'

Lisa and I had stayed up half the night discussing this. 'We have to rule that out,' I said. 'Splitting up means only some people will have access to a doctor. God forbid there are any more accidents.'

We'd known for a few weeks that the navigation system on the *Aderin-Pocock* had failed, so they had been using visual flight rules to follow us down. The fire had forced them to steer away, which was how they ended up in a remote part of the planet.

Ensconced within the relative safety of the *Bondar*, I'd been unaware of the crisis on the *Chawla* until we'd landed. The moment we were on the ground, Devon's voice had erupted from my bunk's speaker, instructing all staff with medical training to report to the airlock and everyone else to stay put.

Georgie bit her lip. 'If you stripped the seats out of your two rovers, could you squeeze everyone in?'

On screen, Tom tilted his head. But Lisa and I had considered this last night. 'With seats in place, each rover can fit up to ten. Without seats – not only would that be a hella uncomfortable ride,' Lisa said, 'there's still no way you could squeeze nineteen people into each vehicle.'

I rested my elbows on the table. 'That's that, then. The only viable option is to stay put until we can get a team to you with sufficient rovers for everyone to drive together.'

On screen, Faz appeared to deflate. I put on my best

reassuring politician face. 'I feel your pain, Faz. I think we all do.'

'We have a responsibility to ensure the safety of everyone we still have,' Lisa said. 'Anyone have an issue with that?' It was a question, but there was steel beneath her words.

No one objected.

Tom rubbed his full beard. 'We've already been living in cramped conditions for twelve months. As much as none of us like the idea of being stuck together for even longer – we've got actual showers and proper toilets in the temporary dome and no one accidentally floats out of bed. We eat our meals with forks and knives and we drink from ordinary cups. Everyone is safe and clean-ish.'

He blew out a breath. 'Still, morale is through the floor. We're all desperate to get to our new home. We've lost friends on the voyage – plus most everyone on Earth. Over the past few days, we've lost more people. We need time and space to grieve, we need to see some fresh faces, and we need privacy.' He stood up, circled his chair, and then sat back down.

'We do understand that.' I poured all the reassurance I could muster into my voice. 'I wish we could magic you home this afternoon, but this is the only viable option.'

'Sorry, has anyone got any snacks? I'm famished,' Georgie said. Mehmet pulled a protein bar from his pocket and tossed it to her. She tore open the reusable wrapping and bit into the bar.

Lisa steepled her hands under her chin. 'Right, let's discuss logistics. How long will it take?'

Iulia bit her lip. 'For regularly equipped rover moving at maximum sustainable speed, including time for battery recharge and to establish and disassemble temporary dome each day, journey can be done in twelve or thirteen days. More passengers and supplies mean more frequent stops for recharging of batteries and oxygen scrubbers. Even allowing for only basic set up of habitat, estimate at least double that for return journey.'

Tom toyed with the drawstring on his hoodie. 'It's not news people will want to hear. Everybody wants to feel like they're doing something, going somewhere – but we'll manage.'

'On the bright side, we can send you some fresh fruit and veg with the rovers,' Lisa said. 'And we'll plan a big dinner for when you arrive. I propose the rescue team should comprise members of my crew plus some from the two ships that landed safely.' Everyone agreed.

'Good, I'll lead. I'll select three of my people to join me. Those of you from *Cristoforetti* and *Bondar*, please select one person from each ship. Good drivers. Level-headed, practical people.'

From the corner of the room, Jupiter softly cleared her throat. I'd practically forgotten she was here. 'Time.'

'Right, thank you, Jupiter,' Lisa said. 'It's important we stick to our schedule. We can't keep letting the power discussion slide, but we'll save it for tomorrow's meeting – following the service.'

*SEACOLE DOME, DEVON ISLAND COLONY, MARS*

I smiled at myself in the mirror above the sink, but it didn't reach my eyes. Brushing my stupid curls out of my stupid face, I repeated the action, trying to force myself to mean it. I couldn't manage it.

I'd always been a cheerful person. My dad used to tell me I was the only baby he ever met who laughed more than cried. Whatever pain and grief life brought, I'd maintained a positive outlook.

When I was twelve, I sat by my mother's side as she died. I remember feeling sad for my own loss and for the pain and grief my brothers and father felt. Still, I was happy my mum was free of pain. I was grateful she had lived a good life. But especially, I knew I had to be strong for my dad and for Cipri, my younger brother. They needed me to hold it all together for them, so I did. I was there for them and I'd be there for Gurdeep now.

I refused to leave this room until I'd reclaimed that.

'One more try,' I commanded myself. Taking a deep

breath, I smiled again. Disappointed with my efforts, I jumped up and down, trying to loosen tight muscles. As I smiled at the woman before me, I told my reflection, 'You can do this.'

'Um... I don't mean to rush you or nothing,' came Brian's voice from the other side of the toilet door. 'Just, I have need of the facilities, you know.'

Putting the smile back on, I opened the door. 'Sorry, just giving myself a little pep talk.'

He shoved me aside. 'Pee first – hug later.' I tossed my toiletries onto my bunk. I was a sucker for bright colours and flashy details, but they didn't seem appropriate today, so I'd chosen my only black dress. But as I looked down at myself, I decided the rainbow polka dots were inappropriate.

I opened my wardrobe-locker-thing and stared at the few articles of clothing I owned. A flouncy, multi-coloured sleeveless dress adorned with teacups, flowers, and cupcakes. A handful of brightly coloured T-shirts with funny sayings. Shorts and cargos. The little red dress that was inappropriate for life on Mars, but which I couldn't bear to part with. I collapsed on the floor. *I will not let myself cry.*

Brian emerged from the loo and knelt down beside me. He put his arm around my shoulder. 'Don't change.'

'But the dots don't exactly give off a sombre vibe.'

'*You* don't give off a sombre vibe. It's not who you are. You are vibrant and colourful and full of joy. You are life and you are alive,' he replied.

Without turning around, I reached up and clasped Brian's hand. 'I just... What am I supposed to wear? Why didn't I plan for this? Didn't it occur to me there would be funerals on Mars? Why didn't I bring any clothes that were even remotely dignified? What was I thinking? Who let me pack this frivolous rubbish? I am a grown-arse woman – thirty-one years old! Why do I still dress like a teenager?'

'Hey, hey, hey.' He stood up and held out a hand to pull me up. When we were both upright, he took a step back so he was holding me at arm's length. 'You dress like you. Ain't nobody nowhere can do it better. You be you and you honour them folk as best you can. Now dry them tears and get outta here. She'll be a'waiting.'

Even in my pain, I had to smile at Brian's mannerisms. The larger-than-life persona he adopted never failed to charm. I took a deep breath and held it as I fanned my face with my hands. Releasing the breath slowly, I rolled my shoulders and jumped up and down a few times to get every-thing flowing.

'You want me to walk with you?'

'Thank you, Brian. I'd appreciate some company on the way to the Scud.' As we stepped out of the flat, he offered me his arm, like a pastiche of an old-fashioned gentleman.

'The who to the what now? We brought Soviet missiles with us?'

'Sorry, the hospital.'

'Ah,' he said. 'We been calling it by the unglamorous designation of the medlab. I like your version better.'

'Helen named it a few days ago.' As we walked, I told him what I'd learned over the past few days about our hospi-tal's namesake, Ida Scudder. The Scud was only one floor down and around the back of the flat we shared with Desmond and two others. 'She was a pioneering physician of the nineteenth and twentieth centuries. An American missionary in India with a focus on providing care to women in poverty. She founded one of the premier medical schools in Asia.'

When we got to the bottom of the stairs, we followed the

curve of the building cluster for about twenty metres until the door of the hospital came into view. 'And here we are. Thank you, Brian. Sometimes I need to be brought back down to, er … Mars.'

'Not a worry,' he replied. 'We do what we can to keep each other sane because the alternative don't bear thinking. I'll see y'all soon.' He hugged me again before continuing on his way towards the Thunderdome.

The ward comprised a sizeable room with pristine white walls and floors. Six beds occupied most of the space, a curtain drawn around one of them. I could hear Nora and Desmond's voices on the other side, speaking in hushed tones. Gurdeep was sitting on the edge of her bed. She was dressed, which I took as a positive sign. The wound on her temple had scabbed over. She wore a long-sleeved shirt, but the edges of a clean bandage were visible at her right wrist. Her trouser leg was pinned neatly at the knee. *Would I ever get used to that?*

She didn't look at me. Her thin black hair had been washed and combed. I ran my fingers through it – careful not to touch the wound – before plunking myself down next to her on the bed. 'Come on, babe. It's time to go.'

Gurdeep turned her face away from me. It killed me to see her so broken. She needed me to be strong for her. 'Babe, we have to go.'

Nora emerged from the curtained area and beckoned me to join her in the office off the ward. I squeezed Gurdeep's shoulder gently. 'Right back.'

'She's pretty low,' Nora said. 'She let me bathe her, change her bandages, and dress her. But she won't interact. She does nae speak more than one word – and most of the time not even that. You'll have a challenge on your hands getting her out the door.'

Helen jostled past me into the tiny office. Like Nora, she was dressed appropriately in a simple black dress. Nora looked elegant in a black short-sleeved shift dress with plum-coloured flowers. Helen wore a black cotton shirt dress. Both looked like they were on their way to a solemn occasion: tasteful and mature. I looked down at myself again. Was that a spot of porridge on my wrinkled spotted dress?

'As Gurdeep's doctor, I feel compelled to point out again that she should not be leaving this hospital for at least a few more days,' Helen said. She tilted her head. 'But as her friend and a fellow member of the provisional government, I understand how important it is for her to be there today. We'll bring her IV drip and we'll keep her hooked up to the monitors. I'll have Frankie bring the ambulance. If anything changes, I'm bringing her right back here.'

I nodded. 'Of course.'

'First, we've got to persuade her to come,' added Nora.

'I'm on it.'

Back in the ward room, I found Desmond sitting on the edge of his bed, finishing getting dressed. He said hello and I caught a flash of his binder – though he was quick to pull his shirt shut with his remaining hand. A tie lay on the bed next to him. *Who on Earth brings a tie to Mars? What a strange decision.*

'Dressing change?'

Desmond nodded again. 'Yeah, just finished. Everything looks good.'

'I can help with your tie if you need,' I said.

'Thanks. It'll be a while before I can manage it one-handed.'

'Oh, I think I know a certain accountant who might be willing to help,' I replied with a wink as I tied a half-Windsor. His skin didn't show a blush, but I could almost feel the heat radiating off him.

'There you go. All done.' I touched his shoulder and smiled, trying to put some genuine warmth in it for him. His curls were buzzed close to his scalp. With the soft lighting and the short hair, his angular features shone like the deepest amber.

'Cheers, Georgie.'

I smiled again, finally feeling some warmth with it, before grabbing a wheelchair from the corner of the room. Gurdeep hadn't moved.

I reached a hand out to touch the unburnt side of her face. 'It's time, babe. Let's go.' She looked away from me. I took her chin and gently turned her to face me. Her eyes were pointed in my direction, but she wasn't looking at me. Not really. 'Sorry, babe, this isn't a request. I know you and I know how desperately you'll regret it later if you don't come today. I'll wait with you for Helen or Nora. But we're going.'

I sat on the edge of the bed with her. A few minutes later, Nora came over and checked Gurdeep's vitals. Helen unplugged the various cords, cables, and lines and connected everything to portable monitors, drips, and an oxygen tank.

Helen helped me lift an unresisting Gurdeep from the bed into the wheelchair – like a sack of potatoes. *Was it only Mars's weak gravity that made her seem so small?* Helen checked everything was okay before we headed out. I pushed the wheelchair; Helen, Nora, and Desmond walked alongside us.

As we exited the Scud, I breathed deep of the herby scents. The bamboo Brian had planted before the rest of us had even left Earth stood tall and graceful across the pathway from the building.

Today's service would take place in the gardens in the Thunderdome. We'd planned a small wake for afterwards. As we arrived, I saw that Brian and Devon had done an impressive job setting up tables for tea, coffee, and bickies. They'd even set out bowls of fresh fruit: apples, figs, and raspberries.

It may not sound like much of a buffet, but it would be at least a mear before we were truly self-sustaining. Still, it was impressive what Brian had achieved in just eighteen months. *What would we ever do without him?*

I heard people approaching and turned towards the airlock connecting to Saca. Mehmet broke away from a group of people walking together. He greeted me with a hug. He too was dressed in a manner befitting the occasion – black jeans and a deep blue turtleneck jumper. *Was I the only one on this whole planet who hadn't brought any adult clothes?*

He knelt down in front of Gurdeep's wheelchair. 'Afternoon, sir. How you doing today?' She wouldn't meet his eyes. He patted her hand then stood up and looked at me again. 'You're doing the service, yeah? I'll stay with her.' I thanked him and kissed Gurdeep on the forehead.

I went off to find the other chaplains. The victims were from different religions and none, so we were all joining forces to lead the community in a single service that blended elements from many traditions. We ran through the plans again briefly as we waited for Lisa's signal. When she texted, we made our way to the front of the crowd and asked everyone to gather round.

Behind the assembled masses, I saw the door to the service room swing open. Lisa and Habi emerged from the building pulling a small wagon with eleven simple brown boxes – the seven victims of the fire and the four who lost their lives on the voyage.

Intellectually, I knew that promession reduced a human body to around twenty kilograms. Still, my stomach muscles convulsed when I saw how small the boxes were.

We led the crowd through the simple ceremony. We all teared up and stumbled through our words in a few places. People shared their memories of the ones they'd lost. Rizwana cried as she spoke about her brief relationship with Gabriel. After that she didn't speak much at all.

When the service was finished, we buried the boxes in the orchard. Brian and his team had dug the holes ahead of time. Each box was moved by the person closest to the victim. Nora, who had known Gabriel the longest, placed her box in the ground. There was no one to carry Sam's box – she had never formed any bonds with anyone on the ship. The only person who seemed to matter to her was the man I so casually stranded on Earth so my wife could join me. My breath caught in my throat as I whispered a thousandth apology to Sam as I laid her to rest.

We would plant a tree above each grave. Brian had suggested oak trees for the seven victims of the fire – to symbolise strength and courage. And he'd chosen graceful birches for the other victims – three suicides and a woman infected with plague. They were all victims of the pandemic that had claimed so many lives on Earth. Birch represented new beginnings.

As soon as we finished the burial, Helen insisted Gurdeep return to the Scud. Her face was passive, her gaze unfocused as Helen wheeled her away.

Iulia sat a few metres away, looking more alone than I'd ever seen her. I crossed the distance between us and sat down. She took my hand. 'Treasure your time with her.' Her voice was so soft I almost didn't hear.

'I will. I do. Oh, Iulia, I'm so sorry for your loss and I'm sorry you couldn't be with him on the journey. Qiang and the others saved us all. There's nothing I can do to make it up to you and nothing I can say but I'm sorry.'

She nodded and raised a hankie to her face, wiping tears away even as more flowed down. 'I know our relationship was not usual, was not conventional. We lived apart so much of time, but we always returned to one another. Like Gurdeep for you, he was my everything, my entire world. We didn't spend every minute together or even every night, but he was always in my heart.'

What could I say to that? 'When is time for babies, I will have his child and I will teach her about her father, the hero,' she said.

I put my arms around her. She dabbed her eyes and whispered, 'His mother's name was Qianru. Is good name, no?'

'It is.' I kept right on holding her.

MEAR 0, DAY 18

976 KILOMETRES FROM DEVON ISLAND COLONY, MARS

I lay in the dark, breathing deeply, steeling myself for the day ahead. When I'd counted to 144, I sat up and heaved my weighted blanket off and slid the bunk door open. The sudden shock of harsh light made me flinch.

Most of the other bunks were still closed. The berth beneath mine was empty, though, implying Brian was up already. With only six of us on this trip, the little hab felt spacious. It was basically a tent-trailer – compressing down to three and a half metres wide when not in use.

Brian was making breakfast. 'Morning, sunshine,' he called out. A groan emerged from one of the bunks.

In the early days on Mars – almost a mear ago – we'd lived in a similar dome for a month while we built Saca.

Brian dropped his voice to a whisper. 'I'm about to brew up a pot of joe. You want?' I gave him the thumbs up before heading into the bathroom.

Once we collected the *Poke*'s crew, this place would feel like one of those comedy snakes crammed into a jar.

Squeezing a glob of toothpaste onto my toothbrush, I squinted into the grubby mirror. I'd grown up on a planet with more than seven billion people on it. How was I struggling to cope with just 149 people on the whole of Mars?

Space. The key was space.

The fifth dome should be open by the time we returned – so at least the *Poke* crew wouldn't add to the congestion. But we'd still be jammed in like beans in a tin.

I put my toothbrush back in its case and plaited my hair. Then I washed my hands again. Dressed and clean-ish, I emerged from the bathroom and sat down at the table. Brian set a breakfast bar and a mug of coffee in front of me. I nodded my thanks. He had an odd smile as he watched me eat. I weighed up whether to ask him what was up, but before I decided, the door opened again.

Lisa and Caoimhe entered the dome. Caoimhe took the first turn in the bathroom, so Lisa dropped into the seat next to me. 'You two ready for the big day?'

Once we were all at the table, Lisa ran through the plan again. We varied the pairings up a bit, but the default was Lisa and Sun in one rover, Mehmet and Caoimhe in the second, and Brian and me in the third. We were sticking with that formation for today.

'We're seventy-two kilometres away, so we should get to the landing site by thirteen hundred. Brian made packed lunches for us,' Lisa said. 'We'll eat as we drive. As soon as we get there, we'll start loading up the rovers and the trailers. We'll leave the *Poke* where it is for now.'

After breakfast, we headed out, leaving the mobile phone mast in place. We'd leave it standing until the ship and its contents had been collected. For now, it would facilitate real-time comms with Devon Island.

I always listened to music as I drove. A lot of people said

they preferred silence, but I found that perplexing; it was never silent. If I turned off the music, I'd hear the engine, the oxygen scrubber, the lights, Brian's and my breathing, plus a high-pitched droning I've never found the source of. It was all distracting and annoying – the music was mine. And it drowned out the other sounds.

We'd been driving for two hours when Brian turned the music down. 'What's wrong?' I asked. 'Did I miss something?' I snatched a glance at him before turning my focus back to the ground ahead of us. He was looking at me with that same funny smile again.

I could feel him watching me. 'Nothing's wrong. I just thought we could talk a mite.'

'Why?' *What was happening?*

'What? Whadja mean why? 'Cause we're … friends, ain't we?'

The pause before *friends* troubled me. 'Are you trying to say you don't want to be friends with me anymore?'

Brian barked a weird laugh. 'What? No, I just... Well, I thought... That is, I had hoped…' His voice trailed off again. I waited for him to continue, but he didn't.

'You're going to have to finish one of those sentences, eventually. I'm not a mind reader.'

'No, you really ain't. Look, forget it. I didn't mean nothing. Just drive.' He reached out and cranked the volume on the heavy metal up even louder than it had been before.

I wondered what I had done to upset him. *Had I been rude? I rarely know when I'm saying or doing something impolite, but I'm aware it's a thing.*

I thought back to the night before in the little temporary shelter. We were getting on so well – sitting together on my bunk, watching *Serenity* for the whatevereth time.

*Huh*. I supposed whatever I did to upset him must've happened this morning.

He'd either tell me eventually or he wouldn't. He'd get over it … or not. It had taken me a long time to learn I couldn't make anyone be my friend.

I focused on the ochre and sepia landscape ahead of me. The route was littered with rocks: from pebbles to boulders larger than the rover. The ground sloped up gently away to my left.

'The composition of the regolith out here might differ from what we have near the colony. I should collect some samples. I might be able to come up with new recipes for my printers, suitable for different applications.'

Brian didn't reply.

———

1,048 KILOMETRES FROM DEVON ISLAND COLONY, MARS

We arrived at the so-called lost crew right on schedule. The small dome habitat was attached to the ship. Unlike the *Chawla*, the *Poke* had at least landed the right way up. The bullet-like shape stood tall against the salmon-coloured sky. It was so much bigger than the ship the advance crew had travelled in.

We suited up, decompressed the rovers, and headed out for the short walk to the dome. Their two rovers were parked near the airlock, looking like bubble-topped vans. A couple of people were hooking trailers up to the back of them. They waved at us and Brian headed straight over to join them.

Sun gazed up at the ship. 'My gosh. It's gotta be, what? Fifty storeys high?'

Caoimhe's laugh was almost a cackle. 'No, I think it's about ten. Maybe fifteen.'

We had two-storey buildings in the domes back at Devon Island. And the domes themselves were taller than that, obviously. I remember visiting my dad's office in Canary Wharf in London. Thirty- and forty-storey buildings were commonplace. They didn't exist on Mars.

'I've not seen anything that tall in – well, since I left Earth. Not since Singapore,' said Sun.

'You saw the ships,' Caoimhe said. 'Both *Bondar* and *Cristoforetti* landed upright.'

Even in her encounter suit, Sun's shrug was visible. 'Had other things on my mind, didn't I?'

We headed towards the dome's main airlock – all of us except Brian. Only two of us could fit inside it at a time. Lisa and Mehmet went first. A minute later, Sun and I entered. Once the airlock pressurised, we opened the inner door and stepped into the dome. I raised the visor on my helmet – and bit back the urge to vomit.

The smell was overwhelming – unimaginable. A mix of unwashed bodies, faeces, ammonia, rotting food, sick. I resisted my body's involuntary reactions. My mouth and eyes watered and sweat streamed down my face. Bile rose in my throat.

I slammed my visor back down to seal out the offensive odours. Closing my eyes, I breathed the clean, beautiful air in my suit. After a few seconds I noticed laughter. 'Oh, come on, Devon! We're not that bad,' came a slightly muffled voice.

I looked up to see my old friend Rosa watching me. I almost didn't recognise her. Her hair used to be long and bright pink – now she had about a decimetre of black roots above faded purple. And it wasn't just Rosa gawping;

everyone was looking at me. Lisa responded before I could form words. 'I'm afraid I'm going to have to differ. I'm with Devon on this one.' She still had her visor open, though. So did both Sun and Mehmet.

At my back, I felt the crank wheel of the door moving and I shuffled out of the way. Caoimhe and a tiny, copper-skinned woman emerged from the airlock. *Charlie?* As they raised their visors, Caoimhe's hand shot up to cover her mouth and nose. Charlie blinked rapidly.

Tom appeared from behind a partition wall with a massive grin bisecting his face. 'Yeah, well, you'd stink too if you'd been trapped in a tent with more than three dozen people for three weeks.' His sand-coloured beard was even scragglier than it had been when I'd last seen him on Earth.

'Hey, buddy, it's good to finally see you again.' Lisa grabbed him and pulled him into a hug. Behind his back I saw her pull a face and blink away tears.

'It's been way too long,' he replied, thumping her on the back. She lifted him off the ground with the ferocity of her hug, spinning him round. 'Man, are we glad to see you,' he added when she set him back down. 'So, what do you make of what we've done with the place?'

The habitat we were in was only meant to be used by such a large group for a day or two. A group of eight or fewer could stay in it indefinitely – not comfortably, but they'd survive.

'With thirty-eight bodies sharing the dome's resources, it's been stretched to capacity,' Tom continued. 'The ship's hygiene facilities weren't designed for use in gravity, so we've set up an extra couple of toilets and a second shower.' He gestured towards the area where we'd had our bunks in the original dome.

Yet again, I felt grateful that I hadn't had to travel on

such a tightly packed ship – and even more glad I'd not been trapped in a tiny stinking dome with so many people for my first two weeks on Mars. *Would I have survived that?*

'Right, everyone. We've got rovers to pack and a habitat to disassemble. Let's get a move on,' Lisa bellowed.

———

As we were packing up, Rosa wandered over to me with the cheeky grin I remembered. 'Hey, you. Long time no see.' Her Mexican accent still brought me joy. No reason for it, I just liked the way she spoke.

'Rosa. How are you doing?'

'I'm good. Looking forward to settling into my new home.' Between us, we picked up an enormous crate and walked it to the airlock. When we set it down, she said, 'I really want to hug you – but I'm aware of how much I stink, so I won't.'

I laughed. 'Believe me, if you didn't stink, I'd accept your hug.'

She clasped her hand to her chest. 'Devon Thornback, you do me an honour. And I'm going to hold you to that – eventually.'

We headed back to the entrance to the ship, where people had been stacking stuff to be loaded into the rovers. When we lifted the next crate, she said, 'Is it all right if I claim shotgun? I mean, I assume you're driving.'

'I'd be glad for the company.' I could use a friend – especially if Brian was done with me.

*28 KILOMETRES FROM DEVON ISLAND COLONY, MARS*

Clicking my mic, I faced the group trudging through the sand almost a hundred metres back. 'You could at least try to keep up.'

Charlie swore at me over the headset.

I climbed over a boulder. Someone cartwheeled past me, moving back towards the lollygaggers.

'Lis, is that you, showing off for us?'

Laughing, I clicked my mic again. 'No, that is the illustrious Dr Sun Gao – physician, water reclamation specialist, amateur gymnast, and all around badass – demonstrating how you all should be able to move on Mars.' I turned myself to face Sun. 'However, as the only extant physician in this stretch of Martian wilderness, please refrain from injuring yourself. These strays we've collected are still rebuilding their muscle mass after a year of zero-G. They can barely carry themselves at this point – I'm not sure they're up to the challenge of carrying you to the nearest rover.'

Sun lifted a gloved hand to her helmeted head in a vague attempt at a salute. 'Yes, ma'am.'

I turned back towards the stragglers. 'How you holding up, Chris?' I'd been wary when the young veterinarian had announced she'd be joining those of us who were hoofing it. The rovers were crammed full of tired, cranky people. With the added demand on the vehicles and air-scrubbers, we could only manage around sixty kilometres a day – so a lot of us took the opportunity to get out and walk.

We staggered the rovers – three drove ahead to set up the next base and two trailed behind the walkers in case of trouble.

The tallest figure in the distant group raised an arm as her voice reached me in my helmet. 'Ka pai, I'll be right. I can handle the jandal – don't you worry.'

Somehow, I'd expected our plague survivor to be tiny. Instead, I'd been introduced to a brick wall of a woman. Chris was easily the tallest of the *Poke* crew – probably about 185 centimetres.

'How come no one asks if I'm all right?'

They were closer now, maybe thirty metres – so I could see the second tallest figure respond to this by elbowing the shortest. 'Come on, Chuck. Everyone knows you can do it.'

Once upon a time, such a statement from Tom would have been intended to goad Charlie into a reaction. But their relationship had shifted on the voyage to Mars. Instead of swearing at him, she punched him in the side – but even from this distance, I could see it was in jest.

'I've walked almost a thousand kilometres – what have the pair of you done?' Chris wasn't exaggerating. Over the past twenty-six days, she and I had walked most of the way – more than any of the others. She was one tough cookie.

The stragglers caught up with Sun and me. I turned back around and resumed walking.

'How much further?' Charlie's voice sounded tired – or maybe just bored.

The plan had been for us all to ride in the rovers the whole way – but that had gone out the window a few hours into the first day of the return journey. In hindsight, we should have known that being trapped in an overcrowded rover wouldn't be ideal.

I popped the display panel on my chest open and checked the satnav. We'd passed the last phone masts this morning – we were close enough now to link directly to the colony.

Sun was quicker to speak, though. 'Just another six kilometres to the final stop before we make it home.'

'Home.' Inside her helmet, Chris shook her head. 'I can't believe I made it.' She linked arms with Charlie and Tom and pulled them forwards. 'Come on. Lunch is waiting.'

---

*22 KILOMETRES FROM DEVON ISLAND COLONY, MARS*

Less than an hour later, we climbed into the rover that served as the airlock. Once it had pressurised, we climbed out the other side into the little habitat. We removed our suits and hung them up before washing our hands and wiping our exposed skin down. Martian dust contained perchlorate. Repeated exposure caused all kinds of nasty effects on the human body.

As we finished, the door slid open again and another group climbed through.

'—and make sure you clean up after yourselves this time. I ain't your mother – if I was, I'd box your ears for treating this colony like a trash pile.' Brian stomped into the nearest bathroom, still in his suit.

Everyone was on edge, but that felt over the top. Brian was normally laidback and easy to get along with. The mood all around had been jubilant when we met up with the *Poke* crew, but it had been falling for four weeks.

I headed to the kitchen area where Devon and Rosa were creating a mountain of sandwiches. 'How you two getting on? That frozen bread is holding up pretty well, eh?'

Rosa turned to face me, a slab of bread in one hand, the other engaged in smearing … something across it. 'This is the last of it. Today's lunch won't win any prizes for quantity or quality. I hope they've got dinner ready for us when we arrive – we'll be starving.'

'They should do. Say, Devon… Any idea what's eating Brian? He's downright cantankerous.'

Without turning around, she replied, 'No, he's been that way since the day we got to the *Poke*. I tried talking to him, but he shut me down.'

'Huh, thanks. I'll have a word with him.' He'd be fine. We needed to get home, have a decent night's sleep, and put this difficult journey behind us. We were all in a heightened state of emotion now. Once we got into the rhythm of our new lives, people's moods would settle.

---

## 1.2 KILOMETRES FROM DEVON ISLAND COLONY, MARS

When I stabbed a button on the dashboard, a professional photo of Davy from her politician days appeared on screen. She picked up on the third ring, replacing the pic with a live image of her as she appeared today: her nut-brown hair falling to her shoulders and her brown eyes bright. 'Lisa? Hey, you almost here?'

'Yeah, I'm just calling to say we're about five minutes out.'

'Sweet. Well, we're ready for you. See you in a bit.'

For almost four weeks, we'd been getting up before dawn to get back on the road. We'd pack everything up, walk or drive for two and a half hours, and then – batteries depleted – we'd stop. The solar panels got hauled out, the tent-trailer was set up, the bodies were fed and rested. Early evening, we repeated the cycle.

This time, everyone was keen to get moving again as soon as the batteries had enough charge – we'd been rolling by fifteen-thirty. And for this final leg of our journey, everyone squeezed into the rovers. We all wanted to get home and be done with this endless road trip.

No sooner had I clicked to end the call, than the colony's comms towers came into view on the horizon. And a moment after that—

'Look,' Charlie shouted – and then within seconds the rover was filled with chaos, like a school bus full of kids excited to be arriving at their destination.

———

Several minutes later, I eased the rover from the large airlock into the garage and we all climbed out. We followed the routine of removing our outer suits, washing our hands, and taking off our shoes. At long last, I opened the door and led my passengers outside into Sacagawea dome.

'Welcome home!' A crowd of smiling people all spoke at once. A ball of energy topped with short blond curls barrelled towards us. Georgie grabbed Tom in a massive bear hug. After a second, she pulled away, waving her hands in front of her face and wrinkling her nose. 'On second thought, maybe I'm not actually that pleased to see you. Wow!'

As the colonists ran and hugged and cried and laughed, Georgie's reaction was repeated all across the open space.

Tom laughed and pulled Georgie back to himself. She hugged him again briefly before leaning away. 'Oh, mate, let's get you to the showers.'

'You offering to join me?'

She punched him playfully on the arm.

'Hey,' I said. 'You think you lot smelled any better when you arrived? Because let me assure you, you most definitely did not.'

'Touché.' Georgie tilted her head.

Tom held his arms up in surrender. 'Right, where you taking us?'

Georgie raised her voice to get everyone's attention: 'Welcome to Devon Island. My name is Georgie and I'll be your tour guide for this evening. If you'll follow me, please, right this way. Our first stop will be the much-needed showers in Hatshepsut dome, which is more commonly called Hatsh. We've arranged for plenty of water, soap, fresh towels, and clean togs for all.'

'Lead on, Macduff,' said Tom, as he fell into step behind her.

I clapped him on the arm. 'I'll see you at dinner, eh?'

Tom nodded. He and the rest of the people from my rover followed as Georgie led them away. 'Once you're all feeling – and smelling – better, I'll take you on a tour of our beautiful city, before finishing up with an evening of the finest dining and entertainment Mars has to offer...' I missed the rest of what she said as she and her entourage moved off into the distance.

I went to my flat in Seacole, grabbed a towel and a change of clothes, then headed out for a shower.

———

Feeling refreshed, I joined the celebrations not long afterwards. They'd arranged things so that each course was served in a different dome, with staggered start times. It was a way of respecting the maximum capacity per dome while also getting the new joiners to explore their home.

In Hatsh, I chatted with Helen and Davy as we sampled two different soups, hummus, a leafy salad, and coleslaw. We moved on to Seacole, where we gorged ourselves on saag aloo, shiro, and ratatouille. Georgie joined us as we headed to Thunderdome for dessert.

As we entered the kitchen, I spied Brian talking to a tall blonde. His eyes sparkled as they shared a laugh. I was glad he'd shaken off the foul mood from earlier.

'Ooh, halva,' Georgie exclaimed. I followed her to the buffet table, excited to enjoy some freshly made sweets.

With our plates and cups full, we headed outside. Through the windows in the dome, the sky was clear and spangled with stars. Someone had set up lawn chairs in a grassy area. We sat in silence for a bit – before I spied a familiar figure wheeling in our direction.

Georgie bounced up from her seat and took her wife by the hand. 'You made it. I'm so glad you came. Here, squeeze in next to me.'

I waited for Gurdeep to get settled before I spoke. 'You look well. How are you doing?' The scar on her temple was barely visible in the dim evening light.

She nodded slowly. 'Getting there.'

Charlie held her spoon aloft. 'You know, I get the whole veggie thing. I do. Meat isn't efficient. But I miss it. This soup is nice. It's fine. But you know what I mean?' She dropped her spoon.

'Hey, if you're not going to eat that—' Rosa reached out towards Charlie's dinner.

With a laugh, Charlie slapped her hand away. 'I am going to eat it! I'm just nostalgic.'

Davy swallowed a mouthful of stew and shrugged. 'I don't mind. I grew up in a province where people think a meal is incomplete without meat, but I'm not fussed.'

Ash held a hand towards Charlie. 'Oh, how grand would this soup be with just a teensy bit of bacon?'

Frankie stabbed a spoon in Ash's direction. 'How can you even think of eating a defenceless pig? Honestly, I've not eaten meat in— Hang on, what do we call a decade now?'

It was a ridiculous conversation.

'I'll tell you, though,' Charlie said as she stabbed a carrot stick into a bowl of bean dip. 'Four-flipping-hundred-and-twenty-one bastarding days of nothing but those tasteless packet meals and protein bars. If I'd had to go one more day without proper food, I would've eaten my fellow prisoners.' She grabbed Rosa's arm and pretended to bite into it.

Rosa pulled back. 'Isn't it funny how all our gossip seems to revolve around food and drink?'

Ash's water glass slipped from her hand as she replied, 'We could talk about who's getting off with whom, if you'd rather?' Frankie leaned back in her chair and grabbed a cloth from the sink, which she tossed to Ash. 'Ta. You'll never guess who I saw Tom shifting the other night.'

Davy scrunched up her mouth. 'Shifting? What even is that?'

'You know, snogging.' Ash's face flushed slightly.

'I can't imagine anything less interesting than what consenting adults get up to behind closed doors,' I said.

Charlie giggled. 'Or in front of them.'

Rosa swiped Charlie's almost-empty bowl from her and licked the remaining soup from it. 'I know, right? I mean, I hope everyone's having satisfactory amounts of mind-blowing sex. But I don't see why I'm supposed to care.'

'Now, if they want me to watch…' Charlie added with a dimpled grin. Rosa threw a carrot stick at her. Charlie caught it out of the air and bit into it.

Frankie leaned back and crossed her arms – brushing against me as she did so. 'I don't want to watch. I'll partici-pate, but if you want a passive audience, get someone else.'

'Hmm… Maybe an interactive audience.' Rosa wiggled her eyebrows. 'You know, judging the players' performance and offering suggestions for improvement. I could do that.'

'But food, though… I could gossip about who's eating what for the rest of my days,' said Frankie.

The door opened and Caoimhe and Korri joined us. 'Oi, sis,' said Caoimhe. 'Shove down.' Frankie budged even closer to me.

Korri grabbed a couple bowls from the cupboard and cutlery from the drawer before he sat down next to his wife. He reached for the tureen at the end of the table, leaning across me for a moment as he did so. 'Let me guess: potato soup again?'

Charlie held up a serving bowl. 'Wuh tessy bee dup,' she replied with her mouth full.

'Bean dip, ooh!' He leaned over me and grabbed a plate full of carrot sticks to dig into the dip. 'Exciting!'

I'd kept up with the conversation to that point, but it descended into a sea of overlapping voices and physical jostling and food scents. It was too much.

*Had the oxygen scrubbers stopped working?* I pulled out my phone and checked the colony's status app. *Nope, just my brain.*

Trying not to draw attention to myself, I bolted from the kitchen. Above the windows in the dome, the sky was inky. I thought about going to my flat, to sit in my bunk in the dark – but then I remembered the three other people I was sharing with. Sometimes one of them brought someone home. Even if no one was in, it would still be full of their stuff and their scents.

I walked without paying attention to where I was going. As I ambled through the orchard, I heard squealing. I spotted two shapes in the twilight: a man and a woman.

'Oh, hey, Devon.' Brian's voice. The woman must be Katya, the tall blonde roboticist. She moved into the light, clutching him possessively. He flinched and ran a hand behind his neck. 'We were just, um…' He stepped away from her, but she pulled him back to herself.

'Never mind. Sorry. I didn't mean to intrude – I'll go elsewhere,' I replied, scurrying away. I wasn't in the right state of mind for conversation.

———

'Devon!'

*Where could I be alone?* I tapped my lip six times as I sped across the ground. After a few moments, I found myself at an airlock, unsure which one it was. I pushed it open, stepped inside, then turned to pull the door shut behind me – only someone was standing in the doorway.

'Hey,' Davy said. She stepped into the airlock with me and pulled the door shut.

Soft strips of night-time lights came on in the airlock as the motion sensors detected our presence. 'Hi.'

'Are you all right?'

I raised my hand to my head, but rather than tapping my lip, I ran my fingers through my hair. 'Yeah, I am.' Despite the words, I shook my head. 'I mean, I'm not. I will be. I need to be alone.'

'Sorry – I'll go.' Her voice was soft. Being alone with her in the semi-darkness… I don't know.

'No, no. It's fine,' I said – and it was. 'I can be alone with you here.' I hoped she understood, but I suspected she didn't. Impulsively, I reached out and touched her hand. The human contact felt like a lifeline in a way I didn't expect.

She accepted my hand. 'Here, I have an idea. You want reduced sensory input, right? Quiet, dark.'

Words wouldn't come, so I just nodded. It was never quiet or dark, but *reduced sensory input* … I liked that.

She nodded, mirroring my gesture. Still holding my hand, she led me through the airlock and out the other side. We walked along the outer edge of the dome to the next airlock. I turned to look at her. She nodded again then keyed in a code and pushed open the door. *Which airlock required a code?* We walked through the airlock and into —

'Oh!'

She grinned as we stepped out into the colony's sixth dome. They must've pressurised it today. Everything was bare. In the dim light, I could see clear across the empty space. The buildings had been delineated in brown under-floor material, which contrasted with the white rubbery pathways that wove elegantly between buildings and airlocks and gardens. The planting spaces were black and empty, waiting to be filled.

It would be ready for inhabitants within the next few days.

Davy led me to what would soon become the kitchen. We sat on the bare under-floor in the relative quiet. Once the motion sensors were satisfied, the lights dimmed and we lay on our backs in the shadows, illuminated only by the starlight pouring through the dome's windows.

Neither of us said anything – for a while. Time always confused me. It felt like ages, but maybe it was only moments. Eventually one of us said something. I wasn't sure who started it, but it felt natural. We talked about nothing and everything.

But then… 'I've read that people with autism —'

'No!' I cut her off with an accidental shout. I jerked away and the lights flickered to life.

'What? You're the one who told me you had autism.' She sat up but didn't say anything further. She touched a hand to her face.

I tried to control my breathing, taking three slow, deep

breaths before I replied. 'No, I didn't say that – because I don't *have autism*.'

She looked at me that way people sometimes did. 'But—'

*Why do I have to explain this to people?* I sighed. Why couldn't people pay more attention to their word choices? Words matter. 'I do not have autism – I'm autistic. See the difference?'

She bit her lip. 'I'm sorry, no. Those two sentences mean the same thing.'

I extended and clenched my fingers repeatedly then tapped my lip. 'Georgie and Gurdeep... They both have the gay, right? And you have the Jewishness? And what about your birth mother? You told me she was cancerous? No, because those statements are wrong. You'd never say those things. People *are* gay or ace or bi or whatever. People *are* a product of one culture or several. Some people *have* cancer or flu or, I don't know, gangrene. Being a thing is different to having a thing. Do you see?'

She furrowed her brows. 'Okay, I think I get you. But having isn't always bad, you know. You have green eyes. I have brown hair.'

'I'd still be me if I had brown eyes and green hair. If I had different clothes, I'd still be me. If I wasn't autistic, *I wouldn't be me*. I'd be somebody else.'

Davy sat still and closed her eyes. After a moment, she steepled her fingers beneath her chin and looked upwards. 'Okay, I think I get you. I'm sorry for being insensitive. And I'm glad you explained.'

I shrugged. 'I want you to understand me. It's important.'

She smiled at me.

I lay back down. 'So anyway, what were you saying?'

'What?' She leaned on one elbow and stroked my hair gingerly, like my dad used to do when I was little.

'I've read that autistic people...' I prompted her.

'Right! Yes, I read a few studies that showed *autistic people* often benefit from having an animal such as a dog or a cat to help keep them – is grounded the right word? I was just trying to learn more about you. Did you ever have a pet?'

I laughed.

Davy stopped stroking my hair. 'Did I say something wrong?'

'No, not at all. It's just I always thought I was allergic to animals. I've never been around them. Before I joined this mission, I had to be tested for all sorts of things. They said I wasn't allergic to anything, so I asked my parents about it. Turns out my mum just didn't like pets.'

We laughed together for a while and then sat in silence.

When she spoke, her voice was soft, hesitant. 'Can I ask you something?'

'Of course.'

'Thunderdome. Does it bother you?'

In the dark, I chuckled softly. 'You mean because I went to all the effort of naming the dome – and now the name has morphed into something silly?'

'I'll tell them to stop. The government, we can step in. I don't know – make an edict or maybe just a memo.'

I chuckled. 'Please don't. Yes, I was annoyed at first. For a few days. But I get it. And actually, it fits. I love seeing how language evolves in our society.'

'It really is changing, isn't it? At the pace it's transforming, I'd almost call it a linguistic revolution rather than an evolution,' she said.

'Like, look at the new dome,' I said. 'Not this one, I mean – the previous one. The *Poke* crew named it after Mary Wollstonecraft. But within a few days everyone was calling it the Craft. Everything here gets abbreviated or altered: the Scud,

Saca, myc. That's myc as in mycoprotein, not Mike, Desmond's partner. Though, I suppose that must be an abbreviation too. Even the *Aderin-Pocock* got abridged to the *Poke*.'

Davy resumed stroking my hair, brushing it behind my ears. 'The congestion gets to you, doesn't it?'

I clicked my tongue against my front teeth. 'We're all squeezed into five domes. When we – the advance crew, I mean – first landed, we focused on getting domes built. Once the rest of you were on your way, we needed the farms to be productive as fast as possible.'

'But now we're here,' she said.

'Most domes have at least thirty people living in them,' I said. 'Funny how it doesn't sound like a lot when you consider the size of the domes, but that's still three or four to a bedroom. So, yeah, I guess I'm feeling a bit agoraphobic.' I bit my lip. 'In the one sense, but very much not the other. A fear of people, not of wide open spaces.'

I screwed my face up for a sec. 'And it's not really a fear – more a sense of overstimulation, of anxiety, of being over-whelmed. Whatever you want to call it, it's definitely what I've been feeling. Tonight at dinner, I had to get out. I needed to be away from people. Away from all the noises and smells and movements and patterns associated with crowds.'

As we lay there in the dark on the floor of an unbuilt building on Mars, I decided Davy was all right.

*THE ANKH DOME, DEVON ISLAND COLONY, MARS*

'Welcome to the White Hart.'

With those words, Charlie cut the ribbon over the door of the planet's very first pub. The Ankh was our seventh and largest dome. The cluster of buildings at its core not only had a larger footprint but also stood four storeys high. It housed more than twice as many people as any of the others, freeing up much-needed space and making the whole colony seem less crowded. Plus … *pub*!

The ribbon was a bit of pomp and circumstance, but it felt like a nice touch.

Charlie opened the door and the crowd queued up to step inside. The menu was simple by Earth standards, but it still felt like a massive undertaking. Frankie had created an IPA, a ruby ale, and a cider. The hops were still Earth-grown ones – but we were working to change that. The apples, though, were 100 per cent Martian original.

Desmond and Mike had created savoury bar snacks:

spiced chickpeas, honey-roasted peanuts, and the obligatory crisps.

The pub had four up-cycled tables surrounded by mismatched chairs and upturned boxes. The riot of colours and textures delighted me. As we passed, Gurdeep ran a finger along a slab of burnt metal taken from the hull of a ship that was perched atop a blue plastic barrel with a crack running through it. Some of the chairs came from the ships.

The space felt warm and welcoming. Too warm – I unfolded my fan and waved it at myself.

Charlie was behind the bar, taking orders, filling them, and accepting payment. Soon the initial rush of patrons had drinks in hand. Bowls of nibbles occupied most of the tables. Gurdeep, Davy, and I sat at the bar, chatting with Charlie as she worked.

Gurdeep raised her glass. 'This was a brilliant idea, Charlie. I'm so proud of you.' Charlie beamed.

I hoisted my own drink and spoke loud enough to be heard around the room. 'To Charlie and the White Hart.' Dozens of people echoed my toast.

'I've come full circle,' Charlie said when the chorus had died down. 'I was a bartender when I met you four years – no, two *mears* – ago. And now I am again.'

'Bar owner,' Lisa corrected as she and Helen joined us. 'On Mars. Hardly the same.'

I tossed a few peanuts into my mouth. 'Heya.'

Charlie threw up her hands and beamed. 'I'll drink to that.' She took a sip of her beer. 'I'm so enormously grateful for the opportunity to be a part of all this. Helping write the rule book on how our society should function was a once-in-a-million-lifetimes opportunity. Best job in both worlds – but now all I want is to be a bartender again. Now, speaking of… What can I get you two?'

Once Helen and Lisa had placed their orders, I called out, 'Oh, hey.'

Charlie looked a question at me, but it was Gurdeep who replied. 'My lovely wife is about to tell you we'd like a few more bowls of those tasty nibbles.' I nodded before spooning the few remaining crispy chickpeas into my hand.

Davy set her glass down. 'Guess what day it is.'

Helen turned to Gurdeep and arched an eyebrow. 'Indeed… How'd your first day back go?'

'First *full* day,' Gurdeep corrected. She'd been balancing half days with physio and counselling sessions for two weeks now.

'I hear you went afară,' said Davy.

Gurdeep nodded in response. I struggled with conflicting emotions. On the one hand, I worried about her. On the other, I was so proud of her. After everything that had happened, I was finally getting my wife back. Obviously, she'd been here all along – but she'd withdrawn into herself. The woman I loved with every fibre of my being had spent months here but not here. A stronger new Gurdeep was emerging.

'I did. *We* did.' Gurdeep sounded tired but thrilled. 'There was a fault in one of the solar arrays.' She held her steel glass in Lisa's direction. 'So, Lisa and I went afară to fix it. It was my first time – bloody amazing it was too. Vast and empty. I stood there gazing up at the sky.' She closed her eyes for a moment. 'Wonderful.'

Helen narrowed her eyes. 'You're walking okay? No difficulties?'

'I'm learning how to walk all over again. Bloody thing is a bitch to get used to.' Gurdeep pulled up her trouser leg to show off the intricate wire cage encasing her prosthetic leg.

The titanium rods and pinions that supported her and enabled her to walk were visible inside the exostructure.

I'd been so worried about her this morning. Was she ready? Was she stable enough on her feet? Did she have sufficient physical strength? Was she mentally up to a full seven-hour day?

I needn't have let myself get so worked up. Helen had declared her physically fit. Her shrink had signed off on her return to work. Nora had gone with her, in case of any difficulty. We looked after our people – we couldn't afford to lose anyone else. Especially, though, everyone looked out for Gurdeep.

'While we were afară, Lisa was telling me about a meteorite that landed yesterday.' Gurdeep looked so passionate. This was the woman I'd fallen in love with so long ago.

'A meteorite? You didn't tell me about this at dinner,' I said.

Gurdeep shrugged. 'Slipped my mind.'

'It was phenomenal,' Lisa said. 'But without much of an atmosphere to protect the planet it's not exactly an uncommon occurrence. Devon and I were out yesterday doing our regular cleaning of the solar panels when we saw it pass overhead. It was a big one – maybe as big as one of our ships – but it wasn't close. Probably landed a few thousand kilometres away. From the solar farm, it was only just visible on the horizon.'

Davy suggested we move to a table that became vacant when its occupants took their drinks outside.

Gurdeep accepted my offered hand, allowing me to help her get into her seat – though I suspected she did so more to appease me than because she needed assistance.

As we settled in, I asked, 'What were you going to say,

Davy? About what day it is? Aside from Thursday, obviously.'

Davy waved her hands. 'Oh yes! I almost forgot. Devon reminded me earlier – today's the day we were meant to land on Mars.'

Gurdeep scrunched up her eyes – then opened them wide. 'The Hohmann transfer window.'

Davy nodded. 'If we'd stuck by the original plan, we would've left Earth a mere two hundred and fifty-nine days ago.'

We sat in silence for a few moments until Davy turned towards Helen. 'So… Any luck?'

Helen blew out her breath and pushed her hair behind her ears. She'd had it cut recently. I didn't understand how she found the energy to look so polished all the time. 'No, I was hopeful about this one, too. He was doing so well – made it to twenty-four days – the furthest yet.'

Her brows furrowed. 'The mice are thriving, though. You wouldn't guess they'd never had a mama. We're going to try inseminating one of them in a few weeks if all goes well.'

Davy's shoulders fell. 'Devon was really looking forward to a puppy.'

I touched her arm gently. 'How is she doing?'

She smiled. 'Much better, thanks. We got our own place when the Ankh opened last week. I wanted to move here' – she waved her hands in the air, a gesture I assumed indicated the dome around us – 'but she was adamant we stay in Thunderdome.' She covered her mouth with her hand and lowered her voice. 'Charlie told us weeks ago she'd be moving out. In the end, I bribed the other couple to go too.'

'You bribed them?' I pretended to be shocked that Davy would go to such lengths.

She chucked a peanut into her mouth and shrugged. 'Told them I'd help them move.'

I raised an eyebrow at her.

'Okay, fine. And I said I'd pay their first two weeks' rent,' Davy added. She waved the incident away, but I laughed. Our society accepted that housing was a human right – everyone had safe, comfortable accommodation. But that only got you a bunk in a shared flat. Those who wanted a place of their own paid extra for the privilege.

Davy raised her hands in mock surrender. 'What? We can have fully automated luxury gay space communism when we find a supply of unlimited resources – until then, we'll have to make do with partially automated queer social liberalism.'

I hoisted my mug in salute. 'Now available in all flavours of the QUILTBAG!' I put my hand on Davy's, returning to the previous topic. 'I'm sure the next embryo will take.'

Helen pinched the bridge of her nose. 'I hope you're right.'

Gurdeep was struggling to keep her eyes open. 'You had enough, babe? Ready to head home?'

Her lips parted slightly and she leaned against me. 'Do you mind?'

'Not at all. I'm pretty tired myself,' I lied. I stood up and offered her a hand. She accepted without fuss. We bade everyone goodnight and I took my wife home.

*ELSEWHERE*

I lay on my bunk, Bible in hand. The twenty-third Psalm stared up at me, but I wasn't seeing it. Around me, the crew were making crude jokes.

They weren't funny.

Their sense of humour was risqué, degrading, and demeaning. Especially Sergeant Cobb – expert mission chief and personal pain in my derrière. I tried again to focus on the pages in front of me, seeking succour from the words I'd read so many times before.

Cobb looked over at my bunk with a sneer. 'Gonna have to toughen you up if you wanna be part of the MENaCE, Seaman.'

I was already part of the MENaCE – Lord help me. No going back now, whether the sergeant liked it or not.

*Therefore, accept one another, just as Christ also accepted us to the glory of God.*

Over the past two years – in training and during the voyage – I'd repeatedly asked them not to be so crude. I'd explained why punching down was hurtful and unfunny. How would they feel if they were the butt of the joke, I'd asked them. I wanted them to see it was possible for comedy to exist without resorting to homophobia, misogyny, racism, other-phobia. At one point, I'd even tried making jokes of my own – ones that weren't based in meanness. All it had earned me was a reputation as someone who couldn't take a joke.

Exasperated, I set the Bible down on my bed. With a sigh, I hauled myself out of my bunk and left the room. I ran a hand over my close-cropped brown hair. I hated it short. Until I joined the coast guard, I'd always worn it shoulder length. I hoped I'd be able to grow it out again someday – though that seemed unlikely.

'Oh no, Cattigan's leaving,' Cobb's taunting voice followed me as I left the room. 'Do you think we said something politically incorrect?'

Raucous laughter echoed from the bunkroom as I rounded the corner into the mess, thinking to get myself another coffee.

My hopes of finding the kitchen empty were immediately dashed. Major Willis and Lieutenant Pearce looked up at me. The major leaned against the worktop. The lieutenant stood a few feet away, arms folded across his chest. I'd interrupted something. 'Hey, Cattigan,' said the lieutenant. 'Are they giving you grief again?'

Yeah, like I was going to rat on my commanding officer. This was probably a test. I bit back the sarcasm that came too easily. It wouldn't solve anything. 'Not at all, sir. Just feeling a bit crowded.'

Pearce nodded. He was tall, blond, and generically handsome. 'With sixteen of us sharing a space smaller than the house I grew up in, it's bound to happen,' he said. He shifted his weight from foot to foot – it was clear I had intruded on a private conversation between the group's leader and his second in command.

'By your leave, sir,' I said.

Major Willis nodded. 'Dismissed, Seaman.'

Growing up in Spokane I shared a bedroom with my two little siblings, so space was at a premium. When I needed to be alone, I would go and lock myself in the bathroom. I'd sit on the can for hours, reading or drawing. Sometimes just thinking. But if I tried that here, someone would chase me out after a minute or two. No, that wasn't the solution to my need for privacy.

Once we got to work on the reactor, there'd be a whole 'nother building I could retreat to – we could all retreat to.

I walked around the habitat. My stride was longer than it had been at home as my feet left the ground with each step. *Would I ever get used to this strange gravity?* It wasn't long before I'd made a circuit of the entire structure. And then I spotted it – the little greenhouse beneath the workbench.

We were growing crops. *Here*! Having lived in urban environments, I found the concept fascinating. The idea that food grew in the dirt seemed alien to me. Food came in packages. Dirt and germs were things we worked to keep food free of – they were contaminants. But they were also part of the food's story.

Because space was at such a premium, the greenhouse had been designed to fit under a double-sided workbench. It had a narrow path between the two planting spaces. I bent down and looked inside. Making a snap decision, I peeled back the clear vinyl flaps trapping the heat and moisture inside and crawled in. There was a little plastic stool in the very centre of the space. I pivoted on my left foot and sat down.

Neat rows of labels on sticks interrupted the potting soil.

Potatoes. Carrots. Radishes. Lettuce. Pots of tomato plants hung from the ceiling. The first tiny green shoots were just beginning to make an appearance.

I wasn't exactly comfortable – seated on the hard stool with my knees up under my chin, I could feel the heat of the lights mere inches from the top of my head. But it was warm and peaceful.

Satisfied with my solution, I removed my phone and headphones from the kangaroo pocket of my hoodie. It was a small sacrilege for a Catholic, but in these times of unease I returned to an old favourite. I called up a series of videos I'd saved for myself by the Sarcastic Lutheran, beginning with *Forgive Assholes*.

Closing my eyes, I let her harsh, nasal tones and soft words wash over my soul. I sat serenely for a time, long enough for the anxiety to ebb away.

I was so absorbed in the tiny world within a world I'd created for myself that I almost didn't notice the lieutenant lifting the greenhouse's flap aside and peering in.

'Cattigan,' he said.

I smashed my head into the low ceiling as I tried to stand up in a space that wasn't even four feet tall. '*Ow!* Sir,' I replied.

He smiled at me, his white teeth perfect and his brown eyes sparkling. 'At ease, Cattigan. I just wanted to see if you were okay.'

I took a deep breath, taking in the ozone-rich atmosphere and the green scents of the plant life around me. 'Yes, sir. I am. Thank you, sir.'

*ACT TWO*

MEAR 0, DAY 304

SEACOLE DOME, DEVON ISLAND COLONY, MARS

Helen texted to ask us to come to the Scud at eleven o'clock. I had a brief panic, but Davy laid a hand on mine. 'If it was anything urgent, she would've asked us to come right away.'

I had a tendency to jump straight to the worst-case scenario in my head.

The moment we arrived at the Scud, Frankie exclaimed, 'She's all cooked.'

I knew what she meant, but I still didn't like to think of anyone cooking a dog. After a brief meeting, we scrubbed up and walked into the nursery. We moved solemnly, like some sort of bizarre gloved, gowned, and masked religious procession. I watched with fascination as Helen disconnected the tubes and unsealed the bag, transferring the puppy to an incubator.

Then Frankie took over, working with her gloved arms inside the clear acrylic. I held my breath as she cleaned her off and examined her. After a few minutes, she removed her arms from the gloves and turned to face me.

Bouncing on the balls of her feet, Frankie said, 'I'm happy to pronounce her fit as a fiddle.' She waved me over before detaching the gloves from the incubator.

I stepped towards the incubator and its occupant, feeling like I was floating – a pleasant sensation, like the first few minutes of our zero-G training flights. The puppy looked so tiny and frail – like a greased tribble. I looked back over my shoulder at the others in their scrubs and gowns. 'You're sure it's okay?'

Helen stood with her shoulders back. 'It's important you bond with her. Since she has no mother, you're going to have to fill that role.'

Frankie's grin was wider than any I'd ever seen on her, smiley though she was. She squeaked as she hugged herself. 'Bare hands, please. We need her to connect with your scent.'

Davy stood in the corner of the room. She smiled at me over her phone as she recorded the birth of the very first Martian. Well, the first proper one. We had plenty of bees and worms and mice.

Every day for the past four weeks, I'd been coming to the Scud, watching her grow. It was incredible seeing her develop before my eyes. The 'womb' was a device that looked like a big zip-top bag studded with different coloured tubes running off in every direction. When I first saw her, she looked like a little prawn in a bag of goo.

At various stages, I thought I saw the beginnings of hair or paws or ears, and then within a few days, they were unmistakeable. From that tiny naked blob, she'd grown into this … this … this… She still didn't quite look like a puppy – just an amorphous ball of shiny black fur. But she was alive and healthy and I loved her.

Nervously, I peeled off my gloves and reached into the incubator. I stroked her – velvety soft – and she licked my hand. Flexing her tiny paws out, she started searching around with her mouth. She made a squeal. I stepped back. 'Oh no! Did I hurt you?'

Frankie smiled at me over the top of the incubator. 'That's a good sign. She's telling you she's hungry. Let's get a weight and then we'll get you set up to feed her. Here, take this.' She handed me a cushion.

I looked up at her. 'It's hot!'

Frankie nodded. 'It's important to keep her warm for the first few weeks. Now put her onto the pillow and bring her over here.' She moved to the other side of the room.

She motioned for me to set the puppy and her cushion down on the scale. When I had done so, she tapped a few buttons and nodded to herself before turning around to face the room again.

'Excellent. She weighs a hair over half a kilogram, which is perfect. The bitch was mostly German shepherd and the stud was a Turkish street dog. I expect she should grow to somewhere around thirty-five kilograms. Big dogs grow in stature for their first— Well, for twelve months. After that they bulk out. She should reach her adult weight in about a mear.'

Frankie motioned for me to pick her up again before continuing. 'We've got some food warming. It's a mix of colostrum we brought from Earth and specially designed formula. You've seen the videos I sent?'

Davy stepped forwards and put her arm around my waist. 'She's been watching and rewatching them in preparation for today.' I leaned back into her.

'Perfect. So you know how important it is that the formula is the right temperature?'

'Between thirty-five point zero and thirty-seven point eight degrees. And I've researched the correct amounts and the timings and how to tell when she's hungry. I'm nervous about the actual *doing* part, but I've got the theory down pat.' I looked at my new charge – she'd shifted on her cushion, exposing russet-coloured paws. Little patches of the same colour were visible on her cheeks and chest. 'Shall we give this a go, Seven?'

Frankie's brow furrowed. 'Seven?'

Looking at her, I smiled. 'It's her name.'

I nodded as I held the bottle to Seven's tiny mouth. I let a drop of the liquid fall onto her snoot. She licked it up then followed her nose to the source of the tasty goodness. Davy rested her chin on my shoulder; she must have been on her tiptoes.

'Eat up, Seven,' I instructed her. 'We need you to grow big and strong. You're the first real Martian – a symbol of new life. That means you have a responsibility to thrive, okay?' In response, she squeaked softly as she sucked her food.

Davy said, 'You've done brilliantly. Thank you so much. I'm just hoping I eventually get a chance to hold her.'

I looked up. 'I always thought I was allergic to dogs.' Davy stroked my hair.

Frankie looked at me but not in the eye. People here were good like that. 'You know how to stimulate her toileting like a mama dog would?'

I nodded and was about to demonstrate when I heard the front door open in the Scud's outer room. Footsteps approached. 'Hey, kiddo,' said a voice from the door of the room. 'Oh! Puppy's come out to say hello. How's the proud mama doing?'

'Isn't she amazing? Look at her—' I turned to show Brian my new puppy. 'Oh! What happened to your face?' Brian's left eye was swollen shut and he was leaning on Katya.

He grimaced. 'Oh nothing, nothing. It's fine. I just... You know me. I couldn't win for losing. Two left feet an' all that. Tripped over myself again. Came to see if someone could have a quick gander at my ankle.'

Katya was watching him closely as he spoke. Something about the way she touched him bugged me. It looked like the kind of *help* my mum always tried to give me after I'd first been diagnosed as autistic. Brian didn't need babying; he was a grown-arse adult.

Helen reacted with a no-nonsense approach. Still clutching my fragile parcel, I followed them down the hallway and peered around the doorway.

'Up on the table, Brian. Let me look at you.' She extended a hand to help him hop up, but Katya squeezed herself in and assisted him. Helen examined his face before turning to his ankle. 'You're a mess. How the hell did you manage this?'

'The poor guy tripped.' Katya spoke for him. 'He fell down the stairs on his way to DownBelow. I always tell him to be careful, but you know how it is. Men, am I right? Always so sure of themselves.' She pinched Brian's cheek, making him wince in surprise. 'You silly old goat.'

Helen scowled. 'Men are quite capable of travelling up and down stairs. Been doing it for thousands of mears. You've not had anything to drink, have you? Been sampling Charlie's wares?'

Brian smiled. 'It's swell stuff, ain't it? But— Ow!' He pulled a face as Helen flexed his ankle. 'No, not today.'

'Hmm. Wiggle your toes for me.'

Brian grunted with effort as his toes moved a couple of millimetres at most. Helen turned to leave the room and saw me hiding behind the door. 'Oh, Devon. It's good you're here. Ask Frankie to set up the X-ray machine. Tell her we'll need images of his face and his ankle. Looks like he's fractured his left zygomatic and his right cuboid.'

'Of course.' I turned and headed back into the office, still clutching Seven to my chest. I repeated Helen's instructions for Frankie.

I set Seven back in her incubator and sat down with Davy to watch her. Within a minute, the puppy was sound asleep. Contented breath sounds rose from inside the device.

*THE CRAFT DOME, DEVON ISLAND COLONY, MARS*

Jupiter and I were on our way to the shop when we spotted Devon pushing a pram.

'Hiya, Devon,' I said as a black nose and big russet lugs popped up. 'Hey, Seven!'

Devon smiled. 'Morning.' The wee dug wagged her tail and tried to climb out of the buggy.

I set my empty shopping crate down to say hello to the puppy properly. But Jupiter beat me to it. She tossed her basket aside and asked Devon if she could hold the puppy. Devon nodded.

'Come here, you.' Jupiter's top swung as she bent forwards, giving me a tantalising view of her cleavage. She scooped the ball of fluff into her arms. 'You are the most adorable thing that ever lived. Oh, thank you, Seven. Those are the nicest nose kisses anyone's ever given me.'

I put my arm around Jupiter's waist and leaned over her shoulder. With my other hand, I reached out to let Seven sniff me. 'What a bonnie wee lassie. You dinnae ken how big a celebrity you are, do you?' She squirmed in Jupiter's arms and then reached out and started gnawing on my finger. 'Oh my, what sharp teeth you have!'

Jupiter laughed. 'All the better to eat you with.'

'You're so fierce, like a big wolf!' I said to the puppy.

Devon looked at us with a crooked grin. 'Watch out – she doesn't have the best bladder control yet. She's just done a big wee, but you never know. Might have more left.'

Jupiter held Seven at arm's length. 'Hmm… Maybe let's not tempt fate too much.'

'Do you two mind watching her while I go in and do my shopping?' Devon asked as we played with her puppy. 'You can put her on the ground – just don't let her wander off. I won't be five minutes.'

'Surely Gurdeep will let you bring her in,' I began before recalling what Devon had just said. 'Actually, erm… I guess maybe dinnae do that until she's house trained, eh?'

The shop had started as a sort of distribution centre where colonists could collect their allotted food and supplies. And it had given Gurdeep a job she could do as she recovered. But it had quickly become more. Artists and crafters brought their wares to sell on consignment. Gurdeep had taken to the business with a natural flare. It seemed to help give her a new sense of purpose.

Devon nodded sagely. 'Good plan.'

Jupiter set the wee puppy on the ground. Seven bounded over towards me, giant paws almost tripping over huge ears. Still watching Seven, Jupiter asked, 'How've you two been coping with her at home?'

Devon's auburn hair gleamed in the weak sunlight as she moved. Or, more likely, it had caught one of the artificial lights. 'It's not been too bad. We'll start working on house training in another few weeks. For now she uses special pads for her toileting. For the first few weeks she had to be fed every two hours, so Davy and I were taking it in turns. She's eating on her own now, but we're still getting up a few times in the night.'

'Sounds like a lot of work,' I said. 'Seven's fine with us. Take as long as you need.'

Jupiter and I sat on the mossy ground playing happily with Seven while Devon browsed. After a few minutes she emerged with her wares. Glancing in her basket, I remarked, 'You really like Ife's spice mixes, eh?'

Georgie's farms struggled to keep pace with demand for variety. In a few years, we should have a diverse array of mature crops, but for now our staples were potatoes, myc, oats, rhubarb, and apples. We had leafy greens and herbs too, but anything that could add a bit of variety to our diet was in hot demand.

'They're great. Ife came over and taught me how to make a few Ethiopian dishes. I love big flavours. It's my turn to cook tonight, so I'm making the recipes she taught me.'

Gurdeep strolled out of the shop to join us. 'Devon, I forgot to mention… The dishes you and Rosa collaborated on are selling like proverbial hotcakes. I'll have a pot of money for you both at the end of the month. Everyone loves the blend of form and function.'

The colony provided every dome with basic dishes and containers, but the tableware Devon and Rosa collaborated on – mainly serving bowls and platters – were stunning centrepieces. Arts and crafts were big in our wee community.

Devon beamed. 'Thank you, I'm so glad people like them.'

The four of us chatted for a few minutes before Devon left and Gurdeep returned to her shop. When we were alone again, she threw her arms around my neck and kissed me.

'You want a puppy,' I said.

She laughed. 'Well, yes… I suppose I do. But what I was going to say was I want a baby.'

'Aye, funny you should say that,' I replied as I took her hand in mine. 'Especially as I'm the one who's going to be doing all the work – at least for the first bit.'

She kissed me again.

———

SOUVESTRE DOME, DEVON ISLAND COLONY, MARS

The next morning, I breathed deeply before opening my eyes. I reached over to touch – *huh, empty mattress*. I grabbed my phone from the shelf above the bed to see if Jupiter left me a note, but there was nothing.

She wasn't in our lavvy either. I threw some pyjamas on and stepped out the door. It was still dark enough in the dome that I could see stars afară. Enjoying the peace and quiet on the balcony, I stood outside in the air for a few moments before heading downstairs to the kitchen. I shivered in the overnight chill. This time of mear, we allowed the outside temperature to drop to twelve degrees.

A soft light emanated from the lounge windows. I found Jupiter sitting on her favourite comfy chair in the corner reading a book. Her masses of curls were constrained in a pretty floral scarf. Santosh and Ash were snuggled up together on the sofa opposite.

'Morning, you.' Jupiter smiled broadly at me. I walked over and perched myself on the side of her chair; she slid her arm around my waist and kissed my cheek.

'I wondered where you'd got to,' I said.

She shrugged. 'Couldn't sleep.' I shifted myself so I was

sitting on her lap. With a sigh, I leaned back into her, wishing we could stay like this forever.

Santosh held the teapot aloft. 'Shall I be mother?'

'Aye, please,' I replied.

'Today's the big day for you two.' It wasn't a question; everyone knew precisely what day it was. The future of the colony was riding on today. On me – well, on my body.

Taking the proffered cup from him, I said, 'Ta. It is, aye.'

'How you feeling about everything?' He topped up the other mugs.

The steam from the tea washed over my face. 'Wow, aye. I'm excited, but I'm also more nervous than I thought I would be. And I wish my mum were here with me.'

I lay my head on Jupiter's shoulder. Helen had picked me to go first partially because of my medical training, but also because she trusted me – we'd been friends for a donkey's age.

I took a sip. It was my own blend of raspberry leaves, red clover, and nettles. An old wives' fertility blend. Almost certainly pure hokum, but it made me feel like I was helping the process. Plus, it was tasty.

Ash sat up and turned towards me. 'How's it work?'

'Very similar to my own origins, I suppose. Over the past couple of months I've been poked, prodded, scanned, jabbed, and tested a million ways from Sunday. The powers that be – that is, Helen – say today's the day.'

'But what about the actual process? Sorry, I don't really know much about it.' Ash made to set her mug down on the table but missed. It bounced and rolled under the sofa, splashing the dregs of her tea everywhere.

Santosh squeezed her shoulder before running to the kitchen. Seeing them together was odd – I'd always thought he was gay. But then, how odd must it be for people to look at me and Jupiter. Two straight women, one of whom had hated and resented the other. *Do I still consider myself straight?* With a shake of my head, I decided I didn't need a label.

When Santosh returned with a towel to clean up the mess, I replied to Ash's question. 'I took a drug to halt my body's production of reproductive hormones. Then I had to take a hormone stimulator for eleven days. After the last one, we waited thirty-eight hours and then Helen collected an egg from me about a week ago.'

His lips curled back and he furrowed his brow. 'Collected … an egg. Does that mean she…' He lowered his hand.

I nodded. 'Up the hoo-haw, aye.'

Jupiter pulled her face away from me. 'Hoo-haw? Is that the medical term?'

'Aye, my love, it is. Or would you prefer fanny? Gash? Fud?' I could nae help a wry grin.

She kissed my cheek. 'Well, I love your hoo-haw. Prettiest one I've ever seen.'

I raised an eyebrow. Santosh and Ash were chuckling at us. 'Anyway.' I felt my face flush. 'To answer your question, aye, it hurt like a bastart. I mean, I dinnae remember the procedure itself, but afterwards…' I sucked air through my teeth. 'It was intense.'

'I'm sorry,' he said.

'Anyway, Helen took the egg she collected and combined it with sperm Jupiter and I chose from the database.'

Ash's eyes widened at that. 'You got to pick the da?'

I smiled. 'Of course. The process was pretty much the same as what my mum did when she had me.'

Santosh already knew this story, but it was new to Ash.

'We used my egg, so the baby's DNA will be fifty per cent drawn from mine. I think we found the perfect sperm donor.' Jupiter encircled me in her arms. 'He looked like he could be Jupiter's brother. Half German and half Ghanaian. The database lets you see pictures of the donor as a bairn.'

'Seriously?' Behind his thick glasses, Santosh's eyes were even larger than usual.

'Yep, some donors have adult pictures, though there aren't as many of those. We wanted someone who was as similar to Jupiter as we could find, so our baby will look like a mix of both of us.'

'A reasonable facsimile, shall we say,' Jupiter added with a cheeky smile.

Ash shook her head as if to clear it. 'I'm about as Irish as they come. But you're both mixed race, right?'

'We're both half white, but even in that we're different.'

Jupiter poured more tea from the insulated pot for everyone. 'My dad, obviously, was white British.' Her father, Nigel, had been the owner of the company that managed the logistics of getting us here and designing the structures we lived in. He'd been exposed to plague before we left, so Jupiter had nae been able to say goodbye in person. The last she'd heard from him had been an email shortly after we'd left Earth.

I was lucky – I still had regular contact with family back on Earth. My mum emailed me faithfully once a week. She was thrilled to bits about the prospect of becoming a grandmother – even though she'd only know my wean through photos.

Jupiter ran a hand over her headscarf. 'Mum was black British – her parents were part of what they called the *Windrush* generation. They both moved from Jamaica. He was a teenager, but my nan was just a toddler when her family emigrated.'

'And I'm half Dutch, half Korean, all Scot,' I said. 'That is, I was born and raised in Scotland. My mum is Dutch. The donor father was Korean. I met him once. Well, spoke to him. He seemed nice.'

It would have been so easy to get lost in my own thoughts at that point, but Ash still had questions. 'So, then what? You picked a donor and then what happened?'

My palms were clammy so I wiped them on my jim-jams. 'Well, the way Helen describes it, she set my eggs and this bloke's sperm up on a blind date. She says she locked them in a room together for a bit of "Netfilms and chill" to see how they'd get on. And now that the embryos have been growing for five days, she's going to pick the best one and implant it in me in' – I pulled my phone from my pocket – 'just over three hours. If any of the others look viable, she'll freeze them in case we need them later. Like, if this process does nae take.'

Ash had a big toothy grin as she reached out to touch my knee. 'That's so amazing. I'm so pleased for you both. I'll say a prayer and cross my fingers and toes and everything else this morning.'

Suddenly, the enormity of the situation overwhelmed me and I felt light-headed. We could be having a baby. Me and this big-haired, loud-mouthed, incredible woman who used to be an entitled teenager with more money than sense. I thought about how much I loved her.

What a funny old world this was!

———

*SEACOLE DOME, DEVON ISLAND COLONY, MARS*

A few hours later, I opened the front door of the Scud and shouted, 'Ye decent?'

'Absolutely never! I'm as depraved as they come,' Helen

replied. She was as nervous as I was, but – as usual – she hid it behind sarcasm.

Rizwana and Leah both stood to the side of the room. Leah nodded. Rizwana greeted us warmly. 'Morning, Nora. Jupiter. How are you both feeling? Ready for the big day?'

Jupiter squeezed my hand tightly – almost too tight – as I responded. 'We're good. Nervous but good. What's up? I dinnae expect to see you until a bit later in the process, if ye ken.' Rizwana had agreed to be my midwife.

'Helen's teaching me about the in vitro fertilisation process – it's amazing. I'd like to be able to help her out while I wait for my first patients.'

Jupiter put a hand on her hip. 'She's not used that awful "Netfilms and chill" line on you, has she?' I looked at her with confusion and bemusement. 'What? I can tell a Helen joke when I hear one.'

'Hey,' said Helen indignantly. 'My jokes are hilarious, I'll have you know. Anyone who doesn't laugh isn't welcome in my hospital. The patient's booty call isn't a necessary part of the process.'

'Haud yer wheesht, yous two nuggets. I'm fashing myself enough already. Can I mibbe request we focus on the task at hand? I need everyone to stay calm to help me get through this. Please.'

Helen and Jupiter both nodded. Rizwana led me to a chair. Part of me felt like bolting out the front door and never coming back. But only part…

Helen smiled – not unkindly. 'Let me just go finish prepping everything for you. We'll be ready in a sec. Leah, can you check her vitals, please, while I show Rizwana how to get everything ready?'

I swallowed my panic as I took my seat.

Davy clutched her coffee like it was the only thing keeping her going. I wondered what people would do once it ran out. Brian had been working on a hybrid strain that balanced productivity with 'taste' – though how anyone could talk about coffee and taste in the same sentence was beyond me. Vile, nasty swill.

She set her mug down. 'You know, when I was a member of parliament back in Canada, I represented more than a hundred thousand people.' She shook her head.

We were alone in the cabinet office meeting room. The others weren't due to join us for – I checked my watch – twenty minutes. The inner wall was dark as there was a minor dust storm afară. 'But?'

She sighed. 'Running a country is so much work – even when that country only has a hundred and forty-nine people in it, don't you think?'

'For sure. Before you arrived, I was in charge of everything on Mars from a day-to-day perspective, but I always knew if there was an issue, I could toss it up the chain – to Gurdeep and later to Gabriel. But now...' I held my hands up. 'The buck stops with us.'

'Us, indeed,' she replied. 'You and me.'

'Do you resent it? That the weight of leadership falls most often on our shoulders, I mean.' I didn't think she did, but I was curious to hear her thoughts.

Davy pursed her lips and breathed out through her nose. 'Resent it? No, not in the slightest. I'm loving it. Honestly, I think I'm just surprised at how much work it is. It's fantastic. I wouldn't change my life for anything – but sometimes I'm amazed at how utterly exhausting it is.'

I put a hand on her shoulder as I stood and went to top up my mug of rooibos. 'Need a refill?'

She handed me her mug and slumped forwards, propping her chin up on her hands. 'Cheers, you're a star.'

When I sat back down with the bevvies, I watched her for a moment. 'I'll run your campaign for you, if you want.'

Davy looked up at me. She closed her eyes then opened them again. 'My what?'

'Oh, come on. How many mears have we known each other? Four? I know you better than you think, Davina Mills.' I wagged a finger at her mercilessly.

The two of us had first met on Earth many mears before. I'd strolled into her dingy little campaign office on Bloor Street on the western fringes of downtown Toronto, sandwiched between a vegan restaurant and a real estate agent's office. I was serving military so couldn't take a visible role in the election campaign, but I wanted to help out behind the scenes. We'd been friends ever since.

'Fine, all right,' she conceded. 'I'm thinking about it. *Thinking*. I haven't decided anything.'

'Mmm hmm.'

Six months from now, we'd hold the colony's first ever election and everything would change. A new leader would be elected. For now, Gurdeep was nominal head of the provisional government, but she let us carry most of the weight. She wasn't intending to stand. Her recovery was proceeding well, but she was different now. She didn't want to be the one to make the hard choices anymore.

A thought popped into my head. 'Hey, did I tell you I've been picking up some weird signals?'

She bit her lip. 'Signals? Weird how?'

Resting my elbows on the table, I said, 'That's the thing – they're coming from Earth. And they seem like they're aimed at us.'

'Nothing weird about that,' she said. 'Devon got an email from her dad last week.'

'Yeah, sure. But these were encrypted. Still, I'm sure you're right. Probably nothing.'

'Sorry, we're not interrupting, are we?' Gurdeep appeared in the room's doorway, a curly blonde burst of hair visible behind her shoulder.

'No, not at all. Come on in.' I stood as they entered the room.

Georgie pulled a folded fan from her pocket and began waving it at herself. 'Geez. Hot in here! You two been steaming the place up?'

At the refreshment station, Gurdeep raised the water carafe. 'Cold water for you, I'm guessing.'

'Cheers, babe.'

It was Davy's turn to be chair. Once all nine members of the government plus Jupiter were present, she opened today's cabinet meeting.

Georgie spoke first, gnawing on a flapjack between sentences. For a moment it put me in mind of the old meetings we had back in the Double Star headquarters on Earth. Georgie always used to bring in a container of Gurdeep's home-baked goods to share. 'One of the compost drums filled up last week ahead of schedule. I've had to redraw the rota, which has a knock-on impact on the whole of food-ag. But we're doing okay.'

Gurdeep reported that her shop was still running out of Ife's spice blends.

Mehmet, who'd found himself serving as our head of safety, ran through a list of the week's incidents. One of the colonists had reported some clothing items had been stolen from her washing line.

He ran a hand through his hair. 'Devon caught Robin running an unregistered, unscheduled program on one of the 3D printers. I spoke to Robin about it this morning. She said —' He snorted. 'She told me she wanted buttons for some clothing she was designing. Fessed up right away when confronted. Said she didn't think using colony resources to create a few buttons was a big deal.'

I crossed my arms. 'How many did she make?'

Mehmet had a bemused grin. 'A thousand.' His words were met with a mix of laughter and incredulity. 'I know, I know.' He shook his head. 'If it had been a dozen, maybe two, I'd have been inclined to let her off with a warning. Needless to say, I charged her for the materials and use of the equipment and fined her on top of that.'

He went through another offence on his list. 'Apparently Dr Sun had a bit too much to drink at Caoimhe and Korri's party last week and broke a chair. I spoke to Charlie about it on the night and again the following day. She's agreed not to press charges as no one was injured. As long as Sun makes her a new chair and buys replacement dishes, of course. Sun is embarrassed – she feels awful about the whole thing. She's never done anything like it before, so no fines.'

Davy raised her eyebrows. 'That it?'

'One more. Domestic disturbance. Called in a few nights ago at about two in the morning. Zoe and Frankie broke up in spectacular fashion, culminating in Zoe kicking Frankie out of their shared flat.'

He pressed his lips together. 'As I arrived, Zoe was chasing Frankie down the street hurling her belongings after her screaming at her. I came around the corner and—' He clapped a fist into his open palm violently.

'Oh God, she hit her?' said Davy.

Georgie shook her head. 'Seriously, have you been living under a rock for the past two days?'

Mehmet held a hand up. 'No one hit anyone. I, however, got hit with a flying shoe as I came around the corner.'

Davy's jaw fell slack. 'Who throws a shoe?'

Mehmet shrugged. 'Zoe, I guess.'

Davy covered her laughter with a hand. 'I'm so sorry, Mehmet. Poor you.'

'Poor Frankie,' added Helen. Zoe was a great therapist, but her own personal life was a disaster.

I reported on the recent dust storms. 'Nothing like when yous landed, of course, but my team are spending extra time afară cleaning the solar panels. Still, the dust we collect in these excursions is useful. As soon as the samples are examined and sorted, Devon puts them straight to use.'

The chairs we sat on, the dishes we ate off, the walls around us, even the floor beneath our feet – were all made of Mars. Devon had done amazing things with the Martian regolith, continually experimenting with new blends and techniques.

Davy nodded at me then turned to the next person on the agenda. 'Helen?'

Helen's thin lips were downturned. 'No major health issues to report this week.' Davy looked like she was about to move the meeting on, but Helen pushed her hair behind her ears and continued. 'But there is something we need to discuss.'

She turned to Jupiter. 'I think this next bit should be noted but redacted from the public minutes.'

Jupiter bit her lip as she looked at Davy, who said, 'Tell us what you have to say, Helen. Then we can decide if any part needs to be withheld.'

Helen pinched the bridge of her nose. 'Brian was in the Scud last night with a broken wrist.' I nodded, as did a few of the others. Broken bones weren't an everyday occurrence, but nor were they unheard-of. 'He said he fell. But his X-ray tells a different story. His arm was twisted. Violently.'

She bowed her head for a moment. 'Nora told me Brian had been in a couple of months back with a broken rib. She said the bruise on his torso appeared to have been made by a boot.'

Her words were met by a collective gasp. Jupiter paused her note-taking and looked up, her brown eyes wide. It seemed Nora hadn't told her that.

For a minute no one spoke. Georgie broke the silence. 'Are you… Are you saying what I think you're saying?' She swallowed.

Helen's long brown hair fell forwards, covering her face. 'I think someone is hurting him.' There was another moment of silence.

Georgie chewed her lip. 'What do we do?' Of everyone in the room, she was the closest to Brian – his friend as well as his boss.

Faz, who'd been silent to this point, looked troubled. 'Is there anything we *can* do? He hasn't made a complaint.'

Gurdeep nodded. 'So. What do we do?'

Iulia played devil's advocate. 'Do we need to do anything? If Brian chooses not to tell us what is happening, is it our business?' Her hair had faded from its characteristic rich, purple black on the flight to Mars back to her natural medium brown, but she seemed to have found something to deepen its hue. *She didn't bring hair dye, did she? Surely not.*

Davy chewed her lower lip for a moment before responding. 'We need to strike the right balance between protecting our citizens and respecting their privacy. But if Brian's in danger, don't we have a moral imperative to act?'

Iulia looked at the diffuse light of the ceiling. 'I agree in theory, but Brian is strong, young man. He is capable to defend himself. We must allow him to do this – I think so.'

Georgie looked more and more uncomfortable as the conversation progressed. Gurdeep put a reassuring hand on her wife's arm.

I looked down at the table. 'Domestic violence isn't always about physical strength. I saw this with one of my best friends in the military. Lee was the strongest, the fittest, the fastest, the best soldier I ever worked with. An amazing person. I remember meeting his husband and thinking what a great couple they were. It was ages before I discovered the husband was kicking the crap out of him on a regular basis.'

I breathed in the steam of my tea. 'I helped Lee find the courage to move out. The husband got it into his head that Lee had left him for me and, well, it got ugly.' I looked at my hands, my short, neatly trimmed nails. 'Anyways, physical strength doesn't make a person immune to violence.'

'Wow. Thank you, Lisa.' Tom reached a hand to his neck and massaged stiff muscles. 'But the truth is, we don't know anything here. We don't want to start kink-shaming if it's consensual or if there's something else going on. Right now what we know is that he has unexplained injuries that may – *may* – have been caused deliberately. The fact they're a couple isn't proof she's guilty.'

Hmm, that was an interesting point.

Mehmet folded his arms. 'Exactly. Violence is a public offence – but we don't know that's what's happening. If...' He shook his hand. '*If* Katya is hurting Brian, we need to understand why he doesn't think he can leave and help him feel enabled to remove himself from danger. He's our first priority. Later, once we've found a resolution that works for Brian, we can look at what to do about Katya. But those are big ifs.'

Faz sighed. 'I know we agreed that there would be circumstances in which we might have to break doctor-patient confidentiality and this is clearly one of those situations, but I don't like it.'

She pressed her fingertips to her forehead. 'I've been handling Katya's counselling sessions, but I don't know Brian well. For her part, I'm inclined to take the accusation seriously. She's—' She smoothed her hijab with dextrous fingers. 'She's interesting. On the surface, Katya's well adapted, genial, charismatic, intelligent. But she can also be manipulative. She was abused as a child and from what I can gather, no one believed her when she tried to raise the alarm.'

*Yikes.* I hadn't known that.

Faz pursed her lips. 'I'll have a quiet word with Brian's counsellor to see if he's said anything that might be relevant. But I can say with certainty that if Brian had ever given her any indication that he was being abused, she absolutely would have spoken to me about it.'

'Brian is still...' Georgie said. 'Well, he's still in love –' her eyes flitted briefly to Davy before she continued '– with someone else. Not consciously, I mean. I doubt he even admits it to himself. But it may be that he thinks he's – I don't know – settling or not worthy or that he doesn't have options. He's my friend. I'll speak to him.' A lone tear glistened on Georgie's cheek.

Faz reached out a hand towards Georgie but didn't touch her. 'Please be careful. If we spook him, he may feel like we're ganging up on him. If he's vulnerable, we don't want to put him on the back foot.'

Georgie beat the air with her fan, blowing a breeze I could feel clear across the room. She said, 'I will.'

*THE ANKH DOME, DEVON ISLAND COLONY, MARS*

Rosa and I were enjoying an afternoon off, sitting in the White Hart. I thought back to the day we'd met, in London at interviews for top-secret jobs. And now, here we were. An asexual autistic physicist and a polyamorous lesbian plumber. On Mars.

When we'd met, Rosa had bright pink hair. Nowadays she used vegetable dyes to add colour, but they didn't last long. Her wavy black hair had a Bride-of-Frankenstein streak, faded to a pale, peachy-pink. Sitting together on the pub's new sofa, we appeared to be a similar height – though if we stood up, I'd tower over her.

Now that I was living with Davy, Rosa and I were rarely able to spend much time together.

We were the only customers in the pub, so Charlie stood behind the sofa, leaning over Rosa's head. Charlie toyed with Rosa's hair as they discussed the possibility of holding another open mic night. Seven, now almost twelve months old and weighing thirty kilograms, was playing with her toy by my feet. Her muscles rippled beneath black and sable fur as she moved.

I was trying to read my book but not really succeeding. Mary Robinette Kowal's *The Fated Sky* was an alternative history novel about a team of astronauts en route to Mars. And here I sat, re-reading the words of a story I'd already read twice before – and lived once. I wondered absently if the author had ever expected people to read her work on the very planet she described.

Still, it was nice just to be sitting there in the calm and relative quiet. It was dust storm season, so the room was dim – the lights turned low and no window screen displays.

It had been about fifteen months since Charlie first opened the pub. In that time, she'd worked hard to improve the atmosphere – to make it comfortable, homey. The whole colony had helped make it happen. Handwoven placemats. Original artwork on the walls. Beautiful stoneware dishes. I loved the way it had come together.

When we finished our juice, Charlie walked with me to the bar to get another round. As she handed over the drinks, the door sprang open and Santosh burst in.

He clapped. 'It's happened!' Seven, still basically a puppy, viewed this as an invitation to play. She got up and ran circles around him, barking happily. Charlie, Rosa, and I all looked at him. I had no idea what he might be referring to.

'Ash had an appointment to get her stitches removed from when she cut her hand, so I walked with her to the Scud. It was quite a scene – Nora had the baby!' Far from his normal reserved self, he balled his fists and flapped them – almost like an autistic stim.

Charlie and Rosa joined him in celebration. All three held one another's hands and waltzed around the pub. Seven followed them, playfully nipping at their heels. I was pleased for the colony and for the future of humanity but saw no reason to dance.

After a few minutes, the three collapsed into a happy heap on the sofa opposite me. 'This calls for a round of something special while you tell us the details,' Charlie exclaimed. She jumped up and ran to the bar, returning about a minute later with a teapot and four little stoneware cups.

'This is a little something I'm trying out. It's based on my nana's recipe for salabat – Filipino ginger tea with lemon. I was so excited to finally get a lemon to work with.' There was a hothouse in Thunderdome where Georgie's team were growing a few exotic trees: lemon, banana, coffee, avocados. Brian had got them started – and the crops were beginning to trickle out, though it would be a long time before such produce became commonplace.

'I hope you like it,' Charlie said as she poured. When she finished, she leaned back, stretching her arm out across Rosa's shoulders. 'So, come on, Santosh. Out with it!'

'Oh, yes, right. Apparently Nora went into labour this morning, just after breakfast. Jupiter called the midwife and then they set out for the Scud. They expected her labour to last a lot longer than it did, but baby wasn't for waiting.' The steam from the tea fogged up his glasses, which he took off and wiped on his shirt. 'Both mum and baby are doing well and resting up. I met Jupiter in the waiting room, she was pacing. Poor girl's beside herself, trying to figure out what she should be doing, only there isn't anything for her to do just now.'

Rosa set her mug down and smacked her lips. 'Do they have a name picked out?'

'Amos. He's got the most amazing head of curly black hair you can imagine.'

The three of them oohed and awwed the way adults so often do when the topic of conversation turns to babies.

And then Santosh whispered, 'I think we're going to go next.'

Silence descended on the pub as we processed that. After what felt like an age, Charlie said, 'You and Ash? You're going to try for a baby?' Santosh smiled shyly as he nodded.

Both Rosa and Charlie squealed their congratulations. I couldn't understand why they were making like it was a big deal. It was logical. Everyone knew that was the idea; if everything worked out well for Nora and her baby, then a whole load of people would try to conceive. Davy and I were making plans too.

Rosa took a sip of her tea then leaned back into the sofa. She chuckled to herself. 'Did you ever imagine, like, say, five mears ago, that you'd be in a relationship with a *woman* and starting a family?'

Santosh looked down at his shoes before taking a deep breath. He set his empty mug down. 'As a matter of fact, yes.'

Charlie's jaw hung slack.

Santosh closed his eyes for a moment. 'I came out to my mum when I was twenty-three. Part of me had always known I was gay, but...' He shrugged. 'I was a shy kid – never dated until I left home. At uni in Cardiff I met a guy. We had a short relationship, which confirmed things in my mind. The summer after my master's degree, I gathered my courage and sat my mum down in the kitchen of our little two-bed terrace in Swansea. I poured my heart out to her, raw and real.'

His left hand shot up to cover his mouth. 'It was the hardest thing I'd ever done – took all my strength. By the time I finished, I was struggling to breathe.'

He stopped speaking and peered into his empty mug.

Charlie put her arm around him and rubbed his back gently. 'What did she say?'

'Nothing. She said…' He waved his hands helplessly. 'She stood up and started making dinner, just like always. No acknowledgement, nothing. Just…' He shook his head again. 'I begged her to speak to me. Without looking at me, she told me to go tell Madhu dinner was almost ready. That was it – conversation over.'

Rosa reached out and touched his knee. He took her hand and held it for a moment. 'The next day an auntie came over for coffee with her daughter. The day after, it was a different auntie with a different daughter. And then another. And another.' He hugged himself. 'Eventually, there was this woman, Lakshmi. We got told in no uncertain terms that our families were losing patience with us.'

Santosh bent forwards in the sofa, his chest pressed to his knees. 'I met Lakshmi for coffee in Cardiff city centre. I cursed myself for my inability to stand up to my family on the walk there. By the time I arrived, I was in a foul mood. The first thing Lakshmi asked me when she sat down at the table was what I had done to earn my family's ire. I looked her dead in the eye and told her I was gay. She burst out laughing.' A chuckle escaped him at that memory. 'I was annoyed with her rudeness, but through gasps of laughter she admitted she was a lesbian.'

Rosa's cheeks dimpled. 'Of course she was!'

Santosh nodded. 'We talked and laughed and had a really good time. It was freeing, just being myself with a woman. No pressure, no expectations, no pretensions. At the end of the *date*, we hatched a plan. We agreed to continue the arrangement in order to get our families off our backs. It worked out beautifully – we were able to use one another as an excuse whenever we had actual dates. Occasionally we met up for coffee or dinner or just to swap stories. I liked her.'

He gazed at the pub's inner wall, its display screens dark. 'We maintained the pretence for six months, but one day she texted me to say she couldn't keep living a lie. Even if her parents never spoke to her again, she had to be true to herself. She'd met someone and —' His shoulders fell. 'I don't know what ever became of her.'

He sighed heavily. 'I moved to Edinburgh, got a job working for Nigel, and met Gurdeep and Georgie. They were like a second set of parents to me. When they offered me the chance to come to Mars, it wasn't a hard choice. Even though I don't really have the opportunity to live the life I'd hoped for, at least people here love and accept me for who I am.'

Charlie put her arm around him and hugged him to herself. He leaned against her as he finished his tale. 'I mean, sure, I'm one of just eight men on the entire planet – and maybe none of them are looking for a relationship with a man. But at least I have the chance to help build a world where future generations never have to make the choices I did.'

He ran a hand through his hair. 'Ash knows, obviously. We became friends when she first joined the mission. It didn't develop into anything more until about twelve months ago. I do love her, which surprised me. That was something I didn't expect, but I do. Mostly it's just companionship, but we both have needs. It doesn't change who I am – I still see myself as gay rather than bi, but I suppose there's a degree of fluidity in all of us.'

Rosa leaned across Charlie and took Santosh's hand again. 'I had a very similar conversation with my family. Well, no, not similar. There was a lot more screaming and swearing and melodrama than your story had. But the outcome was the same in that I moved away and never looked back.' She shook her head.

A crooked grin spread across Charlie's face. 'So you're saying no one on Mars...' She formed a circle with one hand and repeatedly stabbed it with the middle finger of her other hand. Santosh shrugged. He looked at his feet again, but this time there was a grin on his face.

'Davy has sex with Mehmet,' I said. Everyone turned to look at me. Charlie opened her mouth to speak but then closed it.

'Neither of them ever lets on. They don't think I know. I don't mind, though. Mehmet gives her something I can't. I'm happy she has someone' – I shrugged – 'to fulfil her needs. I'm just grateful she comes home to me.'

Santosh looked at me. It was clear he didn't understand why I was telling him this. 'What I mean is, I don't think Ash begrudges you any gratification you seek elsewhere. She might not want to think about it, but she loves you. Ash wants you to be happy and she knows she can't give you everything you need. I don't think she would resent it.'

Reaching out a hand in my direction, he smiled broadly. 'Thank you, Devon. That means so much to me.'

*HATSH DOME, DEVON ISLAND COLONY, MARS*

'What are you thinking?' I stroked Georgie's soft curls as we lay in bed. She'd shaved her head the day we left Earth, but now, a mear and a half later, her hair reached her chin. I'd always worn my hair short, but I'd been letting it grow too. My priorities had shifted. Neat appearances didn't seem as important as they once had.

'I'm worried about Brian,' she said.

'I know, love. I know.' I wished I could take her fears away, resolve the situation.

Brian continued to deny there was a problem. Georgie had tried to speak to him about it half a dozen times. At first, he'd laughed her off, told her she was imagining it. Four months ago, he got angry. He refused to speak to her for a month.

As a government, I felt like we should have been able to solve the issue. *But how?* Brian refused to admit there was a problem. When Mehmet tried to have a quiet word with him, he completely cut him out of his life. And as for Katya… She was convincing. Maybe we *were* mistaken. Brian hadn't been back to the Scud since his broken wrist had healed, so there was that at least.

And now we could have a much bigger problem on our hands. There was an abundance of good cause to be worried.

Georgie twisted in my arms and looked up at me. 'What about you, babe? You wondering how you'll adjust to not being in charge?'

I laughed. 'Not really, no. Davy and Lisa have carried the weight of leadership for the past mear. I haven't been in charge of anything since we left Earth.' My name was listed as the head of the provisional government, but the entire colony recognised that for the fiction it was. But no one else was ready to declare themselves ruler without an election. And I had been the mission leader until the day we launched from Earth.

Georgie made a non-committal sound.

We remained cuddled up a bit longer, enjoying the peace and the soft light filtering in through the frosted window. Eventually, though, we had to get up and face the world. I moved pretty well on my prosthetic leg, but stairs were another matter, so I was grateful we had the rare luxury of a ground-floor unit.

Most of the colony's homes were on the upper floor, above the communal spaces, but Mehmet had made sure we had a few accessible units. Once upon a time, I'd questioned why that was necessary.

I held the kitchen door open for Georgie then followed her. Nineteen people shared this kitchen, so we staggered mealtimes. We were part of the second breakfast shift. Some of the first-shifters were still gathered in the lounge area, lingering with their tea or just killing time before they started work. A couple left as we entered.

'Morning all,' called Georgie cheerily as we walked in. I nodded a greeting. Georgie washed her hands then sat down at the table for a natter.

Korri was standing at the hob, stirring. 'Morning, mate.' I clapped him on the shoulder as I peered around him. 'Ooh, an omelette!' No eggs, of course, but the polenta mix had an eggy sort of texture.

'Morning. With mushrooms and spinach, just how you like it.' We were getting near the end of our Earth-grown polenta mix, but the fields in our domes were inching us closer to true self-sufficiency.

'You're the best,' I said, reaching into the cutlery drawer. I got to work setting the table as Caoimhe, Korri's wife, placed a pot of tea and a bowl of fresh fruit onto the table.

———

Once we'd eaten and cleared up, it was time to get to work. I planned to open the shop for a few hours before the final meeting of our provisional government. Georgie joined me for the walk. I smiled at the increase in temperature as we emerged from the airlock into Seacole.

Georgie, though, pulled out a battered rainbow fan and waved it at herself as we strolled the path to the east airlock. There weren't many people out and about this morning.

As we walked, I marvelled as always at the fecund nature of our colony. I wasn't even meant to be here to see it at all – this miracle our team had created. A green oasis on a red desert planet. The bright white of the pathways had long since faded to a grey-brown. On our left, the clustered buildings in the centre of the dome stood covered in green moss, which helped to filter our air. On the right, the trees in the dome's orchards stood well apart from one another, leaving them plenty of room for growth. The ground extended into DownBelow to provide space for the roots.

Georgie's eyes darted here and there as we walked. While I thought the greenery was perfect, she'd be making notes of plants that needed pruning or watering, crops that were ready to harvest. As we reached the airlock to the Craft, at last we came upon a group of people – I'd started to think the domes had been abandoned overnight.

As the path ahead curved, my shop came into sight – and along with it, a crowd. *What on Earth are they all doing here?*

And then it became clear as Rosa's velvety contralto voice rang out. Within seconds, other voices joined hers. The words brought tears to my eyes.

*For She's a Jolly Good Fellow.*

Almost half the colony appeared to be gathered in front of the shop. That couldn't be true – though it certainly looked it. Our automated controls wouldn't allow us to have more than forty per cent of our people in any one dome at a time. The sensors in the airlocks counted the number of people in and out and alerted us if any one dome was at capacity.

I felt an arm around my shoulder. Georgie was beside me, kissing my cheek. As she withdrew her lips, she whispered, 'Smile or they'll think you're not pleased.' I did as she said, but I was baffled.

'What? I don't —' I reached out a hand to wipe my cheek. 'What's this all about?'

Nora stepped forwards. 'I think it's called an unauthorised gathering,' she said with a laugh. 'Everyone wanted to thank ye for your service over the past however long it is. We've got speeches and gifts.'

'Whatever for?'

Desmond raised his arms wide like an old-school gospel preacher. 'To show our appreciation for all you've done, Gurdeep. If not for you, we wouldn't be here today. This colony, I mean. It's because of you. You made it happen. We are here' – he lifted his hands above his head – 'to say thank you.' He began clapping. Soon they all were.

Without Georgie's arms around me, supporting me, I'd probably have collapsed into a heap. I felt such a jumble of conflicted emotions.

Georgie, prepared as she always was, handed me her phone. In big letters at the top of the screen was a message to me: 'Read these words out.' So I did, because I had no idea what else to do.

'Er, apparently, my gorgeous wife has prepared a short speech for me. Including the words I just read. And these ones too.' I turned to face her and struggled not to laugh through the unshed tears as I made a show of rolling my eyes. I looked at the crowd again. 'But seriously, I'd like to turn your thanks around and give it back to you. All of you. I am so pleased and honoured to have been your leader. I'm beyond delighted with the way this colony has risen to every challenge life has thrown at us.'

I swallowed and nearly lost my place, but I kept going. 'To take a group of ragtag hippies and ask them to pull together to create a whole new nation is the tallest of orders – and it is you who have achieved that. We, many of us, have nothing in common with our neighbours but the desire to build a better society. Through blood—' I faltered then, but Georgie rubbed my arm, infusing me with her strength. 'Through blood, sweat, and tears – using mud, dirt, and our own shit – we have built this land. Long may it continue.' I handed Georgie back her phone and raised my fist. 'To Devon Island,' I roared.

'To Devon Island,' echoed the crowd.

Brian, Devon, and Habi stepped forwards – though I noticed Katya's eagle eyes watched Brian's every move.

'We wanted to get you something that would be useful to you but that would serve as a symbol of the incredibly diverse array of talents, skills, and personalities that have made Devon Island a success,' said Devon. 'It was you who brought us all together and you who've held us together so many times and in so many ways. We wanted to give something back to show you how much we appreciate you. Just about everyone in the colony contributed to this gift in one way or another.'

I looked around, expecting to see someone carrying something – actually, I didn't know what to expect – but no one appeared to be holding anything that looked like a gift. Then I spotted Georgie unlocking the door.

Still in a daze, I stepped into the shop. My shop. A whole new counter had appeared overnight – and there, sitting atop it, was a shiny new espresso machine. Next to it, there were beautiful hand-crafted cups and what had to be twenty kilograms of coffee.

I stood for a minute, mouth agape. And then I examined everything, looked at all the different facets of this wonderful present. So many people had contributed to it – they must have been planning it for months. I'd never been a crier and I didn't want to change that now, but this was testing me to my limits.

And as Devon had said, so many people had taken part: printing the parts for the machine, plumbing it in, carving the handles, growing and roasting the beans. So much work had gone into this. *How did they keep all this from me?*

Something occurred to me. 'Brian, as fantastic as this whole set-up is, you can't keep pace with demand.' Up to now, coffee had been extremely rare. Earth-grown coffee was such a scarce commodity we only brought it out for special occasions now. Martian-grown beans existed, but they were still rare. Or so I thought.

Brian smiled at the floor. 'Well, now, truth be told, I been busy as a one-legged man at an ass-kicking convention.' He grimaced and apologised profusely. 'Um. Sorry. I'm sorry. That's just a figure of speech. I didn't mean nothing by it.'

I re-balanced my weight onto my prosthesis and smiled. Putting a hand on his shoulder, I said, 'It's fine. No offence taken.'

'Anyhoo, I was fixing to create a faster-growing, higher-yield hybrid species coffee tree. It's just come into season. It's maybe not the finest-tasting bean that ever was, but it's better than a poke in the eye with a sharp stick. And there's plenty of it. Well, more 'an none.'

When Brian finished, Georgie cupped her hands to her face and shouted, 'If you'll excuse us now, we need to put this fine machine to work. I, for one, haven't had a decent cup of coffee in months and it's high time we rectified that situation.'

I saluted my wife. 'Yes, ma'am.' Several of us set to work grinding, brewing, steaming, pouring, and handing out beverages. I had made coffee at home many times, but I'd never done it professionally. And it turned out everything I knew was wrong – or so Davy said as she showed me the right grind and how much coffee to weigh out for each espresso.

'I worked as a barista when I was in university,' she said. 'Just one of my many careers.' As she showed me the proper way to do things, she told me about the coffee shop she had worked at.

'And this was in Toronto? No, Montreal?'

She shook her head. 'Nope, though I have lived in both those places. This was in Edmonton.'

'You lived in London?'

'What? No, in Canada.' She looked as confused as I felt. 'I did my undergrad at the University of Alberta, where I grew up. Starting from the summer before university, I worked in a small coffee shop chain. Transcend, it was called. They took their coffee seriously – had their own roastery and everything.' She paused. 'Ours is in DownBelow, in case you're wondering how you missed it. Our roastery, I mean.'

'Ah. I had wondered.'

Davy turned out to be quick and efficient at making coffee and a brilliant teacher to boot. It wasn't long before everyone who wanted one had a cup of damn fine coffee. At long last, Davy and I sat down on the mossy ground outside the shop to enjoy a few free minutes. Seven joined us.

'I hope you win,' I told Davy as I stroked Seven's soft fur. 'And not just because, well ... you know.' Tomorrow would mark the beginning of a whole new era in our colony's history. 'We've done all we can to ensure a bright future.'

Anyone in the colony was eligible to stand for election – so long as they could persuade six people to support their bid. Davy wanted to give it a shot, but none of the others did. Most of us wanted to continue in the cabinet but not as prime minister. A couple of contenders from the community submitted their applications as well.

'Your support for adding more domes is a vote winner, I think. I hope.'

She cocked her head to the side. 'You don't think people

will be tempted by the promise of a reduction in mandatory working hours?'

I shifted my weight from one buttock to the other. 'How the hell would that even work? It's just not a feasible plan.'

We sat in silence for a minute. I swallowed the last of my coffee and asked, 'What are we going to do if Katya wins?'

'Pray.'

MEAR 1, DAY 3

*THUNDERDOME, DEVON ISLAND COLONY, MARS*

We'd constructed this hideout on the roof of our flat ourselves – a sort of grown-up treehouse. At my feet, Seven uncurled herself, covering her face with her paws before relaxing again. She wagged her tail twice then fell asleep.

The roofs were designed to be used. I'd built the little bench and table. Davy really got into the whole gardening thing. Her plants had the space brimming with life. The scents, dry herbal ones and sweet flowery notes, were almost – but not quite – overpowering.

That fine line was key to my enjoyment of this garden. A few months back, she'd grown something with a powerful odour. I'd been unable to articulate what was bothering me. As soon as she'd worked out what was wrong, she'd given the plant away. I watched her work now, checking and pruning things, and marvelled at how skilled she was at anticipating my needs. I tried to do the same for her.

She knelt over the pots, examining each one closely, occasionally plucking a leaf with her fingers or removing a tool from her belt. Her tongue poked out the side of her mouth. She'd let me plait her hair this morning – the tip of the walnut-coloured hair rope poked out under her chin.

'I still can't get over it,' she said.

*Uh-oh, had I missed something?* 'Sorry, what's that?'

She put the plant she'd been holding back down on its shelf and sat back on her heels. 'Ugh, I'm still dwelling on the election.'

'But you won? I get to tell people my partner's the prime minister.'

Davy grinned lopsidedly. 'People? What people? Everyone on the planet knows me.'

I shrugged. 'You never know. We might get, like, invaded. And if they try to hurt me, I can say, "Oh no, please don't. My girlfriend's the prime minister. She can negotiate."'

Davy struggled to stop laughing – and ended up snorting. 'Invaded by whom?'

I picked up my water bottle and took a drink. 'Dunno. Vikings, maybe?'

She hauled herself to her feet and walked the two steps to where I sat with my back against the dome's central column. She gave me a funny look as she sat down next to me on the bench. Seven stood up when Davy did then lay down again with a huff.

'I love you, but you're a nut.'

'Thank you,' I replied. I wasn't good at those words. They were too heavy – but she knew I felt the same. 'I find you acceptable.'

She chuckled. We sat without talking, staring up at the dome's roof. It was peaceful out here.

'I did win the election, didn't I? I really am the prime minister. This is real.'

I nodded. 'You did and it is.' I ran a finger along the edge of her hairline. 'So, what are you dwelling on? Specifically, I mean.'

She breathed in and out before replying. 'Seventy-seven people voted for me.'

'That's more than half the colony,' I said.

'Yeah, it's just...' I felt her forehead muscles tense beneath my fingers. 'And fifty-one people voted for Katya.'

I could never put my finger on why I didn't like Katya. But I didn't get why Davy didn't like her. She had no reason to resent her that I could see – unless she was jealous. *Could that be it?*

'You don't understand why so many people voted for Katya,' I prompted. In the days leading up to the election, Davy had chewed her fingernails until they bled.

Davy chuckled. 'Oh, no. That I get. Katya's popular. She's pretty and smart, fun to be around. She's smooth. People will always vote for someone like that. No, what I can't figure out is the twenty-one people who didn't vote at all.'

The results had been announced at midnight, as soon as the electronic polls had closed. A lot of people waited up. I wouldn't have bothered, but Davy was a walking ball of stress that night, pacing our little flat.

'Almost fifteen per cent of our population didn't bother to vote. That's what I can't get my head around. I mean, sure, we had a much higher turnout rate than most Earth elections. But how can anyone not care who's in charge?'

I couldn't explain it either, so I didn't try. If someone didn't like the candidates presented, surely they had a moral obligation to stand against them or to pick the least-worst option.

'Katya came to see me today. She's still campaigning for the right to attend cabinet meetings – arguing that it's undemocratic to exclude her when a third of the population put their faith in her. To be honest, she's right. I'm all for proportional representation – it seems wrong to exclude her. But –'

I waited for her to continue. 'But what?'

The muscles of her jaw clenched. 'Nothing, never mind. Democracy relies on opposition – otherwise it's just tyranny of the majority.'

'We do have opposition.' She didn't need me to remind her of how the system she designed worked. But this was her way of dealing with things. 'You publish your cabinet meeting minutes and then there's a meeting wherein anyone in the colony can challenge you.'

Davy wrung her hands. 'Scrutiny, transparency, the right to challenge – it all sounds so good on paper. But there are things we can't –' She stood up and paced the small space.

I went to her. Racking my brain for something that would comfort her, make her feel better, I put my arm around her. 'Hey, it's okay.'

She looked up at me then reached her hand up to cover mine. 'It will be.' She took a deep breath then shifted to face me. 'All change ahead, eh?'

'All change. And even more coming.' Looking up at the stars beyond the dome, I tapped my lip. I'd asked the next question quite a few times already, but it was such a big thing I felt like I needed to ask again. 'Speaking of … are you certain about all this?'

She smiled at me. 'I would never have offered if I wasn't.'

'People do, though,' I said. 'They make offers out of politeness rather than out of an actual desire to do things. I can't tell the difference.'

'Let's get married,' she blurted.

'Why?' *Why? Is that really the best I could come up with?* For once, I cursed my own mental inability to behave like a normal person.

She raised her hands to cover her face and bowed her head. 'I'm sorry. I didn't mean to say it like that. I've been thinking it for a while' – *Had she?* – 'but I could never find the right words or the right time.'

The question overwhelmed me. I watched her while I tried to process my own thoughts and kick my brain into gear. My mind was stuck.

She looked up again, shifted one hand behind her neck. 'Once upon a time I would've taken that as a rejection or even mockery. But the better I know you, the more I see this is how you process the world. I can see it in your eyes now, as you stand there, taking it all in, assimilating everything.'

She put her hands on my shoulders and smiled. In my head I thanked her for not touching my face – her hands were still coated in potting soil. 'Because I love you. You're my best friend. You're the most amazing person I've ever known. My everything. I want us to be a family. I want to celebrate our love and commitment publicly with our friends.'

I put my arms around her waist and smiled back. 'Okay, let's do it.'

———

*THE ANKH DOME, DEVON ISLAND COLONY, MARS*

Three days later we gathered in the community centre. In a room that was designed for twenty-four, I counted forty-two who'd gathered to hear Helen speak. There would be a second and a third session later in the week for others.

Nora stood next to Helen at the front of the room with the baby in a sling. In the front row, I clung to Davy's hand.

Helen tried to speak, but there was so much noise in the room that no one heard her. Gurdeep stood up and whistled. The chatter stopped abruptly.

'Um, thank you, Gurdeep,' Helen said. 'And thank you to everyone who's joined us for tonight's session. As you can see…' She held up a hand towards Nora and the baby. 'Amos is healthy and happy and growing like a weed. He'll need jabs of the same cocktail we all take to maintain normal bone mass, but he's growing like we hoped he would.' She tucked her hair behind her ears. 'And that means it's time for more babies.'

The original idea was that each colonist would produce at least one child at some point – whether they were pregnant themself or someone else had their baby. And it seemed people were keen to get on with things.

Helen clicked a few buttons on her tablet, casting a presentation onto the screen behind her. In neat bullet points, it outlined the next steps. 'Each of you who choose to will be given a drug to halt your internal hormone production. Basically, you're going to let me drive the bus. We'll schedule appointments, three patients per week. I don't want you all busting your loads simultaneously, which is why we're staggering the start times.'

The Q&A session afterwards was an autistic nightmare. Everyone had questions, which they all tried to ask at once. Even once Helen asked them to quiet down until it was their turn, people seemed intent on chatting. Donor sperm. Donor eggs. Number of embryos. Failure rates. The words and voices overlapped until I couldn't make any sense of it.

The number of embryos, though… I knew the answer to that question. For most people it would be one at a time.

Multiple embryos could mean multiple births – and that would only be allowed if there was good reason for it. Such as the prime minister being one of the oldest surviving colonists. Davy had turned thirty-seven just before she left Earth. It took them one Earth year to get to Mars, so by now she'd be just about twenty mears old.

When I first joined this mission, I glossed over the baby bit in my mind. But the thought of being pregnant horrified me. I counted myself lucky that Davy was willing to have both our kids.

As our reproductive health expert, Helen had to sign off on any multiple-embryo procedures. And she'd agreed to allow us to try for a pregnancy using two embryos: one from each of our eggs.

At the end of the session, everyone who was ready to go for it was assigned a random number to determine when they would start their treatment.

Minutes later, those who'd signed up received texts with their lottery numbers. Davy turned her phone to me – with a big three on the face. Her treatments would begin this week. If everything went well, we could end up having one or even two of the oldest children on Mars.

MEAR 1, DAY 244

*THUNDERDOME, DEVON ISLAND COLONY, MARS*

As I was heading home after a day of cleaning the solar array, someone called out, 'Hey, Deputy Prime Minister! Why, you're always as busy as a hound in flea season.'

A grin spread across my face. 'Hi, Brian.' I grabbed him in a bear hug. 'I feel like I've not seen you in ages.' I nodded to the woman at his side. 'Georgie.'

'Hey, Lisa. Brian and I just finished work. He's joining me at the White Hart for a drink. Care to come with?'

Before I could reply, Brian added, 'Put on your sitting britches, Lis. Let's chaw the rag a bit for old time's sake.' With his over-the-top turns of phrase, he seemed like his old self again. I hoped this was a good sign.

'Sure, why not?' Though the original eight of us had once been close, I'd barely spent any time with Brian since the rest of the colonists had arrived more than a mear ago.

We chatted amiably as we walked from dome to dome.

As we stepped out of the airlock into Antalya, I smiled at the warmth, but Georgie whipped a fan out of her pocket and began furiously slapping the air with it. 'I swear my hair gets bigger the moment I walk into this dome – and keeps getting bigger the longer I'm in here.' With her free hand she grabbed a fistful of blond curls to emphasise her words.

Davy's new building works had been a smashing success. We'd had three new domes since the election, providing much-needed space for people to spread out. And they all had tropical climes, which brought warm-weather crops out of the greenhouses into the open air under the domes.

Charlie had moved her pub into larger premises in Antalya a few months back. Before we stepped in, I took a moment on my own to enjoy the feel of the daylight lamps shining down on me. I squinted in the dimmer light as I stepped inside. We all washed our hands before heading to the bar.

Brian rubbed his hands together. 'Right, first round's on me. What can I get y'all?'

I assumed Georgie would have juice or water, so I was surprised when she asked him to get her a pint of ale.

My shoulders fell. 'Oh no! I'm sorry.'

She leaned back against the bar and crossed her arms. 'Didn't take. It'll happen when the time is right.'

I squeezed her shoulder. 'It will. Still, I'm sorry. C'mon, let's grab a spot.' We moved towards a secluded table in the corner of the pub.

Georgie picked a seat and dropped into it. 'It's why I was able to persuade Brian to come out.' She shrugged. 'At least Gurdeep had better luck.'

Brian arrived with our drinks after a minute, with Charlie trailing behind him. Charlie made straight for Georgie, her hands behind her back. 'Heya. I guessed your news based on your drink order, so I've brought you two things.'

Georgie smiled sadly. 'Go on, then – what have you got?'

Her eyes widened as Charlie whipped a bowl of chips out from behind her back. 'First off, there's this.' She set the potatoes down on the table and Georgie immediately grabbed a handful.

She popped one into her mouth and asked, 'Wossa secka fung?'

'The second thing is a hug,' Charlie replied, stretching her arms wide. Georgie crammed another load of potatoes into her mouth as she embraced the younger woman.

A couple other early customers walked in and Charlie returned to her post at the bar.

'So, what were those trees with the big-ass leaves out front?' My two botanist friends looked at each other and then at me. 'What? I don't know!'

'Lisa, you been living in an agrarian society for more 'an two mears and you're telling me you ain't figured out what a banana tree looks like yet?'

Georgie's expression told me she shared Brian's low opinion of my gardening knowledge.

'Hey!' I stabbed the air between us with a potato spear. 'I do my shifts in the garden like everybody else. You point me at a plant and tell me what to do to it. Doesn't mean anyone tells me what it is. Besides, I've not had any shifts in the tropical domes yet. You lot keep them all for the … um…'

Georgie smirked as she tossed the last French fry into her mouth. 'The people whose thumbs aren't entirely black?'

'Yeah, okay,' I conceded. 'Fair point.'

'We got a rating system in food-ag. Everybody in the colony has to work in the gardens, but not everyone brings the same—' Brian waved his hands in the air, like he was searching for the right word to finish that sentence. 'Not all y'all have the same level of skill. Some o' y'all been raised on concrete. Folk get graded from professional down on through "keep away from the orchids", if you see what I mean.'

'You're saying you give me the easy jobs? Is that what you mean? 'Cause let me tell you, Bri.' I finished my apple juice and set my empty glass back on the table. 'I don't recall—'

Georgie threw her head back and roared with laughter as Brian waggled a finger at me. 'Easy? Aw hell, no. We ain't give you the easy jobs – we give you the ones you can't mess up.'

Georgie gathered our empty glasses and headed to the bar. 'Cheers, Georgie,' I called as she walked away. 'So that's why I keep getting the gross tasks.' He nodded. 'How am I just finding out about this now? Well, come on – out with it... Who else is a black-thumb? Devon, obviously. Maybe Ash? Girl can't look at a thing without injuring herself on it. She'd find a way to break her arm brushing her teeth if it were possible.'

'Ash, yes – for exactly the reasons you listed. Devon, no. She's solidly middle of the pack.'

'Oh, come on!' I slammed my hands down on the table in mock indignity.

'Devon hates gardening, but at least she can follow a set of instructions. You plucked up all my celery – including the roots!'

I shrugged. 'Like those even look like food! I thought they were weeds.'

'And you once served up sautéed rhubarb greens! Made us sick for days! It's lucky we didn't eat more 'an a few bites.'

'I thought it was the chard you told me to take! And anyways, that was ages ago – before the other colonists arrived.' I rested my elbows on the table. 'And I apologised.'

Brian glared at me until he couldn't hold it any longer and started giggling.

I leaned back into the cushioned seat and crossed my arms. 'Yeah, well, I'd like to see you re-wire a busted tele-coms array.'

'Touché,' he replied when he'd caught his breath.

Georgie returned with the next round of drinks. Once she had sat back down, we all touched glasses. 'Bananas, eh?' Up to now they'd only been grown in the hothouses, so there'd only been a few each season. We all bickered over them like Earth-folks clambering for the last remaining game console on Christmas Eve.

'There'll be more 'an you can shake a stick at a few months from now,' Brian said. 'They'll be commonplace by next year.'

Paxton came in after we'd been there for about an hour, showing off a new hairstyle. 'Didn't Katya do a great job? You found yourself a great woman there, Bri. Gotta admit I might be jealous if I didn't have a great woman of my own.'

I cringed at the mention of Katya's name but tried not to show it. Georgie's eyelid twitched. The hairdo was too retro for my tastes, but Paxton seemed happy.

'Hey, Lis.' Brian was chewing on his tongue like he was deep in thought.

'Yeah?'

'How'd that wind project of yours come out? Any luck?'

I forced air out between my lips noisily. 'Ugh. I knew you were going to ask about that. It is feasible. But the wind turbines would have to be enormous to give us the kind of output we'd need. And the wind speeds—' I waved the words away. 'It wouldn't bridge the power gap. Sorry.'

Georgie put a reassuring hand on my arm. 'I know there's

probably a reason you've not tried it – but what about natural gas?'

My eyebrows narrowed as I studied her. 'Where would we get fossil fuels?'

Georgie tilted her head to the side but didn't say anything.

Brian's jaw fell slack and he stabbed an accusing finger in her direction. 'You thought natural gas meant bottom burps!'

Georgie made several quick shakes of her head. 'What? No!'

Brian and I glanced at one another. 'Sure, of course not,' I said. Her fair skin was pinking up, so I decided to let her off the hook. 'Actually, humans do produce a fair bit of methane and we have looked at how we could extract it from the air.'

'You what?' Brian lifted his hands. 'And?'

'Sorry, buddy,' I said. 'No such luck. Not enough of it to make it a viable option. And seriously, bottom burps? What are you – five?'

'You tried to power the colony with our farts and I'm the one who's a child!' Brian looked at his phone, his whole demeanour changing as he did so. 'Aw, geez. I didn't know it was so late. I better get going.'

Georgie made a face. 'Late? It's not even seven.'

Brian's face darkened. 'Katya worries if I'm not home at a decent time.'

'Decent,' I spat as Georgie's words overlapped mine. 'Oh, she worries, does she?'

Brian raised his hands in a defensive gesture. 'Whatever you might think, she really does worry. That's how love works,' he said. 'Look, don't treat me like a kid. I don't need your pity and I don't need your preaching.' With that, he turned and stormed out the door.

————

*ANTALYA DOME, DEVON ISLAND COLONY, MARS*

Much later that night, after Georgie had gone home to her pregnant wife, I sat with Mehmet at the tables outside the pub. His black hair was getting long again – curling over the tops of his ears. But he was clean-shaven. We enjoyed a quiet drink in the open air under the dome. I had plans to open a radio station and recording studio and I needed his help with the acoustics. Our homes and other buildings provided pretty good sound insulation, but not enough for what I had in mind. Suddenly his phone made a shrill, horrible noise. 'What the hell? That's the emergency tone. Amos once accidentally—' His voice cut off as he pulled the device out of his pocket and saw Brian's photo on screen. He clicked the button. 'Brian?'

As Mehmet answered the call, the screen went dark. I didn't think there was a picture at first, but a richer shade of darkness was spreading across the display. *Where is he? What's happening?* My mind was working on overdrive trying to process what I was seeing and hearing.

'You worthless piece of dirt! Brian, you are so far beneath me I can't even see you. Do you think you deserve me? You deserve nothing.' Katya's disembodied voice shook with uncontrolled fury.

I couldn't believe anyone would speak to a living human being that way. As my hand reached for the airlock, I realised I'd been running across the dome from the moment Mehmet had answered the call. He leapt into the airlock after me. We crossed the distance to the Ankh in two steps.

From the phone in Mehmet's hand, Katya continued screaming. 'You think you can leave me while you're out partying with your slut friends? Just because she's a fat ugly dyke, you think you can do whatever you want with her? Georgie doesn't love you, Brian. No one can love you. I'm the only one capable of loving someone so completely—' She switched to Ukrainian as she continued her diatribe. Mehmet and I crossed the Ankh faster than I would have thought either one of us could move. In between her words we could hear tiny, helpless cries.

As we crossed the final airlock, the one that would take us to their flat in Turing, Katya shouted, 'Who are you trying to call? No one cares about you, you worthless sack of garbage.' Suddenly light spread across the display on Mehmet's phone. Then it went dead.

We arrived at the balcony outside the flats to find a small group of people gathered. Andrea shook his head. 'Something is wrong. I've been trying to get through to you. We've never heard it like this. We've heard them fighting once or twice, but this is different.' For sound to travel between the flats, it had to be roaring. Zoe shook her head helplessly.

I nodded and called Helen. She answered the phone with a flippant joke. 'Helen, it's Brian. Get your kit to Turing now. Bring the ambulance.'

She dropped the attitude straight away. I heard a door slam. 'On my way.' She cut the line.

Mehmet knocked on Brian and Katya's door, softly at first but then harder. After a minute he was pounding on the door and shouting, 'Brian, are you okay, mate?'

I opened my mouth to tell him to use the override just as Katya pulled the door open, clutching her bathrobe at her throat. 'It's so good of you to come. Brian's had an accident,' she said, biting her lower lip. She followed us into the bedroom, where she sat down on the dishevelled bed and crossed her legs primly.

Brian lay on the floor next to the bed. He was convulsing, limbs pointing in unnatural directions. Katya's haircutting shears were sticking out of him, just above his collarbone. I ran to him, kneeling by his head. *So much blood.* I turned to Mehmet. 'I've got him. You deal with her.' Mehmet nodded then led her out the door.

I looked around for something to stem the flow of blood.

Suddenly Helen was crouching by my side. 'His airway's full of blood.' I helped her turn Brian into the recovery position. From behind me, a hand on my arm pulled me aside. Without turning from her work, Helen said, 'Nora. Good, you're here. Lisa, move.'

I nodded to no one in particular as I left the flat. I assigned someone to guard the front door. 'No one in unless Helen asks for them. I mean it. No one.' She nodded.

I walked along the balcony, circling the upper flats, making a note of everyone who was gathered there. They were witnesses – they'd need to be interviewed. My hands were covered in blood. I hadn't seen this much blood since … since … another life on another planet.

Helen and Nora emerged from the flat carrying Brian on a stretcher. 'Everyone get back,' I ordered, creating a cordon using only the sound of my voice.

I helped carry Brian down the stairs to where the cycle-powered ambulance waited. We loaded him onto the trailer. Helen climbed in after him and Nora got into the driver's seat and pedalled off without another word. Helen straddled Brian, elbow deep in the bloody mess.

I wasn't sure what I was meant to be doing, so I gathered up the witnesses and began herding them towards Mehmet's office back in the Craft.

———

*THE ANKH DOME, DEVON ISLAND COLONY, MARS*

Four days later, we gathered in the chapel. Rizwana led us through a beautiful service. As Brian was Christian, it would normally have been Georgie's task. *Normally? What a strange thing to think about a murder. When is murder ever normal?*

Georgie was in no fit state to lead anything. I thought about a different funeral, when Georgie had been Gurdeep's rock. Now their roles were reversed, as Georgie sat with blank, dead eyes through the ceremony.

Several of us spoke, telling stories of Brian's life. Devon told an anecdote from not long after we had landed. We'd taken turns preparing meals for one another as a group. 'It was Brian's first turn to cook. As he was dishing up, he said, "Y'all are mighty brave trying my grub."' Devon's British accent shone through, but the cadence and words were pure Brian.

In my mind I went back to that day, sitting around the table in Saca. He regaled us with tales of his childhood cooking adventures. Devon relayed a culinary delight he'd described that night. 'He said he used to make package macaroni and cheese for his younger siblings. He'd boil the pasta until most of the water was absorbed then mix the cheese powder right into the mushy, water-logged pasta.'

We'd all been crying with laughter by the time he set bowls of what turned out to be a tasty three-bean chilli in front of us.

After the service, we all walked together to Antalya dome. As the procession passed an external airlock, we saw the doors had been emblazoned with graffiti: 'Insert Killer Katya here'.

Over the past four days, the letters KKMD had begun appearing on surfaces throughout the colony. *Killer Katya must die*. For every one we cleaned off or plastered over, two more appeared. I saw the letters carved into the bark of a tree in Thunderdome. Georgie had been furious – not at the sentiment, but at the desecration of a living tree.

Bodies were returned to the ground with as much efficiency as we could manage. But each colonist had a plan for how they wanted people to bid them farewell.

'Brian's funeral plan,' Rizwana said, 'called for the Christian ceremony we just finished. He also requested that the tree planted in his remains be a coffee tree – which is why we're gathered here rather than the cemetery in Thunderdome. He wrote, "I want to keep fuelling the colony long after I'm gone."'

Brian's words collided with the anguish and impotent frustration and raw pain of the moment, overwhelming me. A startled laugh escaped my lips. Beside me, Georgie snorted. Habi made a strangled sort of noise. Even Devon, who'd stood silently sobbing in Davy's arms all day, joined in. Within seconds, the entire group was laughing uncontrollably. Inappropriate giggles were a thing; I remembered learning that at some point in the dim and distant past. A defensive coping mechanism, someone had told me.

The hysterics were cut short by Habi – her voice pitched higher than usual. 'Stop laughing, you bastards. There's nothing funny. How can you laugh at a time like this? A man is dead – don't you get that? He's dead. Brian is— You're all acting like this is some big joke, like he's going to come around the corner, apologising for the misunderstanding.' Beside her, Andrea reached out and squeezed her hand. 'He isn't coming back and you're all sitting there laughing. You should be ashamed of yourselves.'

Andrea enveloped Habi in his arms. He didn't say anything, just held her. Habi's shouting devolved into wordless cries as she pounded her fists into his chest over and over again. Several others went and joined the embrace as Habi collapsed to her knees.

When the storm had passed, Rizwana smiled warmly. 'Brian also asked for a wake with lots of – and again these are his words – cheesy music.'

Gurdeep helped Georgie plant a juvenile tree in the ground above the remains. Georgie's hands shook, but she managed to complete her task. When she finished, I hugged her. She whispered in my ear, 'I loved him, you know. Like my own brother.'

'I know, sweetie,' I said. 'I know. Let's go celebrate his life the way he wanted us to.'

She wiped at her eyes with the back of her hand and nodded. Gurdeep supported her wife as we headed out to fulfil his final wish.

MEAR 1, DAY 283

THE ANKH DOME, DEVON ISLAND COLONY, MARS

'They're ready,' Santosh said. 'If you want to observe, you can return to the community centre.'

I took a deep breath and held it for a few heartbeats. 'Thank you, Santosh.'

He bobbled his head and returned to the building that had served as our chapel, party room, theatre, debate venue – and now courthouse.

Lisa stood up easily and brushed the leaves and detritus from herself. Georgie wasn't quite as nimble – but she got to her feet with more grace than I could manage.

'This was a terrible idea,' I said. 'What the hell was I thinking – sitting on the ground at nine months pregnant?'

Lisa laughed and extended her hands to help me up.

Gurdeep smirked. 'Admit it, you're jealous of my wheels.'

My shoulders fell. For a moment, I *had* envied Gurdeep, looking so comfortable in her wheelchair. 'It didn't seem polite to mention it.'

She'd managed okay on her prosthetic leg until she got to

about her sixth month of pregnancy – and then abandoned it in favour of the chair.

With nary a grunt, Lisa hauled me to my feet. I swept my hands over my tent-like dress to smooth out the fabric.

Georgie pulled a flapjack from a pocket and bit into it as she asked, 'Are we all ready for this?'

Lisa shook her head. 'I'm never going to be ready.' I reached out and took my friend's hand.

'I know.' Gurdeep nodded her head for a few seconds longer than seemed natural. 'I know. But we'll do it together, yeah?'

I nodded my head then grimaced as one of the twins kicked me in my … something. Kidney? Liver? Lung? I couldn't tell and I didn't care; I just wanted it to stop. Clutching my belly, I tried to shush an unborn baby who seemed determined to act out the anger we all felt.

We shuffled into the room and returned to the area set aside for observers, across from the jury. Separation of powers meant we could witness the proceedings but not interfere with them. I looked down at the chair I'd been sitting in before the recess then decided I'd be better off standing. I wasn't sure how long this portion of the trial would run, but I doubted it would be long.

We'd brought three lawyers to Mars – thinking they'd have nothing more exciting to do than drafting and reviewing contracts. Mostly they worked in the gardens with everyone else. They'd dealt with the odd civil suit over the past mear and a half – but nothing like this.

Katya and her defence lawyer sat on the right near the front – the prosecutor on the left.

The room buzzed with hushed voices. After a moment, the door behind us opened and Hiro walked in. Of the three lawyers, she'd been selected to serve as judge. I had no idea how the three of them decided who'd play which role in the trial – I was just grateful this wasn't on me. *Was that an unfair thought?*

Once Hiro was seated, she addressed the people lining the wall to her left. 'Members of the jury, I understand you have agreed a verdict.'

A woman stood up and nodded. 'We have, Your Honour.' Her hand trembled as she held a tablet at arm's length as though it stank. In a way, I supposed it did.

Hiro nodded and Santosh stepped forwards to take the proffered device. He strode to the bench and passed it to Hiro, who looked at it and took a deep breath. 'You're all agreed?'

The jury spokesperson nodded then hastily added, 'Yes, Your Honour.'

Hiro placed her hands flat on the desk and pursed her lips. 'Kateryna Kuznetsova, having heard the testimonies and considered the evidence presented, the jury finds you guilty of the murder of Brian Garcia Lopez.' She laid the tablet down and faced the jury again. 'Members of the jury, I thank you for your service in this most difficult task. You're excused.'

I wasn't sure what kind of reaction I expected from Katya – anger, tears, hysterical laughter, maybe. She showed none of it, sitting with her hands folded in her lap and an impassive expression on her face.

After the jury had filed back out of the room, Hiro addressed the remaining occupants. 'Defendant will be remanded to her apartment in the Craft. We will reconvene on Wednesday morning, when I will deliver the sentencing arrangements.' Before she'd finished the final word, she was on her feet. She bolted from the room, hand pressed against her mouth.

Santosh stood up and looked around awkwardly. 'Well, er, I think we can take that as the conclusion to today's proceedings.'

---

*THUNDERDOME, DEVON ISLAND COLONY, MARS*

After breakfast on Wednesday, Devon took my hand and looked me square in the eye. 'I know you think you need to be there this morning,' she said. 'But you don't. You may be prime minister, but you're not God. Not everything is your responsibility, you know?'

I squeezed her hand. 'I know. But I still feel like I owe it to Brian.'

Devon closed her eyes. 'I get that – I feel the same. But I can't do it. I just … can't.'

'I've got you. I'll be there so you don't have to.'

She smiled and hugged me – though at this stage of my pregnancy she struggled to get her arms all the way around me.

'Oh, gross, no. They're doing it again.' She dropped her arms and backed away, flapping wildly.

This had turned into a playful battle between us over the past few months. It horrified her to be able to see the twins moving inside me. She could stand to feel them kick or flip or whatever gymnastics they were doing, but as soon as their movements were visible, she was out.

I smiled. 'Soon they'll be squirming for real and you won't be able to ignore them.'

'Yeah, in their own skin. That's fine.' She shuddered. 'This,' she said, waving in my direction, 'this freaks me out.'

We headed out together, Seven following. Devon helped

me down the stairs to ground level – and then we began the long, slow waddle to the courthouse. Halfway there, she asked if I wanted to pause to catch my breath.

'It's not even half a kilometre – I can manage,' I snapped. 'Sorry. Sorry, I don't mean to be short with you. It's best if we keep going.'

When we arrived at the community-centre-cum-court-house, I kissed her on the cheek and gave Seven a quick pat on the head. 'I'll see you at lunch, yeah?'

She nodded before turning back and heading for her shift in Saca, Seven at her side. I pushed open the door and headed for the area set aside for observers. Lisa was already waiting – as were a few others, mainly from the advance crew. They'd known Brian the longest. I lowered myself carefully into the seat next to her. No sooner was I down than Gurdeep and Georgie joined us.

There was none of the usual gossip or nattering as we waited for the proceedings to begin. Over the weekend, Katya had been transferred from her apartment to the Scud – suicide watch. Part of me felt like it would be simpler – easier – if she would just off herself and be done with it. But we believed in rehabilitation – *didn't we?*

*Did we still?*

I'd been so lost in my own thoughts, I hadn't even noticed Hiro come in and take her seat at the bench. Everyone in the court was expected to stand for her entrance, but they'd let me off – presumably on the grounds of my pregnancy rather than the fact I wasn't paying attention.

Hiro settled herself at her makeshift desk before nodding.

Santosh spoke to the whole room. 'This is day sixteen of the trial of Kateryna Kuznetsova, Judge Hiro Ito presiding. Please be seated.'

'Thank you,' Hiro said to him before turning to address

Katya. 'You have been convicted on the clearest evidence of the brutal murder of a wholly innocent man. In so doing, you have brought shame upon our entire community.'

She brought her short fingers to her face, pressing her hands together. 'There is but one sentence I can pass upon you and that is life imprisonment. I also had to determine how many mears you will be required to serve before you can even be considered for release into the community. Our colony – however much we may not like it right now – believes in rehabilitation and second chances. But I—'

Her words were cut off by a black-haired woman who stood up and screamed. Paxton's speech was unfocused, unclear, but the words, 'The bitch must die,' rang loud and clear. She made to charge Katya, but she was met by an immovable force.

Without having appeared to move, Santosh was standing before her. Sun, Paxton's partner, raised her hands in surrender. She lifted the flailing woman off her feet and carried her from the room. Sun paused at the door to bow her head in Hiro's direction by way of apology.

'As I was saying,' Hiro continued. 'I warn you, Katya, that you have tested this belief to its very limits. It might be said you trampled right over it. For some in our community, that belief may never be restored. But if we cling to it like it's the only life raft on a sea of trauma, then maybe there is hope for our species yet.'

Hiro took a deep breath. 'You will continue to work your mandated hours as a member of this community. And you will attend your counselling sessions. When not working or visiting your therapist, you will be confined to quarters.'

Putting a lock on the outside of Katya's door was simple enough, but we'd need to rearrange things so her work was closely supervised. What could be passed off to someone else would be. Although we had no evidence that she was feeling vindictive, we'd ensure she'd spend most of her time doing menial tasks that couldn't be sabotaged.

'I find that ten mears is the minimum sentence you will serve. At that time, you will be eligible to apply for parole. If – and I assume you understand the enormous burden I place upon the shoulders of that two-letter word – *if* at that time you are able to demonstrate that you are no longer a threat to yourself or others, your application will be considered. If such application is not successful, or if you choose not to make one, then you will be eligible to make one application per mear.'

Hiro laid her hands flat on her desk. She turned from Katya towards those of us in the back. 'Further, I find that while culpability for this crime lies squarely on the shoulders of Katya herself, it cannot be denied that our government failed to provide the safety net Brian so desperately needed. Therefore, it is my recommendation that there be an independent inquiry into the events leading up to Brian's death.'

She looked directly at me and I felt the weight of her gaze. 'The members of the government have testified to the fact that they had suspicions relating to the ongoing abuse of a citizen. And while they did offer support to Brian and they made efforts to uncover the truth, I find myself wondering: is there anything else they could have done?'

Holding her eye, I nodded my head. It was a question I'd been asking myself for months.

———

Once the hearing was concluded, Georgie hopped up out of her seat and clapped her hands together. 'Right, I say we get some drinks.' Before I could point to my colossal belly, she waved her hands at me. 'Relax. I mean juice, herbal tea, water. I've made a cordial with mint and lemon verbena, if that appeals.'

When Gurdeep had been recovering from the trauma of the landing, she'd withdrawn into herself. She hadn't spoken a word to anyone but Georgie or her therapist for a solid three months. Georgie, it seemed, dealt with the trauma of losing her best friend differently. She'd dialled her personality up to eleven – becoming even perkier, bubblier, and more outgoing than she'd been as long as I'd known her.

The four of us walked back to Hatsh – Lisa and I behind Gurdeep and Georgie. Gurdeep manoeuvred her wheelchair easily along the colony's smooth pathways as Georgie chattered about nothing and everything.

When we walked into their common room, Georgie encouraged us to take a seat in the lounge space. I had to use the window ledge for support as I lowered myself onto the armchair. Lisa sat on the sofa. Gurdeep and Georgie headed for the kitchen to fetch drinks.

A few moments later Gurdeep wheeled into position and Georgie set a tray on the coffee table. She took a seat on the sofa, next to Lisa, and poured drinks.

'Cheers, Georgie.' Lisa shook her head. 'Ten mears…'

Gurdeep rested her glass on her expanding belly. 'It doesn't seem very long, you know?'

Rubbing my hands over my own oversized bump, I replied, 'I know, I know. But then, these twins will be adults by the time she can even apply for release.'

I couldn't help but notice that Georgie went silent when the conversation turned to Katya's sentence. She headed back to the kitchen and fussed with food.

But I still needed to know. 'Are we doing the right thing?'

Lisa shook her head. 'Even the most right-wing among us opposed capital punishment back when it was only theory.'

Gurdeep took a sip of her drink. 'Yeah, but now it's real and we're living it. And some people are re-thinking that attitude.'

'Human rights,' I said, slamming my palm down on the arm of the chair, 'aren't worth the paper they're written on if they don't apply universally.' Georgie looked over her shoulder at us from her position at the counter, a scowl flashing across her face.

Gurdeep looked down at the floor, at her one remaining foot. 'Much as we might hate it, you're right. We can't pick and choose who gets rights.'

I sighed. 'No, we can't.'

Lisa dropped her head into her hands.

Georgie set another tray on the coffee table, this one with apple slices and mini Bakewells that I assumed Gurdeep had made. 'Right. Enough about that, I think.' She held the tartlets up to me. 'So, have you got names picked out?'

*HATSH DOME, DEVON ISLAND COLONY, MARS*

'Come out and face me, you bastard.'

I popped my head round the bedroom door and smiled at Gurdeep. 'He's not a bastard – his parents are legally married and have been for many mears, long before he was a blob in a Petri dish.'

She didn't laugh as she struggled to find something to grip onto to haul herself up off the bed.

'Besides,' I continued, 'he'll face you when he's good and ready.' I offered her a hand to help her up as she glared at me with cold fury in her eyes. She took my hands and together we worked to— 'Nope, nope, sorry.' I dropped her hands and ran for the loo.

I dry heaved into the sink for a minute or two then rinsed my mouth and returned to the bedroom. Gurdeep had somehow hefted herself from the bed into her wheelchair.

My breath ragged, I put my hand on the wall to support myself. 'I'm sorry, babe.'

She pulled a heavy fleece hoodie on over her thermal T-shirt. 'You're still struggling.'

I nodded then leaned down and planted a kiss atop her head. 'Give me a sec, babe. I'll throw some clothes on and we'll walk in together, yeah?'

'Yeah, I'll just keep trying to convince this arsehole his time is up.'

'Our son is not an arsehole,' I called from the wardrobe-dressing room.

'You don't know that,' she shot back.

Two minutes later, I emerged wearing a stretchy sleeveless tunic stitched together by Jupiter using fabric she'd collected from various colonists. Iulia had taught her to sew just after we'd arrived. She'd launched her own clothing line – repurposing old clothes, parachutes, and even storage sacks.

I walked beside Gurdeep as we left the flat and headed for the kitchen. Korri and Caoimhe were busy making breakfast as their puppy zoomed around the room, playing with a squeaky toy.

I felt an overwhelming urge to get down on all fours, to romp and wrestle with Lemmy. At five months old, he seemed to have two modes: fast asleep or full speed. As much as my brain – or possibly my heart – wanted to join him in play, my stomach and every muscle screamed at me not to dare.

Collapsing into a chair, I let my head fall onto the dining table. Gurdeep wheeled her own chair into the vacant space beside me. I put a hand on her knee as she put one of hers on my back.

'Morning,' I mumbled.

Caoimhe walked over to stand behind us. Placing a hand on each of our backs, she said, 'Don't you two worry. I've got you covered.' Although she wasn't part of the care team for either Gurdeep or me, Caoimhe had trained as a midwife before going back to become a doctor. I trusted she knew what she was doing. 'You both just sit there and rest. We'll get everything ready and bring it to you.'

Overwhelmed with gratitude, I raised my head as far as I dared and said, 'Cheers, Caoimhe. You're a star.' I hiccoughed and tasted bile. 'Actually, though … I don't know if I can eat anything.'

Caoimhe rubbed circular motions on my back. 'You need to keep your strength up and you definitely need to stay hydrated. But don't worry. I know what I'm doing.' She returned to the worktop, where her husband was stirring two pots simultaneously. I let my head fall back into my hands.

Beside me Gurdeep grunted, the first noise she'd made since we arrived.

As much as I already loved this baby, I was not enjoying pregnancy. My second trimester would start soon and I hoped things would improve, that my body would calm the crap down. But I wasn't holding out much hope.

Gurdeep's pregnancy, on the other hand, had passed smoothly. At least it had until a few days ago. And then when the due date came and went, she got crabbier and crabbier. Rizwana had booked her in for inducement next Tuesday just in case. Sitting in her wheelchair at the breakfast table, Gurdeep swore at nothing.

I may or may not have drifted off. When Korri set a bowl of congee and a mug of herbal tea down in front of me, I sat up with a start. Caoimhe placed a dish of something different before Gurdeep. Gurdeep scrunched up her nose in almost a snarl. 'Wozzit?'

'Spicy red bowl food,' Caoimhe replied as she turned back to the counter to fetch her own breakfast.

As Korri and Caoimhe sat down at the table, Gurdeep and I both raised our spoons to our mouths. I took a bite of the mild, savoury, soupy rice porridge they'd prepared for me. Bracing for my body's response, I was caught off guard by a torrent of pained swearing from beside me.

Caoimhe bit her lip. 'How long has this been going on, Gurdeep?'

Between curses, Gurdeep grunted, 'Few hours.'

I glared at my wife. 'Why didn't you tell me?'

Caoimhe looked at her watch. 'How far apart and how long do they last?'

Gurdeep clenched her jaw. 'Six. One. Stronger now.'

'You didn't say anything!' Trying to run in multiple directions at once in my panic, I nearly ended up on the floor. Korri caught me with his hands under my arms, steadying me.

Caoimhe had her phone in hand and a chunk of something or other between her teeth. She sucked whatever it was in and swallowed. 'I'll call the midwife. You go fetch your bag of supplies. We'll wait with Gurdeep.'

I nodded and ran. Gurdeep continued to grumble as I left the kitchen. When I opened the door to our flat, my stomach picked that moment to flip. 'Mă rog, now is not the time for this.' Instead of grabbing the bag by the front door, I scurried to the toilet as fast as my fat little legs would carry me. I knelt on the ground for several minutes, clutching the commode's smooth, cold base as I threw up the mouthful of breakfast I'd eaten and all the water I'd drunk over the past few hours.

Between heaves, I cursed and swore like I've never done before. Somehow I was convinced our baby would be born right there in the kitchen before I could get back to my wife.

Little did I know.

When I felt able to, I hauled myself to my feet and ran

back to the kitchen. Halfway there, I realised I'd neglected the very bag I'd gone to get – and turned around again. I opened the flat's door, grabbed it, pulled the door to again – and ran smack into Korri.

My bulky frame moving at speed colliding with his wire-hanger body wasn't much of a contest; we hit the ground with a cacophony of surprised screaming, multilingual swearing, and tangled limbs. He leapt up smoothly – if not gracefully – and heaved me to my feet.

Together, we walked to the kitchen, where I found Gurdeep recovering after another painful set of contractions. Caoimhe had put a mug of herbal tea in her hands, which she clung to like it was the only thing tethering her to this life.

I thanked Caoimhe and Korri for all their help. Korri graciously offered to take my shift heading up the food-ag workers for that morning. I wheeled Gurdeep slowly and carefully out the door, through Hatsh, and into the airlock. Rizwana met us as we exited into Seacole. We got Gurdeep to the Scud – and then waited.

———

*SEACOLE DOME, DEVON ISLAND COLONY, MARS*

Gurdeep's labour was long and difficult. It was awful – I couldn't do anything to take her pain away.

By the time the baby was born thirty hours later, Gurdeep was shattered. I was exhausted. Rizwana, who'd been with us through pretty much the whole thing, was dead on her feet. Everyone had said hello to him, he'd been checked and weighed and declared perfect, and then Gurdeep collapsed. I took the opportunity to pop back home for a quick nap and a shower.

Not wanting to miss more of his first day than I absolutely had to, I allowed myself an hour's sleep. Hair still dripping from my shower, I headed for my lab in Thunderdome. Deep in a locker under a pile of mugs, discarded phones, and bags of muddy clothes was something I'd been working on for months.

I learned to spin using bamboo, which grew quickly and could be harvested without killing the plant. Its fibres made soft, beautiful yarn. Faz had been experimenting with natural dyes. I had selected an assortment of them: a soft gold colour made from turmeric, a bluey-green derived from spirulina, and a beetroot pink. And I'd taught myself to crochet. Using a simple pattern I'd found, I made a baby blanket.

Blasted thing was uglier than sin, but I'd made it with my own two hands.

As I walked back to the Scud, I remembered the first time Gurdeep had taken me home to meet her family. Mrs Singh told me a story, one I later heard her tell many times, but in my mind I heard her tell me again for the first time.

'Such a serious child, my Gurdeep was. Always so sombre. One time she found her father sitting in his favourite chair, trying to solve a Rubik's cube. She walked straight up to him and plucked the thing from his hands. "No, Daddy. Only babies play with toys," she scolded him. Then she walked across the room and gave it to Dalbir, who was only three months old.'

Poor Gurdeep looked like she wanted to sink into the rug listening to that tale for what must have been the thousandth time. Before that day, I loved her, but in that moment I knew we'd be together forever. I promised myself I'd do absolutely anything for her. Twelve Earth years later, I'd shown just how seriously I'd meant that unspoken vow.

As I dashed across Seacole, I felt a twinge of guilt over

the man I'd stranded on Earth so my wife could take his place in the colony, but I pushed it from my mind.

When I arrived on the ward, Gurdeep was still asleep, so I sat down as quietly as I could. The baby was snoozing next to her. In the far corner, Helen and Desmond stood by a bed where a young woman with tawny skin and wavy hair lay unconscious. Tubes and cables connected her to various machines.

Having spent much of the past day and a half in the colony's tiny hospital, it would've been difficult for me to avoid knowing what had happened.

Gurdeep had been resting between contractions when Desmond had called the emergency number. Sun, last night's on-call doctor, went to collect Mike in the ambulance.

Sitting in the small ward I couldn't help but overhear as Helen spoke. 'Sun explained last night that your wife's pregnancy wasn't viable. She experienced what we call a septic abortion.'

Desmond's lower jaw quivered. 'An abortion? What? No, she wouldn't... Why?' I felt a powerful urge to go comfort him, but I figured it was best to let Helen finish.

'Not like that,' Helen continued. 'I don't mean Mike had a termination. No, the baby died. I'm sorry.'

Still on the verge of tears, Desmond nodded. 'We'll try again when she's ready. It'll be okay.' He dropped heavily into the nearest seat.

Helen touched his shoulder. 'Desmond, no. That's what I'm trying to tell you. When Sun scanned her, she found a large abscess in Mike's fallopian tube. We had to perform an emergency hysterectomy. Your wife won't be able to have any children.'

Desmond reached out a hand helplessly and began sobbing. 'What? No, but that's...'

Unwilling to wait any longer, I went to my friend and colleague. I sat down in the seat next to him and gathered him into my arms. Looking up at Helen, I nodded for her to continue.

'Mike should be okay. We've removed the abscess and she's on antibiotics. I don't want to downplay the severity of her illness – she has sepsis. Her recuperation will be long and slow, but with luck and plenty of rest, she should make a full recovery.' She touched his shoulder.

As Helen left the ward, Desmond leaned into my chest. I stroked his back as he cried.

After a few minutes, he sat upright. 'I'm sorry. I don't want to be a downer on your happy day. You should be celebrating.'

I put my arm around him. 'There's time for that. Right now, in this moment, while our wives sleep, I'm here for *you.*'

We sat in silence.

After a few minutes, Desmond said softly, 'I'll do it.'

I looked at him quizzically. 'What?'

'Babies. We're supposed to have two, right? One per person, yeah? That's the rule.'

*Oh!* My eyes opened wide. 'It was, originally – but don't worry about that. And besides—' I bit my tongue. Now wasn't the time to bring up the impact of the power shortages on our plans.

Desmond shook his head abruptly. 'We wanted this. Kids. Big family, picket fences and minivans, everything. Well, you know, whatever the Martian equivalent of all that is. We wanted it all. So, yeah, I'm sure they would make an exception for us—' He leaned forwards and looked me in the eye. 'But I don't *want* them to. I want to have that big family like Mike and I always dreamed. Not yet. Not now – but I will. After we've grieved.' He wiped his tears away with his stump.

He sat back in the hard plastic chair and crossed his arms over his chest. 'I'll have the babies she can't.'

So many questions ran through my mind. *Had he really never had any gender confirmation surgery? Wouldn't pregnancy make for horrible dysphoria? Was there no other way for them to have the family they dreamed of?*

But my questions were my own and the answers were none of my business. I would be the best friend I could be without intruding on his private struggles. 'Whatever you decide to do, mate, know that we all love you and we'll support you. The whole colony, I mean. We're all on your side.'

Desmond clasped my hand. He laughed – a sad, ironic sound. 'You know, my parents said their worst fear for me was that I'd be a lesbian. Not that I'd get sick or die or struggle with addiction.' He looked down at his left arm before waving the stump around. 'Or be injured. No, the worst possible outcome was that I might be into women. Well, the joke's on them – if they're still alive. I'm as straight as the day is long. Just not a woman. If I told them I was married to someone named Mike and that I was thinking of having a baby, they'd build a ship to come to Mars using duct tape and chewing gum, all while singing hallelujah. Ha.' He said the word rather than laughing.

The words stung. 'My father said something similar to me the last time I saw him – and I am a lesbian. I love you, my friend. And we're going to be better parents to our kids than ours were to us.'

After a moment, he whispered, 'Thank you. Truly, thank you. Now, your wife's waking up. Go, be with her and celebrate the birth of your first child.' I rubbed his back before walking back to Gurdeep's bed.

Gurdeep looked up at me with bleary eyes. 'Where is he?'

'Morning, babe. He's right beside you.'

Gurdeep pushed herself up into a sitting position as Nora walked in. Gurdeep reached for our baby. I kissed her on the forehead. As she lifted him, I got my first good look at his little face. *Oh my gosh.* 'Gabriel!'

Nora grinned. 'Aye, spitting image, isn't he?'

I turned to Gurdeep as her eyes filled with tears. 'I'm sorry, I'm sorry, I'm so sorry.' I put my arms around her.

'Shh, babe. None of that.'

'I'm so sorry,' she repeated. 'Can you ever forgive me?'

'Oh, love. It's in the past.' I stroked her back with one hand as the other touched the tight curls crowning his tiny brown face. 'There is nothing to forgive. Not anymore. It's all good now. We're good. He's good. He's healthy and he's perfect. Gurdeep—' I lifted her chin so she had to look me in the eye. 'He's our son. And Gabriel's mum is going to be delighted with our choice of name.'

I rubbed my belly. Another seven months and we'd greet the ghost of another lost friend.

ELSEWHERE

After dinner, Sergeant Cobb ordered us to the briefing room. 'News from Earth.'

The major and the lieutenant were already waiting for us, standing to either side of the room's largest screen.

'Sit,' the sergeant barked as we filed into the room.

When we were all seated, the lieutenant scowled and pressed a button on the keyboard. A man appeared on screen – round-faced with greying hair that had probably once been red. *Interesting.* Usually, orders from home were conveyed to us through the command chain. He wore a marines uniform, bearing a colonel's insignia. 'This is a message for the Mars Early Nuclear and Construction Expedition.'

*The MENaCE, that's us. Dear Lord, what an awful name. What moron came up with that hideous backronym?*

'This is a hard message to convey and one that pains me as much as it will you.' The muscles in my abdomen clenched. It was uncharitable of me to think ill of the man. I begged God's forgiveness even as the colonel continued speaking. 'Unfortunately, the reality of the situation is that it's just not going to be possible to send reinforcements or supplies to you in the next, uh … window.'

I crossed my arms over my chest before I could stop myself. Every bump and groove in the makeshift stool I sat on was suddenly poking me in the butt. In my head, I recited the words that brought me comfort. *The Lord is my shepherd, I shall not want.*

'I want to reassure you, we are not leaving you up there to die.'

Someone snorted.

Almost three years we'd been sitting up here, twiddling our thumbs. The rest of the colonists – along with everything we'd need to stay alive on Mars – were meant to have arrived six months before. They'd postponed that to the next Hohmann transfer orbit period – next year. I couldn't help but remind myself that our supplies would be stretched to breaking point by the time they finally arrived eighteen months from now.

'We are doing everything we can to ensure your long-term safety. The Dowager-President herself is taking a personal interest in your situation.'

*Dowager-President!* I very nearly snorted aloud at that line – but it could be dangerous to express such unpatriotic thoughts. *He makes me lie down in green pastures.*

'Now, I know … I know that you hard-working young men and um … women aren't gonna like this. Hell, I don't like this.'

Behind me I heard Chambers growl, 'I'll give him something he's "not gonna like".'

'That's enough, Private,' snapped Lieutenant Pearce.

What difference did it make? He was part of a planet we'd never see again.

*No*, I chastised myself. *Despair is a sin. Do not fall for it; it is a sin and it is a lie. There is always hope.*

*He leads me beside still waters.*

I forced myself to focus on the screen, to listen to the colonel's words. 'You are likely already aware of the other colony on the planet.'

*Wait, what? Deep breath.*

Judging by the sharp gasps and sudden shuffling around me, I wasn't the only one who hadn't possessed that particular piece of information.

*He restores my soul.*

On screen, the man continued speaking. 'Our analysis suggests this other colony originates in Europe. Their ships launched from Earth in two phases. Three ships departed six years ago —'

'Six years!' The room exploded in a cacophony of angry and confused shouting, everyone demanding to know what everyone else knew. Lieutenant Pearce stabbed a key to stop the video.

Major Willis took a step forward. 'All right, sit your asses down, all of you. I get that it was a surprise. Now get over it and listen to what Colonel Powell has to say. I don't want to hear another peep out of any of you until the video has finished.'

'Sir, yes, sir!' We all chorused the expected words like some sort of shouty call-and-response exercise – though less sacred than the ones you'd find in a church.

The lieutenant punched the key to start the video again. Colonel Powell's face reanimated and his voice filled the room. '—fully fifteen months before the plague, suggesting they had advance knowledge of it. Now, those first ships took off during the, um, Hohmann transfer period. This was the window prior to the one in which our deployment – that's you, folks – began training for your mission.'

It took all my strength not to laugh at that. Six years ago, I'd been so desperate to escape my old life that I was considering joining the military – something I'd always thought was only for … for people like Sergeant Cobb. My 'training' for this eternal deployment had lasted less than a year; it had begun the same week as the plague.

*Join the coast guard, they said. It won't be as hardcore as the army or the marines, I convinced myself. Sure, fine, whatever. But where's the coast, I ask you? Where is the coast? What am I doing on Mars? I leave the entire freakin' planet to escape one pathetic excuse for an abusive ex? What does that say about me?*

I inhaled slowly. *He leads me in paths of righteousness for his name's sake.*

'Additional ships departed from the same launch site in south-west Europe at the very start of the pandemic that devastated our world. Again, this supports our suspicions that they had foreknowledge of the plague. As such, we have reason to suspect they may be hostile to American interests.'

'Of course there are belligerents on Mars and no one thought to tell us,' Chambers muttered under her breath. The lieutenant glared at her and she shut up.

'The fact they departed between' – he looked down at his notes – 'Hohmann transfer windows implies they employed an … um … a ballistic capture flight path.' He looked back up at the camera as he continued. So, our colonel wasn't a science guy.

'That's important because it tells us their flight time would've been longer than our team's – than yours.'

I clenched my jaw to halt the grimace I felt coming on. Two hundred and fifty-nine days in hell. Magnets attempting – and failing – to stand in for gravity. Bizarre and complex suction contraptions for bodily functions. Even less privacy than we had now.

I couldn't prevent a small shudder. These folks spent longer in space? How had they not killed themselves or one another?

'What this means is that even though this other colony left Earth earlier, they've been on Mars just a few months longer than you have. And, as such, it's believed—' Colonel Powell coughed.

*It is believed – by zombies.* I recalled an English teacher back in high school explaining that the simplest way to identify the passive construction was to finish the sentence with the phrase 'by zombies'. If it still made sense, you knew you were dealing with passive sentence construction – and one of its main uses was to obscure the person or people committing the action.

'Ahem, it is believed they're likely in a similar position to your good selves.' *So, running out of food and with no escape. Wonderful. We can all die together. Won't that be nice?*

I forced myself to take another breath. *Even though I walk through the valley of the shadow of death, I fear no evil.*

The good colonel had the decency to look awkward as he shifted his weight from foot to foot. 'It is for this reason that it has been decided' – *by zombies, naturally* – 'that the best course of action is for the two colonies to join forces. Your new orders are to decamp from your position and head for the European colony's site. We've sent the co-ordinates to you.'

*For thou art with me.*

'We estimate it will take you at least a few months to get to them. The rations you have with you were designed to last another eighteen months, though obviously the loss of three of your compatriots' – I crossed myself as unobtrusively as I could. May they rest in peace – 'means the supplies will last you a while longer. Still, it's probably best if you start conserving them now. Hopefully, between the two teams, you'll come up with a way to tide yourselves over. For um…' He swallowed. 'For as long as it takes.'

Corporal Kay stood up, shouting, 'Oh, come on. He doesn't even believe himself! They're leaving us here to die.'

*Thou preparest a table before me in the presence of my enemies; thou anointest my head with oil, my cup overflows.*

*Oh boy.*

*SEACOLE DOME, DEVON ISLAND COLONY, MARS*

'Go, get out.' Helen made a shooing gesture.

'Sure? I don't want to leave ye in the lurch. I'm still on shift for another half-hour,' I replied.

Helen rolled her eyes at me melodramatically. 'What am I going to do – report you to the Health Minister?' She threw her arms up in the air. 'Go on. I don't make this offer every day.' Helen had been less of a workaholic since Rafa came along, but some things never changed.

'I ken. I'm grateful an aw – I am.' I leaned in and kissed her on the cheek, which made her scowl.

She brushed me off, making a show of pushing me. 'Please. I'm practically a married woman. I'm not your plaything. Get off.'

I threw my hands up in mock surrender. 'Aye, I'm going. You'll be there later, right?'

'So long as Ash can refrain from breaking any bones for one night, yes.' We'd all found the clumsiness of Santosh's wife comical and she was always the first to laugh at herself. It had only been recently we'd wondered if there might be a cause for it. Sure enough, Ash met all the criteria for dyspraxia. Having a diagnosis helped her understand why she struggled with her co-ordination and balance. Unfortunately for us, it didn't stop her from injuring herself every other week.

'Cheers, I owe you.' Much to Helen's feigned disgust, I kissed her on the cheek a second time before heading out the door of the Scud. I walked along the faded grey walkway between the gardens on one side and the marbled black and green surface of the buildings on the other.

I made my way to the Ankh. Our largest dome housed a community kitchen open to all colonists as well as a community hall that could accommodate up to eighty – as long as the forty per cent rule was respected. We had 148 adults now, but our total population would get up to more than 300 – assuming we could find a solution to our recurrent power issues.

Today was a celebration day – and, ooh boy, were we going to have a party. Well, as much of a party as parents of infants can have.

As I approached the community kitchen, I spied a frequent visitor to the Scud running through the trees and plants, chasing after something. I followed his movements with my eyes, trying to see what had captured his attention. Aha, a bee!

'Hey, Anders. You shouldn't chase bees, you know,' I told him. 'How's my second favourite boy doing?' In response, the wiggly ball of fluff that was a vaguely Labrador puppy bounded over and licked my outstretched hand. 'Am I very tasty?'

Chris came around the bend into view. Anders rolled over on his back and wiggled all four paws in the air. I knelt down and rubbed his belly.

Chris smiled. 'Wanna see something cool?'

'Aye,' I replied, looking up at her. Chris unclipped the contraption pinning Rafa to her chest and slowly lowered her daughter to the ground. She bent over and offered a pair of steadying hands to the girl – who grabbed them and shoved them aside. Rafa took two unstable steps before dropping onto her bottom. She turned to us with a look of sheer joy and clapped her chubby hands.

I high-fived Rafa then looked at Chris. 'She's walking already!'

Chris beamed. 'As of about an hour ago. Anyway, I'm surprised to see you here so early. I have a hard time believing my fiancée let you leave early. Helen doesn't believe in short working hours.'

I shook my head. 'Aye, she did. What can I say? I'm just that persuasive. You joining us later?'

'Wouldn't miss it,' she replied as she stood back up. 'Come on, you silly beasts. Let's get you back home.'

I waved farewell and headed into the kitchen, where I found Desmond stirring something in a massive slow cooker, his expanding belly pressed against the counter. 'Whatever that is, it smells bloody lovely!'

He smiled at me, but before he could respond I spotted the world's biggest cake. I leaned over for a closer look, admiring the large rectangle, decorated with a vividly realistic Martian landscape. A series of chocolate solar panels adorned one corner of the piece. But the star of the show rose from the centre of the scene – a series of smaller round cake mounds in rich blues and greens – bejewelled with vibrant dots of reds, oranges, purples, and yellows.

'Oh! It's lovely. Hang on… Is that—' I looked up. I turned to face Gurdeep.

'It really is,' she replied with a massive grin. Baking had been her passion on Earth and it was fantastic to see her taking it up again.

Did I dare hope? 'Icing?'

Gurdeep stabbed a pointy wooden tool in my direction and squealed, 'Icing! Buttercream, even.'

'But how?' We'd struggled to find a fat that gave a similar consistency to butter. Both cocoa butter and coconut oil showed potential, but it would be at least another mear before we'd get a large enough yield to test that. Most of our cooking oils came from rapeseed, which wasn't anywhere near solid at room temperature.

'I'm the miracle worker you're looking for,' came Georgie's voice from the front door. She had pushed the door open with her hip. Not only were her arms laden with a huge crate of fruit and veg, but above that, she had baby Adina wrapped to her chest.

'What can I say? *Someone* convinced me that colony morale demanded I grow a batch of milk fat in my lab, so she could have butter. I told her this was far from the most resource-efficient use of my time or materials, but she wasn't having it,' she said with mock consternation. She thrust the basket of produce onto the counter with a grunt.

'It is a special occasion after all,' replied Gurdeep, as she put her arms around her wife's prodigious waist.

I adored their gentle banter. Adina reached up a sticky hand and pulled a fistful of Georgie's curls into her mouth.

'You know Davy agreed with us on this,' said Gurdeep.

Georgie's face was sceptical. 'Do I, though? Do I really? All I saw was a politician reluctant to alienate voters by taking sides.'

Gurdeep smiled. 'There has to be a difference between living and surviving. Someone wise once told me that, but I'm struggling to remember who it was.' Gurdeep tapped her lip.

'Gurdeep, that cake is stunning. Honestly, it looks incredible. Thank you so much.'

Gurdeep faced me, one arm still holding her wife, pride evident in her smile.

Desmond cradled his bump with one hand. 'As fascinating as this is, I thought it might be a good idea to get dinner finished before the guest of honour arrived.'

'Spoilsport,' Georgie replied. She turned to me. 'Shall we go see about setting up the buffet tables?'

'Absolutely.' We walked through to the large community hall as the front door opened and a whirlwind of black-haired excitement burst through it. Amos ran straight for me, shouting a semi-coherent stream of consciousness. He leapt up into my arms.

'Mummy! Mama said I get presents today and cake,' he squealed.

Jupiter reached out and touched my hair then leaned in to kiss me hello. A lot of people said having kids dulled the fire in their relationships, but it certainly hadn't done so for us.

'Aye, ye will indeed. Lots of presents and the greatest cake in the history of Devon Island. But not yet.' I sent him off to play in the corner with his books and toys, where Mike was already sitting on the floor with Little Gabe.

'We've just been to the gym.' Jupiter wiped sweat from her brow with the sleeve of her hoodie. 'I don't understand how he still has so much energy.'

Georgie and Jupiter and I got to work setting the tables

and chairs up for tonight's big celebration. The first ever baby born on Mars was turning one today. One mear – 669 days. Since then there had been dozens more babies added to our colony.

But my Amos would always be the first.

MEAR 2, DAY 86



'What? Why would you think I don't like it?' What a bizarre thing for Rosa to say. We'd been friends for mears and I loved her music. She had teamed up with a few others to make the most incredible punk covers of songs from our childhood. They were fantastic.

'But you never come to any of our shows, silly,' said Rosa as we climbed the stairs to my flat. 'If you like our music, why don't you come support us? It's okay – you can just say it's not to your taste.'

After spending the morning with her bandmates, we were on our way to pick up Seven. There weren't many places my dog wasn't allowed to go, but Lisa was adamant the recording studio remained one of them.

Upon seeing me, Seven leapt up and did her happy dance. 'Come on. Time to go.' She did two full twirls before following me out the door.

Seven greeted Rosa by butting her hand with her head.

Rosa obliged, patting her. She wasn't the dog's biggest fan, but they seemed to get on all right – for my sake, at least.

'Anyway, back to our previous conversation,' I said as we walked south, towards Seacole. 'I adore your band. Seeing you play in the studio means I get to focus on the music. When I go to shows in the White Hart, I'm surrounded by people talking and eating and drinking and all the various sights, sounds, and smells that go along with that.'

'But,' Rosa replied as we stepped out of the airlock. 'I've been at the pub with you plenty of times.'

I could never understand why this was so difficult for allistics to understand. 'Yes! I like going to the pub with you or with Davy or with, I don't know, whoever. I just get uncomfortable if there are too many people or if there's too much going on.'

We walked in silence for a few minutes. Eventually we crossed into Lovelace dome, which was always a pleasant shock to the system. The tropical climate meant it was about four degrees warmer than most of the other domes.

Lovelace dome was like an assault on the senses – but in a good way. Bananas and lemons and coconuts and avocados. Brian's much-loved coffee plants thrived here. I reached out to stroke a few palm fronds as we walked towards the cluster of buildings.

Out of nowhere, Seven barked up a storm and ran in frantic circles. She loved to play and frolic, but this looked more like panic. She doubled back every two or three steps. After a few seconds she looped around and nipped me on my ankle. I didn't know what it was about, but I trusted Seven; she had senses I didn't. Grabbing Rosa by the arm, I sprinted after my dog.

Rosa screamed at me, trying to claw her arm free. 'What are you doing? Let go of me!'

Just as the words were out of her mouth, a horrible alert sound filled the dome and the park lights flashed red. Seven ran to the community kitchen, still barking frantically. I followed her there, dragging a confused Rosa with me.

The moment we shut the door behind us, deadbolts thunked home and the 'no exit' sign above the handle lit up. It wasn't quite eleven in the morning, so the space was empty.

I looked through the window to see Lisa turning mid-stride to run for the airlock instead of the kitchen. She must have been right behind us. I hadn't known she was there – though I couldn't have held the door for her anyway.

When the system sensed a failure in life support, it gave a thirty-second alert before closing and sealing all building exterior doors. After sixty seconds, the airlock doors sealed themselves. Lisa needed to get there before that happened.

Watching Lisa's progress through the windows, I scrambled along the outer edge of the living room. I looked on in impotent horror as she tripped and fell. She got back up and raced in the direction of the nearest airlock, the one leading to Antalya.

Around her, dust and plant matter and discarded toys were all lifted into the atmosphere towards... From my vantage point inside the building, I couldn't see the top of the dome, but it was evident there was a breach. As I reached the corner of the room, Lisa disappeared from my view.

I dropped to the floor, letting my head fall into my hands. Her chances of making it weren't good. I pulled my phone from my pocket. The screen was covered in alerts. In all the noise and confusion, I hadn't even felt it vibrate.

Lovelace dome is experiencing a loss of pressure. Seek shelter in the nearest building or vacate the dome immediately.

This is not a drill. Enact your emergency plan now.
Warning: oxygen levels in Lovelace are critically low.

Another alert popped up before I finished reading the ones already there. This one – rather unhelpfully, I thought – said Lovelace was now in lockdown.

A trapdoor in the ceiling opened and a ladder dropped into the middle of the living room. It took me a few seconds to parse what I was seeing as Charlie and Mehmet climbed down through the opening. Mehmet wore boxers and Charlie had only a tiny pair of knickers on. Both had unkempt hair. Mehmet carried Ysabel in one arm. Charlie was crying.

Rosa ran to them. 'My baby!' She plucked her daughter from Mehmet's arms. Balancing her on one hip, she leaned into him. Mehmet encircled both women in his arms. Charlie kissed Rosa so hungrily, it looked like she was trying to swallow her. Mehmet held them and kissed the top of Charlie's head.

I buried my hand in Seven's thick fur.

In the event of a depressurisation event or life support failure, the buildings were equipped to keep the dome's residents – plus a margin of error to account for guests – alive for up to three days.

Anyone locked inside would need to be able to move between units – which is why whenever the deadbolts on the exterior doors and windows closed, the locks on the small doors connecting the units opened.

'It was awful,' Mehmet whispered. 'We woke up to the sound of the alarm. I thought it was a drill. We were already inside, so there wasn't anything for us to do.'

Charlie wiped her face with her bare arm. 'After a few seconds, I got up and looked out the window. Henri was chasing Renaud through the garden. The baby seemed to think this was all a game. Iulia was helping Henri, both of them trying to catch the poor babe,' she said between snorted sobs.

Mehmet picked the story back up, clutching Charlie. 'When the dome tore, Renaud flew. He just—' He stopped to catch his breath. 'He was there and then—' He covered his face with his hand. After a few seconds he continued, wiping his face. 'Henri and Iulia both shot up off the ground after him. But when the air was gone, they fell back to the ground. It…' He gripped the back of his neck with his hand. 'It was horrific.'

We stood there for a few seconds – in shock, I guess. Rosa, Charlie, and Mehmet locked in an embrace; me standing awkwardly to one side.

Davy would be wondering where I was. I looked at my phone – seven missed calls in the last three minutes. The state I was in, I'd missed them even though I was holding the device. It buzzed again. Davy's face popped up on screen, so I clicked to accept. She would only call if it was urgent – I hoped there wasn't another emergency elsewhere.

'Hi,' I began, unsure where to go from there.

'You're okay.' Every muscle in Davy's face was clenched.

'I am. Seven went nuts. We followed her to the kitchens. Er, we're there now.'

Her eyes went wide. 'You're in Lovelace?'

'There are at least five of us locked inside. Six with Seven,' I said. 'And er … Lisa, she…' I realised I didn't know how to tell her that her oldest friend was probably dead, so I started with Iulia, Henri, and Renaud. Davy's face was ashen.

'Wait, what did you say about Lisa?'

I looked down. 'She didn't make it to the kitchen in time

... the bolts ... before she could... She ran for the airlock, but I ... I don't know if she made it.'

She swallowed twice, seemingly incapable of forming words. After a moment her eyes darted away and she said, 'Hang on, Helen's calling. I'll patch her in.'

Helen's face appeared on my screen, stacked above Davy's. 'Davy?' Her voice was pitched even higher than usual.

'Helen, Devon's in Lovelace. She says she believes we've had three, possibly four casualties. I've had confirmation that five people escaped through the airlocks to neighbouring domes and Desmond's team are stuck in an exterior airlock. What more can you tell us?'

Helen bit her lip. 'Do your figures include Lisa?'

I confirmed she was the possible fourth casualty.

'One of the suits just locked onto Lisa's phone. It's sending out data, but the life signs are weak. Devon, do you know if Qianru was present?'

Mehmet put his arm on my shoulder as he stepped into my phone's field of view.

'No, Renaud was the only baby outside,' he said. Both Davy and Helen heaved visible sighs of relief.

'Nora and I are en route to Antalya dome now.' As she said it, I noticed the background was moving behind her. 'And I've sent Frankie to the south airlock to free Desmond and his crew.'

It occurred to me Desmond had to be about eight months pregnant. 'Is he okay?'

Helen nodded. 'Yeah, I spoke to him. He was leading a team working in the garden near the airlock, so they all headed straight for it when the alarms sounded. Aside from being trapped, they're all right. Frankie will hook a rover up to the afară side of the airlock to free them all.'

Mehmet grabbed his jaw in his hand and gripped it so hard his knuckles went white. 'I should be with Frankie.'

Davy looked like she might be sick. 'I know. I feel the same, but we've all got our roles to play. Having an engineer with Frankie is a good plan, though. Helen, send Gurdeep with her, please.'

Helen pursed her lips. 'Sure. Nora and I will focus on getting Lisa out. We'll see if there's anything we can do for her.'

'I'll say a prayer for Lisa,' said Davy.

Helen swore at her and told her not to bother. Then she cut the connection, leaving me on the line with Davy.

Mehmet walked back to where Charlie, Rosa, and the baby were.

'Devon, I need you to tell everyone to sit tight,' Davy said. 'This could be a long one. We're two engineers down. Lisa and Mehmet should be leading the recovery efforts. I'll get the other engineers onto it. We'll see how quickly we can get you out, but it might be a couple of days. Keep me updated with what's going on there and I'll keep you updated from this side.'

She clamped her jaw shut. It made me sad to see her so worried.

'And, Devon.'

'Yes?'

'I love you,' Davy said.

'I know.'

ACT THREE

MEAR 2, DAY 95

*THUNDERDOME, DEVON ISLAND COLONY, MARS*

I shoved a packet of flapjacks into my pocket and headed out into the pre-dawn stillness, zipping up my jacket as I walked. This time of mear the outside temperature normally dropped to twelve degrees overnight, but with the power issues we had now, it was allowed to go closer to freezing. I intended to sort that today.

Since the decompression just over a week before, I'd had trouble sleeping. Kept waking up in a cold sweat. That must be why I'd let time get away from me this morning. Normally, I was a stickler for my routine – I got up at the same time, got ready, got the kids ready. Breakfast ran like a well-oiled machine.

But the last few days had been a struggle. I was edgy and my brain felt foggy. It took ages for me to fall asleep, only to wake up again in a cold sweat two hours later. Every time I closed my eyes, I saw a hole in the dome – which was weird because in reality I'd never seen the damage.

Yawning, I emerged from the airlock into Saca, my mind

still on the events of the prior week. I had to admit, going anywhere without Seven made me nervous now. It wasn't just that I missed her presence, much as I did, but rather that I'd started being paranoid that I would die if she wasn't there to keep me safe. But she couldn't come afară.

After the accident, those of us in Lovelace had been trapped indoors overnight. As soon as we were freed, I'd taken Seven straight home to bed. By the time I returned to work a few days ago, the torn dome panel had been replaced. The psychological damage to the colony would take a lot longer to heal. I'd had two counselling sessions already and we hadn't even begun to unpack the trauma.

As I reached out to open the door to the garage, I realised I'd been flailing my arms – stimming. I hadn't noticed I was doing it – not even counting the movements. I wasn't embarrassed of my stimming, but it wasn't a good sign that I hadn't been aware of it.

The rover was parked in its usual spot, cleaned and ready. I was due to meet up with my team in DownBelow in – I checked the time – twenty-four minutes. Twenty-four was a good number.

*Come on, Devon, it's an auspicious start to the working day.* Great, now Lisa was giving me pep talks inside my own head.

I pulled open the door and inspected the rover's interior, removing a forgotten food container and placing it in the sink in the corner of the garage. If no one came to claim it before I returned, I'd deal with it later. Once I'd finished the inspection of the vehicle – inside and out – I selected a suit from the cupboard. I put my right foot in and – *what the hell?*

For the last week, my brain kept trying to persuade me I was hearing the sound of rushing air. But I was pretty sure I could tell the difference between real and imaginary whooshing. I smacked my ear with the heel of my hand, but the noise and sensation both continued. Sucking in as much air as I could, I scrambled to put my suit on, jamming the helmet on and slapping seals shut. *No, no. Not again. I'm not going to die today.*

The airlock door swung inwards. *What? It's not yet seven o'clock in the morning. No teams should be afară.*

Two people in filthy suits walked in. My eyes took them in, but my mind refused to process what I was seeing. Inside my sealed suit, my heart raced and I struggled to slow my panicked breathing. *Why were their suits blue instead of yellowy-green?*

The taller one took a step towards me; I stumbled backwards.

'Hello,' he said. 'My name is Lieutenant Pearce. I represent the 583$^{\text{rd}}$ RED HORSE squadron, the—'

He turned to his companion. 'I don't think she speaks English, Seaman Cattigan. Try French.'

*Semen? Did he just call that person Semen?* I opened my mouth to speak but nothing came out.

The other person was shorter and slighter, but I couldn't tell whether they were male or female. Their lower lip quivered inside their helmet.

'Bonjour. Je m'appelle matelot Cattigan. Voici mon commandant, le lieutenant Pearce.' *Why are they speaking French?*

The taller one spoke again. 'Try German, Seaman.' *Is Semen the person's name?*

'Guten Morgen. Ich heiße—' My hands flapped in front of me.

The lieutenant turned to his companion. 'I don't think it's a language issue.'

The power of speech finally returned to me. 'I speak

English. Sorry, you caught me off guard. I, er, I wasn't expecting anyone. Obviously, I mean, why would I anticipate strangers in the airlock?' Their suits had the wrong number of pockets and an odd texture.

'Yes, ma'am, I can understand that. Now, if you don't mind, I think it's probably best if I speak with your CO.'

This morning was not turning out how I expected and my brain kept rejecting all the evidence presented to it by my eyes and ears. 'My what?'

Inside his dirty helmet, he smiled broadly. The light wasn't bright enough to reveal many details, but he had perfect teeth. 'Who is in charge around here?' He spoke slowly, enunciating every syllable and emphasising them with gesticulations. I remembered being spoken to this way on Earth sometimes.

I nodded. Good idea. Yes, I should take these two aliens – for want of a better word – to Davy. She'd know what to do. I hoped.

'Davy. Yes, I'll take you to— Whoa, whoa, whoa? What the hell are you doing?' The man was moving towards the inner door. His companion remained rooted in their original position.

The lieutenant put his hand on his hips and sighed dramatically, which made me giggle somewhat hysterically. Daniel had made the same gesture last night when I refused to give him the toy Yana was playing with. I caught my breath. 'You can't go out there like that.' I waved my arm at him, trying to indicate his dust-covered suit.

And then I spotted the thing I should have noticed first. I let rip a multilingual stream of profanity that would have made my mother cry. When I finally got my tongue back under a degree of control, I spluttered, 'Are you ... weapons?

Have you … armed?' I flapped my hands wildly, trying to get my brain and mouth to work together.

'Guns,' I shouted. 'You brought guns into our colony. Holy mother of goat and sweet baby cats, what on Mars are you doing?' I backed as far away from the pair as I could, putting the rover between us. 'Is this an invasion?'

Through the vehicle's bubble dome, I saw the tall man make a show of setting down his weapon. 'Seaman,' he growled, not taking his eyes off me through the windows of the vehicle. 'Put your weapon down.'

My view of the smaller individual was partially obscured by the rover, but I saw them bend down. There was a noise of something clattering to the ground.

So many questions danced through my mind. *Who were they? Where had they come from? How long had they been on Mars? Why were they here, now, in our colony? What did they want from us?* I didn't dare ask them. I'd probably only succeed in mangling everything together and asking them when they were from or how they wanted us.

They sounded American. Or maybe Canadian. I'd never tell Davy – or Lisa, for that matter – but I couldn't tell the difference. Except French-Canadians. Obviously Caoimhe and Frankie sounded different from the rest of the Canadians and the other French speakers. Henri had…

*Stop it*, I commanded myself. *You have more pressing matters to think about than people's accents.*

I moved out from behind the rover and unclipped my helmet. Slowly, keeping an eye on the interlopers. 'We can't leave the garage in afară-wear. The whole of Saca would be covered in toxic dust.' I removed my suit as I spoke and hung it in the blast cupboard – it was still clean, but I figured it was simplest to demonstrate what to do. I turned around to see them both still standing there in their suits, blank looks on their faces.

'Perchlorate? Chlorine? Come on, get your kit off.' I closed the cupboard door and pressed the button to start the unit. I pointed at the clear door of the cupboard so they could see the process. My suit shook. If I'd been afară, we'd have seen dust falling to the grate below. Then it swayed as it was hit with a blast of high-pressure forced gas.

The tall one – the lieutenant, pronounced loo instead of lef – held both hands up, palms out. He slowly moved them towards his helmet, which he lifted off. I was punched in the face by a smell so overpowering, I retched. I thought of the flapjacks I'd brought, grateful I hadn't eaten them yet. Head down over my knees, I heaved onto the grated floor.

Rotten flesh and unwashed bodies and putrescence and… I coughed and waved my hands in front of my face. 'Okay, change of plan. Drop your clobber where it is. Someone who doesn't have a sensory processing disorder will come back and deal with it later. I'll take you to the showers. While you're in there, I'll call Davy to come to us. Deal?'

The lieutenant laughed heartily. 'Yes, ma'am.' They both stripped off their suits and left them where they fell. Beneath them, they wore – what would you call them? Combat fatigues? That's what they said in the films, anyway. Camouflage get-ups covered in pockets, gadgets, and badges. Little American flags on their sleeves. Even without the bulk of the excursion suit, I still wasn't sure whether Semen was a man or a woman.

The lieutenant moved towards the door again.

'Ah, ah, ah!' I walked to the sink and began the process of washing my hands, counting out the seconds. When I got to thirty, I grabbed a towel from the cupboard and moved out of their way. I motioned for them to do likewise.

Once their hands at least were clean, I took them to the door leading out to the main body of the dome. I changed into my regular shoes then turned back. 'Oh, erm, I guess you'll need to go barefoot. Wait, you don't have more weapons, do you? Like, in the films they always have knives, guns, and whatnot in every pocket.'

'No, ma'am. No more weapons. Scouts' honour.'

'Good. Thanks. Okay, let's go.' I turned the handle to open the door and they both gasped. 'I know, I'm sorry it's so cold.'

'Whoa!' Semen seemed to be doing their best impression of Keanu Reeves in *Bill & Ted*.

As a light flickered on overhead, the lieutenant exclaimed, 'It's so green.'

*I mean, everywhere in Devon Island is green. Why is that such a surprise to them?*

It was still early and only a handful of people lived in Saca, so we didn't encounter anyone on our walk. I grabbed some towels and soap from the cupboard before showing each of them to one of the dome's shower rooms. I gave them my code to turn the water on, hoping I wouldn't have to pay for all the excess.

As I pushed the door to the kitchen open, I pulled my phone out and dialled Davy. Her face appeared on my screen.

'Devon, are you okay? That's a stupid question – you're calling. Of course you're not okay. What's happened?' She frowned and squinted at her phone. 'Are you in the kitchen?'

I paced around the room as I spoke. 'Hey. Erm, yeah. I'm okay. I'm just... Oh, are you at the crèche? That's a good idea, yeah.'

'What's a good idea, Devon? What's happening?'

'I need you to come to Saca immediately. Like, right now.

Get Tom to bring some of his clothes. Or maybe some scrubs from the Scud. Yeah, do that. Two sets, please. One big, one sort of my size. Just get here quick as you can, okay? Please?' My voice cracked on that last word.

Figuring I should probably make myself useful, I hopped onto the power-cycle to give the batteries some juice. I ran through the morning's events in my mind as I waited for Davy – and for the two soldiers. *That's what they are, right? Soldiers. Have I just walked an invading army into our colony and shown them to the showers?*

After not many minutes, the door from the utility area swung inwards. The lieutenant peered his head around it. 'Um, ma'am?' He stood dripping wet, holding the towel around his waist. He was sort of blandly good looking – though his eyes were sunken and there was an angry bruise spreading across his torso.

I leapt up off the bike seat. 'Sorry, geez. That was quick.' I sniffed the air, still getting a whiff of stink. 'Are you sure you're clean?' I got off the power-cycle and walked towards him slowly.

With his free hand, he rubbed his wet hair. 'I didn't want to take advantage of your hospitality. Water's a precious resource.'

'I'd much rather you didn't stink.'

He chuckled. 'Yes, ma'am. I'll, um, get back in and do a more thorough job. I'll let Cattigan know to do the same.'

'Who?' This day was really getting away from me. I wasn't exactly at my shining best.

'Seaman Cattigan. My colleague.'

'Oh, yeah. Sure. Them too.'

The lieutenant tilted his head oddly. He turned to go, but just then the front door opened. Davy and Tom walked in. Davy was wearing Daniel in a harness contraption on her back. Tom held Rafa in his arms. As usual, Yana insisted on walking, Seven by her side. Both adults stopped dead in their tracks, jaws falling slack.

I was grateful for Seven's calming presence, but I wondered why Davy brought children to meet the soldiers.

Yana marched straight up to the lieutenant and yanked on his towel. Seven stuck her nose under it, sniffed him, and sneezed ferociously. He looked down at them both and chuckled. 'Excuse me. Do you two mind?' Then he strode across the room and held his free hand out to Tom. 'You must be Dave. I understand you're the OIC.'

Tom stared down at the hand, dumbfounded. Somewhere in the back of my head I remembered handshaking being a thing. But surely that died out mears ago. *Was he from the past?*

Davy blinked twice before she recovered herself. 'I'm Davy. I'm the – the prime minister. This is my colleague, Tom. He's our minister for education and children's affairs. And I see you've met my wife, Devon.' She held a hand out in my direction. She unclipped the pouch and set Daniel on the sofa.

'Welcome to Devon Island. Um, oh, Tom, you should probably give the man some clothes.'

Tom set Rafa down next to Daniel and handed the man the stack of folded cloth he held.

'Thank you, sir. My name is Lieutenant Pearce. Now, um, if you'll excuse me, Devon – it was Devon, right?' He turned to look at me. *Oh crap, in all the excitement, I think I'd forgotten to introduce myself. My mother would be appalled.*

'Yeah, sorry. Probably should've mentioned that.'

'Not a problem, ma'am. I think it's fair to say we bush-whacked you.' He turned back towards Davy. 'I'm sorry for dropping in unannounced. We, um, we didn't know how to get in touch with you.' He looked down at his body then added, 'Your, um, wife expressed concern about the way I smell, so if it's all right with you, I'll take a couple more minutes with that fabulous shower you've got and be back with you as quick as I can.'

Tom took a few steps in a sort of box waltz. 'I'll put the kettle on, shall I?'

Davy nodded. 'That sounds like a good idea. Are you — Hang on, I gather there's more than one of you. Is that right?'

'Cattigan is still in the shower. The rest of my team is outside.' He must have meant afară, because there definitely hadn't been anyone else outside the kitchen. *Wait, there were more of them? More soldiers?*

Davy's jaw clenched. It was a tiny tell. Most people wouldn't notice it, I didn't think. But when she was worried, a little muscle just below her ear stood out. 'How many of you are there?'

'Just seven of us left, Madame Prime Minister.' Somehow, he seemed to shrink as he said it.

'Please, just Davy will be fine.' There was that muscle again. 'Do you have a means of contacting them from here?'

'Yes, ma— Yes, Davy. I've got a radio in the pocket of my fatigues. Shall I call them in?'

Davy crossed her arms over her chest and then uncrossed them. 'Yes, of course. Tom, would you go to the garage to meet them, please? Perhaps call Li— no, Gurdeep to assist you.' Lisa was still in a coma.

'No weapons,' I said. Judging by everyone's faces, I'd probably spoken more loudly than the situation warranted. 'They had weapons.'

Davy raised an eyebrow at me and held it as she turned to Pearce. 'No weapons, please, Lieutenant. Devon and I will make tea and put some refreshments together while you finish in the bathroom.'

He saluted her before leaving the room.

Moments later, the other person from the garage emerged from the shower wearing fresh green scrubs. They were a bit shorter than me and thin. Short brown hair and hazel eyes. A few freckles were scattered across their face.

'Um, good morning. My name is Cattigan. Um, please call me Jamie. The lieutenant said I should assist you as you see fit.'

'Hi, Jamie. Welcome to Devon Island. I'm Davy.'

'I'm Devon. Sorry, I should have mentioned that.' Oops. 'She's the prime minister – my wife, the prime minister.'

Catching sight of Seven, they danced across the room. 'Oh my gosh. You have a dog. May I?'

I nodded. 'Of course, her name's Seven.'

They let her sniff their hand and then sat down on the floor in front of her. Seven graciously accepted the fuss. Yana was fascinated by the newcomer. She climbed into their lap and poked them in the eye.

MEAR 2, DAY 95

SACA DOME, DEVON ISLAND COLONY, MARS

'The water will shut off automatically after three minutes,' said the peculiar, tall woman with the red hair. 'But it's okay – just this once – to turn it back on again. Use the same code.'

She raised an eyebrow. Having avoided eye contact so far in the whole surreal situation, she made a point of looking us each in the eye as she repeated the instructions to start the water. It was clear she thought we needed it. The way she looked at Pearce – like he was an idiot child – I had to bite my cheek to keep from giggling.

She turned to go then thought better of it and looked back at us. 'Sorry, the water's cold. Power, you know.' She shrugged and left.

The lieutenant and I were in separate bathrooms. No sounds emanated from the other side of the wall. The bathroom was clean – not the cold, sterile sort you'd see in a fancy hotel. Clean like a much-loved home.

Up near the top of the wall – against what looked like a frosted window, but it must have been artificial lighting – there was a row of plants. One of them was peppered with small violet flowers. This place must be some kind of paradise.

*A shower! A shower big enough to dance in.* I sat down on the can and cried.

I hadn't had a real shower since we'd left our base six months earlier. Six months of standing in a trickle of icy water in a bathroom the size of what you'd get in an airplane. Six months of us all being cooped up in a high-tech camper van. Eighty per cent rations. Zero privacy. Driving at night, recharging the solar batteries during the day.

Four years ago, sixteen bright-eyed and optimistic soldiers left Earth with the hope of building a new life for Americans. Three died in the first year – two accidents and a suicide. Six months ago, we'd split the group – eleven desperate people left our base in search of what we thought was an equally desperate group. Today, seven skinny, starving, malnourished, dehydrated, and hopeless people arrived in paradise.

Death had claimed seven of our people in total. Chambers died four months ago – appendicitis. She'd been my only friend on the team. Without her around, I'd been so tempted to follow — *Dear Lord, please forgive me.*

*But if we confess our sins to Him, He can be depended on to forgive us and to cleanse us from every wrong.*

Oh boy, did I need cleansing. Physically and spiritually. I wiped the tears from my cheeks with the backs of my hands. My filthy hands.

I stripped off my scuzzy, grimy clothes and stepped into the shower. Just below the control panel, someone had carved four letters in neat handwriting. KKMD. I wondered what that meant.

Letting the tears flow freely, I scrubbed and lathered and rinsed and repeated. The water was warm, not cold. The dirt and the stink gradually sloughed off, but the psychic stains would take more than one shower to purge – glorious though the shower may be.

*Blessed are those who mourn, for they shall be comforted.*

The bar of soap the woman had given me smelled faintly of mint and … maybe lemongrass? Whatever it was, it was heavenly. I wanted to stay in the shower all day. When the water shut off, I switched it back on again. And then one more time. That was probably enough. *Nine minutes wasn't too long, was it?*

And then it hit me: I had no clean clothes. *What am I supposed to do now?*

I could smell my rank uniform from here. She didn't want me to put that back on, did she? Surely not. But… Wrapping the towel around my chest, I cracked the door open an inch. I looked up the hallway and then down it.

Was that the lieutenant's voice in the distance? Had he found clothes somewhere?

'Just seven of us left, Madame Prime Minister,' I heard him say.

*Prime minister? Was that sarcasm? It had to be. No, that didn't make sense. Surely, I misheard.*

I could hear a faint reply, but the speaker must have been further away, as I couldn't make out any words.

'Yes, ma— Yes, Davy. I've got a radio in the pocket of my fatigues. Shall I call them to come in?' *Was Davy a woman?*

Again, I couldn't hear the reply. But then, just faintly, I heard another voice. 'No weapons.' It might have been the strange woman. 'They had weapons.'

A moment later the door in the hall swung outward, and the lieutenant appeared wearing only a towel, closely followed by a slender man with a beard. Water dropped from Pearce's damp blond hair onto his body. His smooth, pale skin glistened in the hall's dim light.

I blushed when he turned my way. 'Tom, this is Seaman Cattigan. Seaman, this is Tom, he's part of the colony's um … their government.'

Through the crack in the door I nodded at the man. 'Hello. It's nice to meet you. This is a wonderful place you have here.' Tom wore plain khaki pants, not entirely dissimilar to the ones we wore. But that's where the similarity ended. He had paired them with a well-worn T-shirt with a faded print and old stains. On his feet, he wore flip-flops. His fair, thinning hair was longer than the military would permit but still short.

Tom smiled warmly. 'If you bring your dirty clothes to the end of the hall, you'll find a laundry room. Just drop them on the floor. Someone will get to them in a bit.'

The lieutenant stepped toward me and held up a neatly folded stack of well-worn green fabric.

Hiding myself behind the door, I reached for the soft, cool cloth. I offered a nod of thanks, not trusting myself to speak, lest I burst into tears.

The lieutenant said, 'Seaman, get dressed and go help the women in the kitchen. Do whatever they tell you to until I return.'

'Yes, sir.' When I had closed the door, I leaned against it and brushed away the tears that were threatening to overwhelm me again. This place was heaven.

*I will give thanks to You, Lord, with all my heart; I will tell of all Your wonderful deeds.*

The pale green fabric turned out to be hospital scrubs. I put them on then carried my reeking pile of dirty clothes to the laundry as instructed. Once I'd washed the stink of them off my hands, I went into the kitchen.

The odd woman – I really should have asked her name – was there along with another woman. They were facing away from me. The strange one was removing jars from the cupboard; a brunette was rummaging in the fridge.

'Good morning. My name is Cattigan.' They didn't seem like military. 'Um, please call me Jamie.' How long had it been since anyone had addressed me by my first name? 'The lieutenant said I should assist you in any way possible.'

The woman at the fridge stood up and turned to face me. Her face looked warm and open – she seemed like someone people would instinctively trust. 'Hi, Jamie. Welcome to Devon Island. I'm Davy.'

The redhead screwed up her eyes. 'I'm Devon. Sorry, I should have mentioned that.' She took a few awkward steps in my direction. 'She's the prime minister – my wife, the prime minister.'

Across the space, there was an area set up like a living room. Movement caught my eye. By the far door, a dark shadow on the wooden floor shifted. A German shepherd walked toward me. 'Oh my gosh. You have a dog. May I?' She looked like the dog I had as a child.

Devon nodded. 'Of course, her name's Seven.'

I held out a hand to let her sniff me. She put her head in my hand and I sat down on the floor in front of her. My knees were going to give way if I didn't. She stood regally before me as I buried my hands in her soft, warm fur.

The day – which was already pretty surprising – got even weirder when a small head popped up from the couch. A child approached from the same area. She had masses of wavy brown hair. I'd guess around a year old.

She toddled right up to me and jabbed a finger in my eye. It was a tiny but very human thing and it filled my soul with joy. I booped the child on the nose, still petting Seven with my other hand. The toddler squealed with glee.

'That's Yana, our daughter,' said Devon. Another child climbed down off the couch and moved to join us. 'Oh, and here comes Rafa – she's Tom's.'

Rafa was smaller than her friend but looked a few months older. Early to be walking so steadily on her feet. She climbed into my lap. I looked into her brown eyes. 'Sorry, I need to go help in the kitchen.' I made to disentangle myself, but Davy stopped me.

'You're helping beautifully already, Jamie. Why don't you keep an eye on the kids while Devon and I make — Hang on, I didn't ask. Are your team likely to be hungry?'

I swallowed and rubbed my nose, determined not to cry. Even with food as scarce as it was, they were willing to share what they had. 'We don't want to be a bother. You need your rations as much as we do … more, in fact, with all the littles.'

I saw Devon mouth the word *rations* like it was an alien language.

The door from the shower area swung open and the lieutenant stepped in. His eyes fired straight to me on the floor. He opened his mouth to speak, but Devon cut him off. 'We asked Jamie to help us by watching the kids.'

Davy addressed the lieutenant. 'How about you chop some veg with me while we chat, eh? What would your team say to a fry-up?'

'A what?' He shook his head. 'Sorry, ma'am. That is, we'll eat anything.'

I looked up from where I sat playing pat-a-cake with Yana. Rafa climbed onto my back, giggling. 'Don't forget Sergeant Cobb is allergic to eggs.'

Devon turned around from her position at the kitchen counter and replied, 'That won't be an issue.' I wondered what she could mean.

Davy pulled a load of veg from the fridge and set it on the counter. 'I'll call Mehmet to get someone guarding both the kitchen door and the door to the utility area. No one comes in here until I'm ready for them. The lef— Sorry, the lieutenant and I have some things to discuss.'

She pointed a fresh carrot at Devon and then at me. 'Can you take Jamie with you afară? We need the farm up to full capacity by this afternoon or else our guests will need to have a go on the cycles.' I couldn't even begin to understand what half those words meant in context.

Looking back at Devon, Davy continued, 'But first, can you take the kids to the crèche, please?'

Requests, not orders.

Devon nodded. 'Sure, I can do that.'

'Yes, ma'am,' I added.

'Enough of the "ma'am" business. Please call me Davy.'

I started to reply, but the door opened again. Two women walked in. The first was tall and broad-shouldered with brown skin and fine black hair. A scar ran out and up from the corner of her eye. The second was shorter and rounder with long, tangled, curly blond hair. The former had a tiny bundle wrapped in cloth bound to her chest, while the latter had a baby with deep umber skin kicking fat little legs against her belly.

The blonde one's eyes were wide as she spoke. 'Lone Starr here only rocked up in a Space Winnebago!' I couldn't place her accent – maybe eastern European – but she punctuated each word with a wild gesture. I bit my cheek to keep from laughing; it wasn't hard to guess who she meant.

Tom and the lieutenant followed them in. 'Hang on, what'd you call me?'

The blonde turned to Pearce. 'Oh, you heard me, Lone Starr.' Something about the way she said it made me doubt anyone would ever call him anything else ever again.

He scratched his head. 'Lone Starr?'

The dark-haired woman shook her head, her shoulder-length hair swishing with each movement. 'I mean, it *is* a Space Winnebago. And if you think my wife is going to let you off without a *Spaceballs* reference, you've come to the wrong Mars colony.'

Tom looked over at Davy. 'The rest of the team are in the showers. By the look of them, they could all use a good meal.'

As I stood up, the two toddlers each grabbed one of my hands, the small gesture of acceptance melting my heart. We walked to the sofa, where I noticed another baby with a shock of bright red hair – it was pretty obvious whose child this was. This one looked about the same age as the other two, just less adventurous.

Devon said, 'This is Daniel. He's ours too.' Daniel licked a teddy bear. 'Right, Jamie. Time for us to head to the crèche and then we're going afară. I grabbed some fruit and flapjacks for breakfast. We can eat as we drive. Sound good?'

I had no clue how anyone could eat flapjacks in a vehicle. Maybe without butter or syrup? Still, a morning in this green paradise where people called me by my name? It didn't sound good, it sounded like a dream. Granted, it was a dream that had started out pretty strange, but it had improved dramatically since then.

———

*THE CRAFT DOME, DEVON ISLAND COLONY, MARS*

Six hours, two square meals, and multiple pills and needles later, the lieutenant contacted me using Devon's phone and ordered me to the colony's civic centre. Devon agreed to walk me there from the amusingly named Scud. The whole colony was like a maze.

We'd come to be fast friends over the course of the day. When she explained she was autistic, it helped shed some light on the events of the morning. And then when she told me how Seven had saved her life ten days before, it made me want to hug both her and the dog. Somehow I didn't think Devon would appreciate that, though.

The meteor shower that killed three of their people and seriously wounded another had also killed two of our team – including Major Willis. Walking through the brightly coloured domes, seeing all the healthy-looking people, dogs and toddlers frolicking in the greenery, birds singing in the trees, it was easy to think this place was utopia. And yet, from what Devon had said, they'd been plagued by many of the same troubles we had.

She touched buildings, leaves, and trees as we passed them. Their colony had lost people to suicide, accidents, diseases. She'd lost a good friend, too.

'And here we are,' she said. 'I'll see you at the dinner tonight, yeah?'

'Absolutely.' I waved goodbye then turned and walked into the building she'd indicated. An African-American woman… *Wait, that can't be right.* What were you supposed to call people of colour if they weren't American?

Anyway, a young woman with curly black hair greeted

me. 'Hi, you must be Seaman Cattigan, yes? My name is Jupiter. I'm Davy's chief of staff. It's lovely to meet you.'

'Likewise, but please … call me Jamie.'

She nodded her head. 'Jamie, excellent. Your team are all in our meeting room just through there. I'll see you at dinner.'

'Yes, ma'am.'

'Oh my days, you're adorable. See you.' She turned and headed out. I opened the inner door she'd pointed me to and walked in.

'Seaman Cattigan. How good of you to join us.'

I saluted Sergeant Cobb. 'Yes, ma'am. Sorry, ma'am. I came as quick as I could.'

'Sit your ass down, Seaman. The lieutenant is waiting.'

I did as she bid, taking the one remaining seat at the smooth, black conference table. Cobb sat down next to me.

At the head of the table, the lieutenant stood up. He too was wearing borrowed clothes. He'd managed to shave and buzz his hair since I last saw him. 'Corporal Kay is still in the clinic being treated for an infection, so this is us for now. As you've all no doubt seen by this point, this colony – Devon Island – is not quite what we expected. They are not a military outpost but consider themselves an independent nation.' A small chuckle escaped his lips.

'Although they lost a good deal of crops last week in the meteor shower – along with three members of their group – they are a self-sufficient colony. They operate as a democratic state with a mixed economy.'

He leaned forward and laid his hands on the table. 'I've made a tentative agreement with their leader. I was able to exchange messages with Colonel Powell back in Washington and he's given the plan his blessing. But of course, it's conditional upon support from the Dowager-President. It's been proposed' – *by zombies*, added my brain – 'the MENaCE join this colony in the interim. We'll be non-voting residents, but I will participate in certain aspects of their – um – government as your representative.'

He stood up straight, hands clasped behind his back, and took a deep breath. 'We will be bound by their laws and customs, but you will continue to report to me. In essence, we will be in their society but not of it.'

Well, that sounded familiar. *Do not be conformed to this world, but be transformed by the renewing of your minds.*

'We will be assigned jobs and added to their rotas. They've made some space for us to bunk in.'

The lieutenant shifted his weight from one foot to the other and back again. 'Two members of our company will remain at the base to look after things. We'll swap out every six months. Thankfully, with fewer people and supplies to transport, we'll be able to make the journey in about two months.' He crossed his arms over his chest, his muscles straining against the short-sleeved scrub top he wore. 'OPSEC remains a priority. Under no circumstances are you to discuss the nature of our mission or what the base comprises with any member of Devon Island colony. This order comes direct from the Dowager-President. Not a peep.'

After a few more organisational matters, he assigned us all phones connected to the colony's comms array. Without that, we hadn't had any means of contacting them before our arrival. They used phone numbers, not radio frequencies. 'Now, our first assignment will involve building two new apartments to accommodate us. For now Sergeant Cobb will show you to your billets. You are free to rest up until the dinner scheduled for eighteen hundred hours this evening, when we will join in a banquet they've planned in our honour in the dome called the Ankh.'

He shifted his stance. 'Dismissed.'

*The Lord Almighty will spread a wondrous feast for everyone around the world – a delicious feast of good food, with clear, well-aged wine and choice beef.*

Though if I understood things correctly, we'd never see beef again.

SEACOLE DOME, DEVON ISLAND COLONY, MARS

'That's it. I hereby pronounce you all better. You'll need to take it slow, but you're well enough to be discharged. I advise easing yourself back into work over the next few weeks.'

The bed I was sitting on had been my home for six weeks. 'Thank … you.' It was still a struggle to get the words to flow properly. 'Caoimhe. Thank you, Caoimhe.' *Better. Only a brief hesitation that time.* I could form words and sentences coherently in my head, but I still struggled to speak fluidly.

She bent forwards to touch my knee. 'Hey. Your body was without oxygen for almost three minutes. By the time Helen pulled you out, your heart had stopped.' She lowered her voice and leaned closer. 'Don't tell her I said this, but it's a miracle you survived at all.'

I nodded.

She smiled. 'You're doing well – remember that. Keep focusing on building your strength and stamina. Try not to do too much too quickly. Stick with the physiotherapy, but you're ready to start reinserting yourself back into life. And speaking from a purely selfish perspective, I think you should start by putting your efforts into cooking rather than engineering and maintenance. Who cares about emergency alerts or being able to breathe?' My doctor waved her hands wildly to brush away such mundane ideas as physical health. 'All I really want is a good burger – and no one makes a better myc burger than you.'

'Word.'

I turned towards the voice that had spoken from across the room. Only two of the ward's six beds were occupied. Desmond lay propped up in his bed. Mike, his wife, sat on a chair next to the bed, bouncing Qianru on her lap.

'Sorry,' Mike added. 'Didn't mean to eavesdrop – but Caoimhe is one hundred per cent correct. No one makes a better burger than you, Lisa.'

Desmond looked happier than I'd ever seen him. He'd walked into the Scud with a strained look on his face yesterday evening as I was heading to the toilet. He'd given birth three weeks earlier than expected – but baby and parent were both healthy.

Desmond caught me looking at him. He grinned and winked. 'What's the matter? Have you never seen a grown man chestfeeding his newborn baby before?'

I chuckled at that, but before I'd thought of a retort he continued, 'I dunno. Did you try one of the burgers Lone Starr made last week?' He licked his lips.

'Lone Starr?' The Americans were the biggest news to hit our colony in ages – but I didn't remember any of them having such a silly name.

'The lieutenant in charge of their group. Georgie dubbed him Lone Starr on account of the Space Winnebago and it's kinda stuck.'

'Lieutenant?' That didn't make sense. I was surprised that such a junior officer would be in charge of a RED HORSE unit. Surely, there should be at least a captain – probably a major.

Caoimhe nodded. 'I heard their senior officer died in the same meteorite strike that injured you.'

'So much loss.' I shook my head. *When would it end?*

Caoimhe touched my shoulder. 'All the more reason for us to keep going.'

I pulled my sweater on. 'So, what are they like?'

Desmond shrugged. 'Lone Starr's all right – only called me ma'am once. I doubt he'd ever knowingly met anyone trans before. He was a perfect gentleman when I explained.' He affected a stern face. 'Ah can't say ah unnerstan, but ah respect your right to live as yer see fit.'

Caoimhe and I both burst out laughing. Mike turned to her husband with a dumbfounded expression. She shook her head. 'What on Mars was that? Was that really you trying to do a Boston accent? What kind of monster have I married?'

Desmond lifted the baby away from his chest and closed the hospital gown. He hefted the newborn to his shoulder, patting it gently on the back. 'Hey, don't even go there. I've heard your attempt to mimic my South African accent.'

Mike ran her fingers through Qianru's fine brown hair. 'Point made. Maybe neither of us should ever do accents again.'

Desmond laid his head back on the stack of pillows. 'Deal.'

I took that as a sign he'd run out of energy, so I turned back to Caoimhe just as Nora walked into the room.

Nora had a canvas bag over her shoulder and was wearing civvies. 'Right, you both.' Looking at Caoimhe she said, 'Helen's arrived to run the show here for this evening, so we're off the hook.' She turned to me. 'And you've been discharged, so it's time for all three of us to hit the road. Come on, I'll bring one of the ambos and give you a lift home.'

My new apartment was in Antalya. Someone had moved all my stuff while I'd been in hospital. I'd have to return to Lovelace to face my own fears – but not today.

'All right,' I said.

We left the Scud and walked slowly along the path. I used a cane to steady myself rather than accept the ride. Caoimhe was meeting Korri at the White Hart, which was next door to my new digs, so she walked with us. Her dog, Lemmy, trotted happily alongside us and Nora rode the bike that pulled the ambulance.

Antalya wasn't far, but I was cautious of not over-exerting myself, so I climbed into the back of the ambulance after a few minutes.

Twenty minutes later, we walked through the door of the pub. Although I hadn't planned to go in, I wasn't ready to be alone yet. I may as well sit on the pub sofa as the bunk in my room.

Caoimhe went to the bar to place our order while Nora and I found seats.

Nora made a beeline for the piano. She sat perpendicular to it, facing me on the sofa close by. She played absently with one hand as we chatted about nothing. I looked past her out the window at the lush banana and lemon trees.

When Caoimhe brought our drinks over, Nora turned her back on the group and played more earnestly – a tune emerging from the formless notes. As the song took shape, she began to sing. Her music wasn't to my taste, but she did have a beautiful voice: haunting and melodic.

'Oh my days! You know I hate that song. Don't you know any other ones?'

We all turned towards the pub's front door. The voice was loud and brash but playful. Jupiter – holding Amos by the hand – crossed the bar and plunked herself down at the piano next to Nora.

'Hey, Jupiter. It's your song. I sing it for you.'

'I know. And I love you. But oh, how I hate that song.' Jupiter leaned over and kissed Nora.

'Mama,' said a small voice next to them.

Both women turned to look at their son. He was the oldest of the many babies born on Mars, about three years by Earth standards, but not even one and a half mears.

Nora turned from the piano keys. 'Aye, Amos?'

'I would like a drink, please.' He was so small – it shocked me how clear his words were. Jupiter led him to the bar to place their orders.

'So, how are things? What've I missed while I've been stuck in bed?'

'Puh-lease,' said Nora. 'Ye've had visitors every single day. And we all ken how well news travels in this place. There's unlikely to be much of anything you've not already heard.'

I waggled my head back and forth – but that made me dizzy, so I stopped. 'True, but a lot of what was said I heard while I was under the influence of a cocktail of drugs.'

Caoimhe waved dismissively. 'Excuses, excuses.' She paused as Jupiter and Amos joined us and settled in. 'Anyways… Here's a bit of gossip for you. The day after they arrived, Lone Starr went to Davy and said they had one thing to offer us that we *clearly* didn't have.'

I frowned sceptically. 'What's that – uniforms? Meat?' I snapped my fingers as a thought occurred to me. 'Actually, they don't have a magical source of unlimited electricity, do they?'

Jupiter snorted, but it was Caoimhe who responded, continuing her story. 'As if. No, he said they could offer us the services of their chaplain – since we *obviously* didn't have one of our own.'

Nora struggled to contain her giggles. 'Apparently, he told her Jamie would hear our confessions.'

Jupiter scrunched up her lips, then pursed them, and back again. I figured she was weighing up what she was allowed to say. 'He, er, he offered to have Jamie lead a service for us. Davy was pretty gracious about it. She said Georgie would welcome Jamie to stand in for the regular Wednesday night service.'

She took a dainty sip of her juice. 'Lone Starr stood there for a moment, blinking. But in the end, he was as diplomatic as she was. "I'd appreciate that, ma'am. We've not had the opportunity to take communion since we left our base. We'd be grateful to join with you in the sacraments." And it was a particularly nice service, more people than usual.'

The pub was growing busier. When a family with a toddler came in, Amos clambered down off the sofa and wandered off to play with the child. Nora moved from the piano bench, curling up with Jupiter on the sofa, in the space their son had vacated.

'The first few days after the incident were pretty dark,' Nora said.

Jupiter nodded. 'Yeah, figuratively *and* literally. With half our solar panels damaged or destroyed, we needed every bit of power we could get our hands on just to keep things going. We let temperatures fall almost to freezing in most of the colony. Put the lights out inside homes – everything we could think of.'

Nora looked at me. 'It's a good thing our fridges get their chill from the planet. Even still, we were manning the power-cycles pretty much twenty-four/seven until they got the replacement solar panels in place.'

She lifted her glass to her lips. 'It only took a couple of days to repair Lovelace dome last month – at least structurally. And Devon led the team that repaired the solar farm, so we're back up to full power. Davy announced today that Mike would step into Iulia's former role as the colony's finance minister.'

I'd been advised of both of those facts when I regained consciousness. Devon had returned to work as soon as she could, printing components for the new solar panels. If the damage to the solar array had been more extensive than it was, the long-term devastation to the colony would have been irreparable.

Caoimhe stroked her dog. 'With Desmond being on leave since his close call, Korri took charge of some of his work.' Desmond was the head gardener for the three warmer-weather domes. Korri and Georgie split the rest of the habs. 'Korri's been, um – il a de la broue dans le toupet.'

I laughed at the old French-Canadian idiom. Something about beer in the hair. Her poor husband must be absolutely swamped. 'Korri told me we lost all the crops in Lovelace. Everything. Fruit, veg, fibres, trees, oxygen scrubbers, the algae ponds and myc vats – even the bacteria in the soil died.'

Jupiter grinned as she wagged a finger at me. 'While you've been snoozing, we've all been hard at work replanting crops.'

I had a sudden recollection: Brian telling me I was a black-thumb, not fit for handling live plants. My shoulders fell at the bittersweet memory. *Iulia. Brian. Gabriel. Qiang. And that was just the people I counted as friends. How many more had to die before we figured ourselves out?*

Nora leaned across the table. 'It'll be okay.' She shook her head as if to clear it then smiled sadly. 'Anyway, enjoy your hot chocolate while you can. Prices are about to skyrocket.'

All I could think was: *what difference does it make?* Even I would gladly sacrifice all the chocolate on Mars if it meant people could live out their natural lives. But Jupiter mistook my silence for failure to grasp the economics. 'Supply and demand, innit? The bottom has fallen out of our supply, but demand hasn't changed.'

Caoimhe set her glass down. 'Korri says it'll probably take about two mears to get a halfway decent crop of cocoa beans. Maybe a mear for pineapples and twelve months for the first bananas. Coffee would've taken at least a couple mears to become anything close to productive, but we have Brian's faster-growing variety. Korri's optimistic in his time-lines, but there's still going to be a tropical food famine for a bit.' She shrugged. 'Sorry.'

Jupiter leaned her head back and groaned melodramatically. Most of the time, it was easy to forget just how young she really was – but every now and then the mask slipped. 'Oh my days, Caoimhe. If you lot are putting people into comas now, where do I sign up? I never agreed to this,' she said.

Caoimhe laughed at her. 'I can't believe you don't trust my husband. If he says there will be coffee, there will be coffee – otherwise he'll have to fight me.'

I chuckled at that image. 'Personally, I don't give two hoots about coffee – nasty, vile swill. I like chocolate, but what I really want is bananas. And pineapples!'

Caoimhe shifted topics abruptly. 'So, how soon until you go back to Lovelace?'

'I don't know,' I answered honestly. 'It's not rational, but the thought of going in there scares me.'

Nora put her arm around my shoulder. 'No one will make you do anything you're not comfortable with.'

'Thanks, I know.' I took a sip of my now-lukewarm chocolate. 'I kind of feel like I should just get back up on that horse even though I'm anxious.'

'This is nice, having a bit of a clavardage,' said Caoimhe.

Both Nora and Jupiter gawped at her. 'A what?' they asked in unison.

This had been a good evening, but I was tired. It was time to go check out my new apartment – and in particular, my bed.

ANTALYA DOME, DEVON ISLAND COLONY, MARS

'Here you go, mate. A pint of Mars's finest lager. Well, I say a pint. It's half a litre, obviously. Devon still insists imperial measurements are stupid, so she refuses to make actual pint glasses.' I set the beer down in front of Tom.

'Cheers, Georgie. Skål.' The steel glasses made a dull clink.

'Noroc,' I replied with a smile. 'Enjoy that – it's on Charlie. She sends her best wishes. Though she did add a few unkind words about marriage, which I won't repeat.' This was what passed for a stag do in Devon Island: two people having a drink in the White Hart.

Tom tossed his head back and laughed. 'Never one to miss an opportunity to speak her mind, our Chuck.' He took a drink then set his glass down. 'I didn't give her enough credit in the beginning. Underestimated her. To my shame, I even tried to make her feel bad about who she was – all because I didn't have the courage or the strength to be who I was.'

I took a long pull of my deep amber ale and sighed happily. 'Never let Helen get you up the duff, Tom. Forty weeks of pregnancy. And then nursing… This is my first drink in a mear. I can't tell you how much I've missed this.' I leaned my head back and savoured the taste – as the sweet malty flavours receded, the bitter hops came to the forefront.

Tom chuckled. 'Thanks for the advice. I'll bear that in mind. Gurdeep's on baby duty tonight, I take it?'

'Indeed. And she's got her hands full with the pair of them, I'll tell you that.' We sat in companionable silence for a minute until he broke the spell.

'It's not my first,' he said softly. He searched for something to hold in his hands – the way he used to fiddle with cigarettes or pens.

I took another sip of my beer and popped a handful of root veg crisps into my mouth. I set my drink down and proffered the bowl of savoury goodies. He declined. I had a feeling I knew some of what he was about to tell me – and had guessed more.

Tom ran a hand through his thinning hair. 'It's been so long since I've told this story, in full at least. All in one go.' He closed his eyes for a moment. 'I was married. Mears ago now. We were young, so very young. We met in undergrad, like you and Gurdeep did. Both of us were involved with a "Refugees Welcome" group.'

He wiped his mouth and laughed at his younger self. 'I had joined partly because I was a young idealist with delusions of changing the world – and partly because I figured it would be a good way to meet women. Audrey joined because her family had escaped to Denmark from Cameroon a dozen years prior.'

Tom slumped forwards, supporting his chin in his folded hands. 'We fell madly in love pretty much from the moment we met. Even now, I still love her.' I reached across the table and touched his hand.

'After we finished undergrad, we got married,' he said. He waved his hands around. 'Big, traditional wedding: church, marshmallowy dress, tuxes, flowers everywhere. The whole thing. It's what we wanted. Well, at least, it's what our moms wanted.'

He removed his phone from his pocket and clicked a few buttons, before turning it to face me. I pushed my glasses back up my nose and accepted the device. It showed a smiling couple. The younger version of the man before me wore a black tuxedo with a white satin waistcoat and a teal tie. An enormous herbal boutonnière adorned his lapel.

A startled laugh escaped my lips before I could stop myself. 'Oh, Tom. I'm sorry. I don't mean to laugh. I shouldn't mock, I really shouldn't. But your hair! What were you thinking?' Tom shrugged. 'How much work did it take to make your hair look that messy?'

He raised his hands, palms upwards. I looked back down at the image on his screen again. Next to young Tom stood a beautiful woman with warm brown skin and a round face. Her petite frame was engulfed by mountains of tulle and white lace. They gazed adoringly at each other, as if they were oblivious to the photographer's presence.

Our photographer had posed us in a similarly contrived manner. Flashing a quick *wait* gesture, I pulled my own phone out. It took me a few seconds to find what I was looking for. I studied it for a moment before wordlessly handing it to him.

'Is this…?' He reached out to take my device, eyebrows raised. I nodded as he accepted it. The photo I'd handed him was one we didn't often show people – it felt too intimate.

Both Gurdeep and I considered it a favourite, but it was only for us. Usually.

We stood facing one another, my fingers on Gurdeep's cheek, our faces nearly touching. My curls – dyed pale pink for the occasion – were piled on top of my head and spilling over gracefully. I wore a white satin dress with rainbow ribbons stitched into the hem. My beautiful bride wore a tasteful black suit and black shirt with a brightly coloured tweed bowtie.

In the picture, Gurdeep smiled shyly at the youthful me – it looked like she was on the verge of tears. I had my head thrown back in riotous laughter. 'The photographer told her to whisper something dirty in my ear. Poor Gurdeep! She was so embarrassed – you know how private she is.'

Tom looked me in the eye and handed the phone back. 'What a beautiful memory.' His eyes brightened. He drained his beer. 'When I look back now I cringe – but we thought it was amazing at the time. The perfect day – the most beautiful everything.' He shook his head and laughed nostalgically.

I picked up our empty glasses. 'Same again?' He nodded, so I headed to the bar for another round. When I returned with two more pints and a couple bowls of chips, he continued his story.

'We moved to Germany. I did my PhD and she got a job working in politics. Being separated from our families and friends took its toll on our relationship.'

He tossed a chip into his mouth. 'But everything changed again when Florent was born. I was determined to be the best father ever – and the best husband. I loved them both more than I thought possible. Once I finished my PhD, I got a job offer working for a big mental health clinic in the US. Audrey wasn't sure about the idea of living in America, but...' A tear formed in the corner of his eye.

I reached across the table and touched his shoulder gently. 'It's okay. You don't have to tell me anything you don't want to.'

'I know.' He nodded. 'We moved to Illinois just after Florent's first birthday. The first few months were a whirlwind – everything was new and different. I worked long hours while Audrey was home with the baby.' He sucked in a deep breath.

'Eventually, I realised Audrey was unhappy. Our life in suburban Chicago made her miserable. But instead of doing something that could have taken her sadness away, I pushed her. To do more, to get out of the house, to meet people, to make friends. Never once did I put myself in her shoes, imagining how miserable the lifestyle I'd dumped on her would have made me if our roles had been reversed. All I could think was that she should be happy for me.'

He downed half his pint in one go. 'For me,' he repeated with a bitter laugh. 'As if my career and my life and my progress should be enough for her. That's not a mistake I'll make this time.'

'I know,' I said softly. 'You're not that man anymore.'

'We fought like cats and dogs. She'd snipe at me when I got home and I'd bellow at her about what a mess the house was or how she hadn't done anything all day.' He jabbed both hands into his own chest. 'Here's someone working in mental health, and yet I couldn't see what a deep depression my own wife was in. Or I was too selfish to care.'

He took a sip of his beer. 'One day, I came home from work to find the house dark and quiet – a note on the kitchen table. She'd taken Florent and was going to stay with her parents in Copenhagen.' He closed his eyes. '"I love you, Tom, and nothing can ever change that, but right now I also hate you." I just…'

His words dissolved into tears. He laid his head on the table. I got up and shuffled around to the other side and put my arms around him. Several minutes passed.

'I drank myself to sleep that night in the dark. I awoke the next morning bleary-eyed and confused, with some bastard jackhammering inside my skull. When I realised the sound was my phone, I picked it up and looked at the screen. It was the police.'

He plucked at his shirt sleeve. 'You know how people talk about the last words they spoke to someone? You hear people saying, "The last time I saw my dad I told him I hated him" or "The last words I said to my daughter were that if she left she wouldn't be welcome back"? People always regret if their last words to someone were ones of anger or betrayal.'

That struck a chord. The last words my father had spoken to me were almost exactly those. *I should try messaging him; he might still be alive.*

Tom drained the rest of his pint and slammed the glass down. 'Whoops, sorry. Sorry.' He waved his hands in apology. 'The last time I saw Audrey, that morning as I was getting ready for work, I refused to speak to her. She tried to kiss me goodbye – I turned my face away and left.

'A white supremacist. He, um … he wanted…' Tom shook his head. 'I don't know what he wanted. But he murdered my wife and my son. Their driver too. I lost myself. Didn't so much quit my job as just never go back. Packed a few things and ran away. Never even went to the funeral. Instead, I flew to Korea and took a job teaching English to rich teenagers. I drank too much, took too many pills, slept my way across east Asia. Tried to forget.'

He picked up the empty glass and made to take a drink then set it back down. 'And that's where Nigel found me.'

I put my hand on his. 'I'm so glad he did,' I said.

He wiped his nose on his sleeve. 'I won't forget Audrey or Florent. But, I guess, somehow I moved on when I wasn't looking. They're my past. It's time to focus on my future.'

———

*HATSH DOME, DEVON ISLAND COLONY, MARS*

Four days later Tom and I stood in my flat. 'Come on,' I urged him. 'You're going to be late for your own wedding.' He fussed over his hair and tried to straighten his tie. I focused on trying to get his daughter, Rafa, to put on her dress while she ran around the flat, squealing. I wasn't sure whether she was crying or laughing.

'I want everything to be just right,' he said. 'I need it to be perfect.'

Giving up temporarily on my battle with the toddler, I took his hand and turned him towards me. I reached up and put my hands on either side of his face. 'It won't be perfect, because nothing in life ever is. But it will be exactly right because you folks are right. You're in love. And you've made an amazing child together – even if she is driving me up the wall just now.'

I patted his face. 'Now come on, let's get you to the church.'

'Don't let Helen hear you call it that or she'll cancel the wedding.'

'Fine, let's get you to the multi-faith chapel.'

He pulled a face. 'I'm not sure that's any better.'

'The multi-faith-and-no-faith-at-all chapel?'

He raised his hand and made a wibbly-wobbly, maybe-maybe-not gesture.

'How about the community hall, which sometimes doubles as a chapel for those of any or no faiths?'

'Better,' he conceded. We turned and headed out the door.

———

*THE ANKH DOME, DEVON ISLAND COLONY, MARS*

I took my place at the front of the chapel – whatever Helen thought, in my mind it was a chapel – and looked out over the small crowd. Looking down at my hands, I touched my wedding ring. A simple band: one side sand-blasted titanium, the other pale oak. Wood and metal. Dark and light. Technology and nature. Bound together.

From the door, Jupiter gave me the thumbs up. I clicked the button to start the music and signalled for the crowd to stand.

When Jupiter pulled the door open, the first to walk through was Rafa. I'd managed to get her into her dress and braided her wavy hair. She carried a bouquet of brightly coloured flowers and a few white daisies.

Chris was next, her brown hair flowing loosely over bare shoulders. She wore a simple, strapless cotton sundress with a bold print and carried a bouquet similar to Rafa's. Her smile filled the room with its warmth and brightness.

Finally, Helen stepped through the door. She looked like a goddess – with her smooth black hair swept up in an elegant chignon. I touched my own sloppy curls as I admired her. She wore a deep purple dress with a high neckline and a fitted bodice. The calf-length skirt was full but slit high up her thigh, revealing delicate yet muscular legs.

Once they were all standing before me, I motioned for

the guests to be seated. Although I'd memorised the entire ceremony, I looked down at my notes to collect my thoughts.

'Beloved, we are gathered here on this joyous occasion,' I began. I spoke the agreed opening paragraphs then paused for a deep breath. 'And now I'm going to tell you all a story. Some of you know it, but I promise I'm not giving any secrets away. I've discussed this with Tom and he's all right for me to tell it.'

There were a few puzzled faces – Lone Starr in particular – as I continued. 'Once upon a time – so very long ago, and yet not – Tom turned his back on all this. He walked away from us' – I shrugged – 'in what could be described as a somewhat dramatic fashion.' Helen expressed her trademark sarcasm with a single raised eyebrow. I heard a few soft chuckles from those who remembered the shouting and the shattered glass.

In the early days of planning the colony, we had proposed bringing no men at all. Tom had felt all the hard work he'd put into our new life slipping away from him. It had been Helen who suggested we skew in favour of women while still including some men.

'And honestly, with the benefit of hindsight, he was right to do so. We were heading down a path that wasn't the right one for the colony. And Tom brought us back from the brink. We thought we were facing a terrible choice, but Tom made us see that a third option was possible – and isn't that the most beautiful metaphor for today?'

I looked him in the eye and then out at the congregation. 'I speak for myself when I say this, but I suspect I also speak for these beautiful ladies too, and in fact for the wider community: we are so very glad you're here with us. We're grateful that you reconsidered your decision to leave. We're pleased we were able to reach a compromise that worked as well as this one has. And we're forever delighted that you are a part of this colony. Make no mistake, Tom, you are the heart of this community. You are the quickest to show your emotions and the freest with your feelings – and we are all the better for your presence.'

I paused while Tom wiped tears from his cheeks. Helen looked to him and then rolled her eyes – but she couldn't hide her own joy. Rafa had begun to fuss, so Chris picked her up and balanced her on her hip.

I waited until they were all ready. 'And now the important part. Tom, please take your brides' hands for this bit. Do you, Thomas Nielsen, take Helen Souza and Christine Ngata in the sacred bond of marriage?'

Sobbing, Tom managed to respond, 'I do.'

'Do you promise to love, honour, cherish, and protect them both?'

'I do.'

I repeated the sacred words with Chris and then with Helen, who were both smiling and clinging to one another's hands. Helen had her free hand around Tom's shoulder and Chris stroked his face.

'Well, then by the authority the three of you have invested in me, I hereby pronounce you married. You may kiss the, er… spouses.'

And by golly, the three of them made a good go of it.

———

Later on, once the hall had been rearranged and redecorated for the reception, a man approached me, drink in hand. 'That was a beautiful service, ma'am.'

'Enough of this ma'am business. I've told you – call me

Georgie.' I gave him a wry smile. 'Or you can make up a nickname for me and try to make it stick, Lone Starr.'

He winked at me. I'd never had any interest in men, sexually speaking, but from an aesthetic perspective, my gosh, he was stunning. I'd estimate about 185 centimetres tall. Blond hair, lively brown eyes, perfect lips, and cheekbones a supermodel would kill for. He looked like an angel. The muscles rippled beneath his fitted uniform shirt.

'I've never been to a polyamorous wedding ceremony before. It was … nice.'

I raised an eyebrow. 'Polyamorous? Look at you learning new words! But alas, no, very much not. There is nothing polyam about Tom, Helen, and Chris. They are completely monogamous – well, polygamous, I suppose.'

He blinked rapidly but recovered himself. 'There are three of them.'

I nodded. 'That's right.'

'But…'

I continued, 'And I congratulate you on not calling it a bigamous wedding, but polyam would mean it was an open relationship and it is no such thing.' His brow furrowed. 'Helen and Chris… They're both Tom's wives, yes?'

'Yes, ma'am.'

I let the ma'am slide. 'But Helen is also Chris's wife, yeah. And vice versa. In the same way Gurdeep is my wife.'

He nodded, his forehead still creased.

'Now, if you look over there.' I tried to be subtle as I drew his attention to a pair of people a few metres away from us. 'You'll see Charlie rather unsubtly coming on to Jayne Cobb.'

He wagged a finger at me. 'Ah, see now, firstly, Sergeant Cobb's first name is —'

'Oh, I know what her first name is. She's still called Jayne Cobb.'

His brow knitted together even tighter than before. 'You know what? I'm not even going to ask. Anyway, secondly, I can assure you Sergeant Cobb doesn't swing that way.'

I threw my hands up in surrender. Maybe my gaydar was way off on this one. 'Huh. Well, whatever. What I was going to say is that Charlie is in long-term relationships with both Mehmet and Rosa. The three of them live together and raise their daughter together. But their relationship is complex and non-exclusive. That's what polyam looks like. Or, what it looks like for them at any rate.'

We both sipped our drinks.

'Huh, I guess I do still have a lot to learn. You do get how strange your colony seems to outside eyes, though, right?'

I grinned at him over the top of my glass. 'You don't have outside eyes. Not anymore – not after living amongst us for eight months. You're one of us.'

Lone Starr moved his head from side to side. 'Well, yes and no. Mostly yes. But also mostly no.' He drained the rest of his glass and leaned in close. Lips brushing my ear, he whispered, 'What I really hear you saying is that Charlie's fair game.' He backed away, setting his glass down on the nearest table. 'If you'll excuse me, ma'am.'

I chuckled to myself as I picked up his empty glass and carried it through to the kitchen. Then I went in search of my beautiful wife.

MEAR 2, DAY 406

*107 KILOMETRES FROM DEVON ISLAND COLONY, MARS*

I tossed an ice boulder into the skip and then instinctively raised an arm to wipe my brow – only to slap my helmet's faceplate. *Oops.* Sweat trickled down my cheek, so I turned my fan up to max, the cool air feeling delicious on my overheated skin.

After checking the weigh scale's display, I clicked the button to activate my mic. 'That's it – we've got enough. Great job, everyone. Let's load this onto the trailer. We don't want to be doing that in the dark tomorrow morning.'

Rosa hopped up into the crane's cab. The crane, telecom tower, and small habitat were permanent fixtures at this site. A group trekked out about once a mear to bring ice back to the colony to top up our water supply. We operated as near to a closed loop as possible, but water recycling was never quite a hundred per cent. Plus, each new colonist – baby, adult, or animal – increased our needs. This wasn't the first water mission I'd joined – but it was my first time leading one.

The four of us guided the skip onto the flatbed trailer as Rosa operated the controls. Once it was in place, she jumped back down and brushed herself off.

'Cobb,' I said over the network. 'You and I will secure everything. The rest of you, please head in and get started on dinner.'

As Rosa passed, she touched my arm. Sound waves travelled directly between our suits. 'Don't let Jayne order you around, eh? She's not the boss here. You are.'

Inside my helmet, I nodded. 'We'll be fine. No worries.'

She nodded back before heading for the habitat with the two other members of the team.

Cobb's voice crackled to life in my helmet speaker. 'You a pitcher or a catcher, Red?'

My eyes narrowed. 'What?' Red was obviously a reference to my hair, but the rest... I understood it to be a sexual reference – but not one that applied to two women – especially not in a professional context. 'Sorry, what?'

Cobb rolled her eyes at me. 'You know – baseball?' She turned and walked away.

I reckoned she must be making social conversation – if a bit of an odd choice of topic. 'Er, no, I've never played. It's not really a thing in England. And I'm not a sportsy person.' *Go on, ask her about herself,* my long-dead mother chided me in my head. 'Are you a fan?'

From two metres away, Cobb appeared to study me. She tilted her head – the same gesture Seven made when she didn't understand something. Cobb reached into the storage space under the trailer and pulled out a coil of rope. She hoisted it in the air. 'Don't be a dumbass, Red. Do you want me to throw the rope to you or do you want to toss it to me?'

'Why didn't you say that?'

She squinted at me before walking around to the other

side of the trailer. Without warning, something came hurtling through – well, through the not-air – over the top of the skip. I caught the carabiner deftly then pulled the rope as tight as I could. I felt rather than heard the click as I secured it to the side of the trailer.

'Ready for the next one?'

I nodded my head – then remembered she couldn't see me. 'Yep, towards the front, yeah?'

———

After dinner, we sat on our sleeping bags, all huddled around the heating unit in the centre of the dome. Someone had painted flames on its ceramic surface.

Rosa set the dishwasher to run then walked the three steps from the kitchen to where the rest of us were. 'They're not s'mores, but they'll have to do.' She set a tray down on the floor then dropped into a casual pose in front of it. 'Hazelnut flapjacks – get 'em while they're cold. Everyone for tea?'

I passed the plate of nutty squares around as Rosa poured and distributed mugs of spiced rooibos.

Kay raised her mug in one hand and a flapjack in the other. 'Better than our last road trip, hey, Sarge?' I didn't know either woman well, but Jamie had told me some horror stories from their trek across Mars – how they'd been certain our group had been left up here to die. Just like they had.

Cobb tore off a bit of flapjack with her fingers. Before popping it into her mouth, she replied, 'You've gone soft on me, Corporal. Time was, you could work sixteen-hour days without needing your government-mandated tea break and complimentary granola bar.'

The corporal turned her mug slowly in her hand, staring into it. When she looked up, she had an odd smile. 'It wasn't a tea break we needed – it was adequate food, hygiene facilities, healthcare, and a government that didn't write us off as casualties of a non-existent war. In fact, if we'd had that, maybe more of us would still be alive.'

Cobb raised her hand, stabbing her index finger at Kay. 'That's not—'

Rosa used the tablet that operated the controls to cut the overhead lights, plunging us into darkness. Then she activated a small spotlight and pointed it up at her face, making her eyes sparkle.

Grinning mischievously, she said, 'My abuela was the best storyteller – and this is my favourite of her tales.'

Rosa looked around the room until everyone was paying attention. Cobb crossed her arms defensively, but people were looking at Rosa. 'When she was a little girl, her own grandmother always used to speak of that time she died. It was just … this thing. No one in the family ever gave any detail.

'My abuela said she'd always assumed it was a momentary thing – you know?' She thumped her hand to her heart and sat frozen in place for a few seconds. Then she inhaled noisily. 'Before someone did CPR or something. But when she was fifteen, she was doing a class project on family histories, so she decided to interview her.'

When she paused again, the only sounds were of five people breathing and the dull hum of the machines keeping us alive.

'The pair sat down with an old-fashioned tape recorder. "Tita," my abuela began. "Tell me about the time you died." Tita crossed herself.'

Rosa took a sip of her tea. 'Then Tita said, "Are you sure you want to hear that?" My abuela nodded. "Measles. It was measles that killed me the first time." Now it was my abuela's turn to cross herself. "Back in nineteen thirty-eight, there was an epidemic. Young and old – everyone caught it. I remember being sick in my bed. And then…" Tita shrugged and tipped the ash off her cigarette. She didn't speak for a moment. My abuela thought she wasn't going to say more.

'But then, she said, "I don't know, Nieta. I wish I did. I woke up under a pile of bodies. The weight on me was crushing. It was crawling with maggots. Human waste and bodily fluids had soaked through everything. I scratched and pulled hair and dragged myself to the top of the mound. It was a quicksand of corpses – and I was alone, fighting to get to the top."'

Rosa leaned back on her elbows and took a bite of her flapjack, like she was finished.

Kay leaned forwards. 'Come on, Ro. You can't leave us there! What happened?'

Rosa shrugged. 'At that point in the story, Tita got up and ran from the room, crying.'

'And then what?' demanded Frankie.

'And then she died.'

'What?' shouted everyone in unison.

'Tita died again that night, never having finished her story.'

Frankie clicked her tongue. 'Gimme that. Good start, but now it's my turn.' Rosa passed the tablet with its spotlight to her. Frankie balanced it on the floor in front of her, so it directed the light upwards at her face, casting eerie shadows.

'My father – Papa Felix – tells this story best, but I'll give it a whirl. My great-pépère was American. He and his brother crossed the border as draft dodgers in the Vietnam War. Papa Felix said he was never sure how long ago this … incident was. Great Uncle Max never gave the same date twice.'

She dropped her voice low – both in volume and pitch. The effect was immediate; people leaned forwards, straining to see her. I doubted they were even aware they were doing it. 'Max took one of his girlfriends up to this national park in Maine.'

Kay fidgeted in her seat. 'You never said you had family in the US. Was it the Appalachian Scenic Trail? We used to go there when—'

Rosa swatted playfully at Kay. She let her fingers linger on Kay's knee for a few seconds. 'Cut it out. Let Frankie tell her story, you goof.'

Kay raised her hands in surrender. 'Sorry. Carry on.'

Frankie, still cast into weird contrast by the spotlight, nodded at them. 'So, Max and this girl – they go in through the visitors' centre. The park ranger gives them his spiel. Papa Felix could never remember the whole thing, but the part he always included was this super-cheesy line.' She put on a gruff, masculine-sounding voice and jabbed her fists into her sides. '"Take only pictures – leave only footprints." Max had heard it a million times already, but I guess he never knew it was a warning.'

Frankie took a sip of her tea, leaving her audience hanging. Ghost stories weren't really my cup of the aforementioned beverage, but I admired her skill – getting the audience hooked and then making them wait.

She set her mug down on the floor and paused, like she was trying to remember where she'd left off. 'She's kind of a scrapbooker, this girl. Keeps taking things as they walk –

pulling pinecones off trees, picking berries, gathering twigs. Old Max – well, Young Max, I suppose – arched an eyebrow at her.' The light caught Frankie's own raised brow. '"What?" she says with a laugh. "It's just a piece, right?"'

Frankie ran her hand over her trousers, smoothing out the fabric. 'After a day of hiking, they arrive at their campsite. They pitch their tents and get a fire going. Eventually, they head to bed. Separate tents – I dunno, maybe one of them was in the closet or perhaps they were just prudes. Whatever. Anyways, in the middle of the night Max wakes up because he hears the girl screaming. So, he runs out to check on her.'

Frankie shifted her weight like she was struggling to get comfy. Rosa and Kay were both at the edge of their seats – metaphorically, at least – their fingers inching closer together with every heartbeat. Even Cobb looked captivated.

'Come on,' said Rosa. 'Don't leave us hanging.'

'He finds the ranger standing outside the girl's tent. Max points his little flashlight at the guy and the light catches something in his hand.' Frankie snatched the tablet up from its spot on the floor and waved it around wildly. She must have set this up in advance because when she turned the light back her way, it caught the glint of a knife.

'It's the glint of a knife,' she said, her voice low and gravelly. Rosa leapt off her sleeping bag and into Kay's, pulling the fabric up over her head.

Frankie dropped her voice even lower than before, barely a whisper, running a finger along the blade of her knife. 'There's also something in the guy's other hand – something small, but it's dripping. He realises he can't hear the girl anymore. Before he can say anything … the park ranger turns to him and smiles. "What's the matter, Max? It's only a piece."'

Kay did a full body shudder. Rosa popped her head up from under the sleeping bag and slid an arm around her waist – at which Kay screamed and jumped into the air.

Still sitting cross-legged on the floor, Frankie bent from the waist, bowing low over her legs. 'Thank you, thank you. A collection basket will be passed around shortly.' I assumed she was kidding – I hoped she was kidding.

Kay crawled forwards and grabbed the tablet. Instead of shining it at herself, though, she directed the light in Cobb's direction. 'Go on, Sergeant. Tell us your idea of a horror story.'

Cobb crossed her arms over her chest. 'Corporal.' It was more of a growl than a word.

Kay turned the light on her own face, balancing the tablet on her knees. 'The good sergeant once told me that the scariest thing she could imagine was spending the rest of her life in a hippie vegan lesbian commune. Starting each day by singing kumbaya and ending with a group hug.'

I narrowed my eyes. 'You mean us? But we don't sing kumbaya or do group hugs. And I'm not a lesbian.'

Still hugging herself, Cobb scowled. 'Yeah, sure. You're a regular machine.' She scoffed. 'I mean, you – yeah, you are. You're basically a robot, Red. But this whole—'

Rosa leapt to her feet, stabbing a finger in Cobb's direction. 'Don't you dare talk to Devon that way. I'm not going to sit here and let you insult my friend.'

Cobb got up and stomped off in the direction of the airlock. 'Fine, don't.'

This was my responsibility – I couldn't allow anyone to go afară alone, especially not after dark. I caught up with Cobb as she was putting her suit on.

As I reached for my own suit, she snarled. 'I don't need a babysitter.'

I didn't reply – I just continued getting dressed. She was moving faster than I could, so I hopped backwards until I was blocking the airlock.

Cobb slapped the seals on her helmet and took a step. She was probably trying to appear menacing – I gathered the others were intimidated by her. But I didn't budge.

'Fine, you want to walk with me, you knock yourself out. But don't expect me to wait for you, Red.'

As soon as I'd sealed my helmet, I stepped aside. Cobb cranked the door and we climbed into the tiny airlock.

Neither of us spoke while it depressurised. She grabbed the handle and pummelled it open. As soon as she was afară, she picked a direction and began marching. I followed.

We walked in the dark, our helmet lights illuminating only about a metre of ground ahead of us. Overhead, the sky was a diamond-studded expanse of rich velvet. With no air to carry sound waves, the only noises were the ones inside my suit: my heart pounding, the blood coursing through my veins, my breathing.

In spite of the impetus for the moonless hike, it was peaceful. After a few minutes, Cobb's pace slowed. When we'd been walking almost half an hour, she came to a halt.

She bent forwards, hands on her knees. 'There's no structure, no order, no chain of command. How do you people function like that? It's always' – she raised her voice to a nasal drone. I couldn't tell if she was doing an impression of anyone in particular – 'please this and if you wouldn't mind that. If it wouldn't be too much trouble? How are you *feeling*?' She emitted a wordless roar.

Clicking my mic on, I said, 'I make my own order, establish my own routines. They don't have to be enforced from above.'

She closed her mouth and studied me.

'I'm agreeing with you. Mostly. I need structure. And order. But I prefer to create my own. What I like most about Devon Island is that I can stick to my routines, apply order to my daily life – but I have the freedom to do so in ways that work for me. You can do the same – the only thing you can't do is demand others conform to your structure.'

She put her hands on her hips and tilted her head.

'Come on,' I said. 'We've got enough oxygen to make it back – but not much to spare.'

I couldn't hear her movements, but out the corner of my eye, I saw she'd fallen into step beside me.

At length, she clicked her mic back on. 'Do you know what day it is today?'

'It's mear two, day four-oh-six,' I replied. I tried to recall if there was anything particular about today. My eyes widened as it struck me. 'The Hohmann transfer orbit.'

'Bingo. Our colonists were meant to land today. If everything had gone to plan, we never would have needed to join your colony. The fallback date, I mean – the original intent was to have them on Mars two years ago. More than one of your *mears*.' Her voice dripped with scorn on the last word. 'We shouldn't need you.' She shook her head but kept moving.

After a while, I said, 'I'm sorry. I'm sorry your people weren't able to keep their promises. And I'm sorry you've struggled to adapt to our way of life.' The light in her helmet cast her face into relief, so I saw the muscles in her jaw clench. I raised my hand in a gesture that I hoped conveyed a combination of surrender and defence. 'I don't mean that in a condescending way. Genuinely – I know how hard it can be to have to change to fit in with other people's expectations. If

I ever make you feel unwelcome or like you need to be someone other than your true self, please tell me.'

'You're okay, Red.'

'Yeah, I know,' I replied.

*THE CRAFT DOME, DEVON ISLAND COLONY, MARS*

The dim lighting cast us all into shadow. 'So, are we all agreed?' I clung to the hope I wasn't signing my colony's death warrant.

Both Georgie and Tom looked away. Gurdeep covered her mouth with her hand and stared blankly at the table's surface. A faint scar cut a graceful line from the corner of her right eye, like some sort of macabre eyeliner. Jupiter was poised, ready to record the vote – only no one could bring themselves to do it.

Lone Starr's expression was pained. This must be as difficult for him as for the rest of us – and he didn't even get a vote.

I focused on my breathing. 'We all hate this. It may mean the beginning of the end, but it's a sensible precaution while we work to figure things out. We've all known this day was coming. Hopefully, we'll find an alternative soon and we can reverse this decision.'

No one met my eye. I pointed at the numbers on my

tablet. 'There are a hundred and forty-seven original colonists remaining plus eighty-eight babies and children. We have seven members of the MENaCE with us as well as two more at their base. Add to that the six people who are currently pregnant and our total population is two hundred and fifty. That's it – that's the magic number. We agreed this ages ago.'

Helen ran her hands over her swollen belly and stared at the ceiling. She was only about two weeks from her due date.

*How can we do this to our fledgling nation?* I shook my head. 'Without a new power source, each generation will need to lower the cap. The RTGs meet a portion of our electrical needs, only they're dying – slowly but steadily. The solar farm supplies us with ample power.' Looking each person in the eye in turn, I added, 'Except when it doesn't.'

I closed my eyes again. 'Such as now. Ninety weeks a mear we have all the power we need – but the remaining six weeks are a struggle. Some mears are worse than others. Every time there's a dust storm, we lose power capacity. We can keep building solar panels, but we can't rely on them all the time.' I rolled my neck to stretch out some of the tension. 'We're still dependent on those RTGs and we have no way to make more of them. Look, we've debated this and debated it until we're all sick of the sound of our own voices. The fact remains, until we find a solution, our ability to sustain ourselves is going to fall over the coming generations.'

Lisa set her hands on the table. She was the electrical engineer in our group. 'Look, you had to leave Earth earlier than intended. If you'd had longer to prepare, like we planned, there'd be more of them.'

Tom ran a hand through his already messy hair. 'But what about—'

Lisa had a long, slow fuse – but she was nearing the end

of it. She stabbed a finger in Tom's direction. 'Don't you dare say solar panels to me, Tom. Don't even.'

He deflated under her icy gaze. 'But…'

She shook her head – tiny, rapid motions. 'We've got power to last us several generations and solar is reliable *most of the time*. But we need to prepare for the worst-case scenario. Solar will continue to be unavailable several weeks per mear, so we can't plan a future depending solely on it.'

A quick glance at Lone Starr told me how uncomfortable he was. I felt for the guy. He'd led his crew on a nightmarish journey across Mars, in search of salvation – only to find that while our colony's impending doom was less imminent than their own, it was still very much a factor.

'Right, folks. It's time to vote. I say it's better to limit our colony's size than to condemn it to failure. So… No more babies until—' I pursed my lips; this wasn't a time for mincing words. '*Unless* we sort out a plan to cover our long-term electrical needs. Yeah or nay?'

———

*LOVELACE DOME, DEVON ISLAND COLONY, MARS*

This afternoon's cabinet meeting was still weighing on my mind, but I was determined to enjoy the evening. Charlie and I had planned this catch-up ages ago – and I'd already had to put it off once. The two of us had become good friends on Earth when she'd been my deputy in planning for the colony's culture and economy. But I hadn't had much time to socialise since getting to Mars.

After giving the thermos a good shake, Charlie poured us both cups of apple mojito. The cold steel tingled my finger-tips as I steadied the glasses on the blanket. We sat in the open air of the orchard in the Ankh – beneath the starless sky as the dust storm afară raged above us.

'To childfree nights,' Charlie said cheerfully.

In my heart, I cringed, but today's decision wasn't public knowledge yet.

Forcing myself to smile, I hoped she couldn't read my expression in the pale light of her phone screen. She was much too good at reading people.

'I'll drink to that.' We touched glasses.

'And to Brian,' she continued. 'Wherever his soul may be, who blessed us with the recipe for the mojito.'

I admired the cup's texture – it was easy to grip in spite of the liquid condensing on its surface. Another of Devon's little touches. 'To Brian,' I agreed. We clinked our glasses once more and I took a long drink.

Charlie smiled as she watched me. Even in the murky light, I knew her eyes sparkled and her dimples were forming.

Touching my lips with the glass, I asked, 'What?'

She chuckled. 'Remember how restrained you used to be? You were wound so tight, I was sure you'd eventually go —' She made an explosive noise and waved her hands around chaotically. 'You're a lot more —' This time she let her hands float on imaginary waves in front of her.

I brushed her jibe away. 'Sure, I'll grant you that. Brian would've had a colourful saying to describe how uptight I was. A stick in the mud?'

'Oh, please. Brian would have had some phrase about … I dunno: possums and ploughs and probably a hat.'

I snorted. 'Fair. His sayings were inscrutable and yet he always seemed to convey his meaning clearly enough.'

Charlie held up a finger as she took a long drink from her

glass. 'I'll give you a phrase, though. You needed to get some. A serious boning.'

'Maybe.' I swallowed most of my mojito in one go.

She peered over the top of her steel glass. 'Speaking of which, are we expecting you at ours this evening?'

My heart raced. 'I've no idea what you mean.' *Mehmet hadn't told her about our arrangement, had he? He'd always assured me it was strictly between us.*

Charlie replied with a noise somewhere between a sceptical grunt and a chortle. 'Oh, I know.' She tipped the contents of her cup into her mouth.

There was a rustling sound behind us. 'Oh gosh, I'm so sorry. I didn't see you there.'

I turned towards the familiar voice, grateful for the excuse to change the subject. 'Hey, Jamie.' Jamie and Devon had been close since the day they'd first met – but then, it was hard to think of anyone who didn't consider him a friend.

Charlie hoisted the thermos above her head. 'Join us, Jay. We got mojitos.'

Jamie dropped into a cross-legged pose across from us on the edge of the blanket. 'Thanks. That sounds nice.'

'How's it going?' Charlie poured three little cups of mojito and handed us each a drink. In the mear since the MENaCE joined us, Jamie was the one who'd acclimatised most easily. Much of the time, it felt like he'd always been here.

'Yeah, thanks,' he replied. 'Just out for an evening stroll.'

I took a sip of my drink. 'How's Rosa coping with being pregnant again?'

'All good – she revels in it.' Charlie looked away.

Their baby would probably be the last one for a long while. 'That's good,' I said.

Jamie touched the leaves of a nearby daisy. 'I just love babies – don't you?'

My eyebrows climbed unbidden towards the invisible roof of the dome. 'Spoken like someone who's not had to do a two a.m. feeding.'

Charlie reached out her glass once more and clinked it against mine. 'I hear you there, sister.' We both downed more of our drinks.

Jamie lifted his glass to us then took a sip. He coughed and spluttered. 'Wow, that's um… That's good.' He shook his head. 'But seriously, what's it like to be pregnant – if you don't mind me asking?'

I almost choked on my rum. 'Sorry?'

Jamie clutched his cup to himself. 'What? Surely, it's just a human thing, right? Everybody wonders – it's human nature. Everyone longs to know the feeling of growing a… What it's like to… What? Why are you looking at me like that?'

I raised my hands to – I don't know, I guess to defend myself against a question I didn't know how to answer.

Charlie blew a raspberry. 'Aw, hell, no. Nope, nope.'

Both Jamie and I looked at her. Jamie's mouth hung loose. 'You've never been pregnant?'

I grimaced at the question – Charlie might not want to answer. But she surprised me. 'Oh, I've been pregnant. Hated every second of it.'

Jamie opened his eyes wide and covered his mouth with his hand. 'Oh no, I'm so sorry. Did you…'

Charlie waved the question away. 'It's funny. Funny-strange, I mean – not ha ha. Losing the baby was awful. It was –' She slapped the air in front of herself, like she could banish the painful memories away. 'Physically, psychically, spiritually, emotionally – in every way, awful. But … but it was a revelation.'

She leaned back on her arms. 'When I was growing up and figuring myself out, I knew I was attracted to people of all genders and none – but I never stopped to ask myself *who I was*, you know?'

Jamie pulled his head back. 'How do you mean?'

Charlie frowned. 'So, I've never looked at a man and thought I'd like to be him. I've never felt like I was a man. But I guess I always took for granted that I was a woman. It's only recently that I've started to realise that most people – cis, trans, gay, straight, male, female, whatever, and what have you – most people feel a connection to their own gender.'

I nodded, but Jamie looked startled by a statement that was – to my mind, at least – pretty innocuous. It would be hard to disagree with Charlie's assertion. And yet…

'Do they?' Jamie scratched his head. 'Really?'

This was all getting a bit much for me, so I polished off the last of my drink.

Charlie extended both hands towards him. 'Exactly! My own gender was always just there – a fact but not an important one. Not relevant to my daily life, you know?'

Charlie's thermos was empty, so she reached into her bag and pulled out a small bottle. When the phone's light caught it, it glowed gold. 'I guess we're drinking the rum straight now.' She raised the bottle in offer, so I held my cup up to her.

Charlie poured out a generous amount for all three of us. 'I never gave it any thought, because it seemed like the least germane, the least salient thing about me. You know?'

'I'm sorry,' I replied. 'Much as I love you, Charlie, I don't understand.' I drained the shot of rum.

'Well, I think what I'm saying is I'm non-binary.'

I set the empty cup down on the blanket next to me. 'Yeah, I get that. And I don't mean any disrespect at all. But I don't understand.'

She leaned forwards defensively. 'What's to understand? It's me. This is who I am.'

Jamie was watching the back-and-forth like a tennis match. I waved my hands in surrender. 'Hey, hey. I mean I don't understand because I have no frame of reference to relate – but I don't need to understand, you know? I accept you for you. I can't grok what it is to be non-binary any more than I can what it is to be a man. But that doesn't mean I can't love you for you – as you.'

Charlie put her elbows on the blanket and stretched out over them – sort of a yoga cat pose. I was in no fit state for even thinking about yoga. Jamie was still watching us – the way Daniel sometimes did – observing everything but saying nothing.

'I'll take it,' she replied from somewhere under her own hair. 'And I love you right back.'

MEAR 3, DAY 97

THE CRAFT DOME, DEVON ISLAND COLONY, MARS

I swallowed the last of my sandwich and buzzed.

The speaker activated as a voice said, 'Come on in.' I pulled the key from my pocket and unbolted the door. Katya greeted me with a smile, her shoulder-length blond hair perfectly coifed. My stomach turned. 'Morning, Georgie,' she said cheerfully. 'How are you?'

'Get a move on,' I replied.

She stepped through her door and joined me outside. 'How are the kids doing? Are they letting you get any sleep?'

'We're emptying the toilets this morning,' I replied.

Jayne Cobb met us at the bottom of the stairs and the three of us headed north-west, towards Thunderdome. I breathed a silent prayer of thanks for Cobb's presence.

She rubbed her hands together. 'Ready to head Down-beneath?'

I squinted at her. *Was that a joke?* The MENaCE crew had been in Devon Island for a mear. 'DownBelow. It's called

DownBelow.' I may have raised my voice a little when I added, 'Brian chose the name. You never met him, Cobb, but he was my friend.'

Katya touched her hand to her chest as we stepped into the airlock.

I filled the void by telling Cobb about DownBelow. 'The area under the colony is home to the guts of our habitat system. The overhead pipes carry clean water, wastewater, and air. There are miles and miles of cables.' As we stepped into Thunderdome, I ran my fingers over the letters KKMD that had been carved into the airlock door.

'Thought you didn't use miles,' Jayne grunted.

*This is going to be a long day, I thought* – not for the first time. 'Not as a unit of measurement, we don't. But some figures of speech endure despite the underlying meaning being lost.'

She crossed her arms over her broad chest and shrugged.

I continued talking as we approached the service building. 'Most of the machinery needed for living – and dying – on Mars is down there. And obviously, that's also where the composting drums for the toilets and garburators are.'

I made a broad, sweeping gesture. 'In many ways, Down-Below is a foil to the domes. Above is lush and green – and swelteringly hot. Sure, the manmade stuff may be faded and worn.' Running my hands over my thin grey top with its faded pastel dots, I said, 'This shirt was once a black dress with bright jewel tones. But the habitat we've created is alive with colours, textures, smells, and sounds.' As if to emphasise my point, a bird flew overhead in a blur of bright colours.

Cobb's body language was – not exactly hostile – disinterested, perhaps. Bored, maybe. But I had to keep talking or else Katya would. 'By contrast, DownBelow is dim and grey.

It's shielded from afară, but it's not pressurised or oxygenated. We hold the temperature to six degrees to protect our compost.'

As we entered the lift block, I ran out of things to say, which gave Katya an opening. 'Adina and Little Gabe are both toddlers now, right? How are they doing? I heard there's a new art centre in the crèche for the kids. Do they like it there?'

Thankfully, it was too awkward to talk as we climbed down the service ladder. When we got to the bottom, I grabbed suits from the locker and threw one at each of my … colleagues. 'Put these on.' Once I had my own suit on, I tapped out a rhythm with my gloved fingers as I waited for them to finish.

Before I could fill the silence, Katya started speaking again. 'These things are such a pain, don't you think? Do you want any help with yours? I always think it's so much easier when you help one another,' she said. I crossed my arms over my chest.

We headed into the airlock. While we waited for it to depressurise, I continued my pointless drivel.

'With two hundred and forty-seven humans – and three more on the way – plus assorted dogs and wildlife, we create a whole lot of excrement. And food waste. Even without the kind of waste we tolerated on Earth, there's still a lot left over. Apple cores. Nutshells. Coffee grounds. Husks and rinds.'

When the light turned green, we emerged out the other side of the airlock into DownBelow proper. I switched my mic on. 'Obviously, we use our veg scraps in stock – but after the broth is made, the veg is still there. So, it all goes into the garburators and from there, into the composting drums.'

I made the mistake of holding my tongue while I retrieved the first dolly – a giant lidded bucket on wheels. Katya seized the opportunity to start talking again. 'So, Jayne ... it is Jayne, right?' In DownBelow's dim light, I couldn't see Cobb's face, but she didn't reply. 'Am I right in thinking you've not been on compost duty before?'

Rather than let her continue her prattle, I resumed my needless lecture on the composting system as I led my charges to the first vat. 'The liquid matter drains out – siphoned off to the wastewater treatment equipment – so only solid matter goes into the composters. No one likes having to empty them, but it's a fact of life. Without them we'd die. We all take our turns emptying them out.

'Drum one, Katya. You know what to do.' I turned my back on her and continued my speech over the headsets, filling the silence to prevent her from doing so.

'Cobb, over here. We'll head to drum two. We'll do it together and then you should be able to manage the next one on your own.'

We walked to the next vat along. 'See, this is how you connect the composting drum to the hatch in the front of the dolly. Then you press the button to make the composter expel the contents. Once it's done, we'll inspect the contents for dangerous bacterial content, suboptimal pH, contaminants, or what have you.'

As we worked, I carried on talking as much as I could, but the moment I paused—

'Oh, look at this,' Katya said in my speaker. She sent an image she took with the helmet's camera. I flipped my suit's chest panel down and looked at the screen – a metallic toy robot. 'I call that a win. Do I get to keep it?'

'Drop it in the contaminants bucket.' Turning towards

Cobb, I added, 'Occasionally we find larger objects – kids' toys are pretty common. Wood ones don't matter. They decompose along with the rest of the contents. But some materials can leach badness into the humus.' She arched an eyebrow. 'Yes, badness – it's a technical term. Anyway, we have to fish those items out. One time, there was a drum with mercury particles. No idea how that happened, but almost a hundred kigs of humus had to be disposed of. Can't let it contaminate the food supply.'

Jayne's lip curled into a snarl. 'What the hell are kigs?'

I stirred the thick mixture as it poured into the bucket. 'Kilograms, Cobb. Isn't it about time you got used to metric already?'

Jayne grunted.

———

*THUNDERDOME, DEVON ISLAND COLONY, MARS*

After four infuriatingly long hours, we'd finally finished our task. We gathered up our tools and climbed into the decontamination chamber. First, it blasted us with pressurised gas to blow away any dry gunge. Then it rained soapy water on us, which we used to scrub one another's suits. Then clean water for rinsing. Lastly, we were hit with another blast to dry us.

My voice was shot from my non-stop blithering.

We stepped into the airlock before the final climb to the surface. As soon as the light went green, Katya unlatched her helmet and lifted it off. 'Oh man, it feels good to breathe real air again, don't you think?'

Jayne and I both crossed our arms over our chests.

'Regulations state that helmets are not to be removed until we've exited the airlock,' I said.

Once we were out, we escorted Katya back to her prison. I didn't even have the energy to talk over her.

'I know we didn't actually touch anything with bare skin, but I always feel gross after a compost shift, don't you? I can't wait to have a shower,' she said.

She continued yammering until she swung her door shut, locking herself back in her prison. The moment it was closed, Jayne turned to me.

'No idea why you folks didn't just push her out an airlock. That woman's a monster.' She shrugged and bounded down the stairs. I stood on the balcony for a few minutes, staring out at the gardens below.

---

*THE ANKH DOME, DEVON ISLAND COLONY, MARS*

Fifteen minutes later, I opened the door of the chapel. Jamie came straight over and put his arms around me. After a moment, he walked back to the room's side table, where a teapot was waiting. He poured me a mug. 'Liquorice and honey tea. In your text, you mentioned your voice was raw – this should help.' He sat down on the chapel floor. 'How did it go? You got through it, I see.'

The tears overwhelmed me and I broke down crying in a way I'd not done for mears. Dropping to the floor next to him, I realised I hadn't cried this freely when Brian died.

As my sobs dwindled, Jamie asked, 'Are you ready to forgive yet?'

'Whuh?' I looked at him, aghast. *How could he ask that?* 'I can't. I can't. I won't. She doesn't deserve it. She doesn't even *want* it.' I inhaled and held the air in my lungs for a few moments. 'Adina has his eyes.' I twisted the ring on my finger.

Jamie put his arm around me. 'So I've heard. But it doesn't matter whether Katya wants your forgiveness,' he whispered. 'You don't forgive someone for *their* benefit. Forgiveness isn't earned – that's redemption. Forgiveness doesn't mitigate the wrong. It doesn't negate or devalue it. It isn't about her – it's about you. It's about letting go of the hate – it's about you moving on with your life.' He shifted to face me. 'But it wasn't her I was talking about.'

I sucked back snot. 'But who— Oh.' I ran my sleeve across my face. 'Me. You're saying I need to forgive me.'

Tilting his head to the side, he smiled sadly.

Sniffing, I replied, 'I know. I don't want to know and I don't want to agree. I don't want you to be right, but I know you are. About everything. But I'm not ready yet.'

'That's okay,' he said. 'You will be.'

I sat back, wiped away my tears, and let out a yell of frustration.

'Thank you,' I said, taking Jamie's hand. 'You're a beautiful soul.'

'I'm here to help – anyway I can.'

Shaking my head, I laughed. 'Ugh, what a ridiculous day. But I did it. I got through it. You know, Jayne told me she would've put Katya out an airlock. I've never believed in capital punishment – but in that moment, I could've pushed Katya out to the surface myself.'

Jamie furrowed his brow. 'They don't get it. The whole MENaCE crew... They can't understand why you'd keep a murderer alive.'

That didn't surprise me, though it disappointed me. 'There was a trial. She was found guilty. But we hold life in too high a regard to throw it away – it wouldn't bring Brian back.' I shook my head again. 'And yeah, I get the irony of me being the one to say that. But it's true. I'm not ready to forgive her, but—' I took a deep breath. 'I will absolutely defend her right to exist.'

*THUNDERDOME, DEVON ISLAND COLONY, MARS*

Faz bent low over the table, breathing in the steam from her mug of mint tea. She pushed the tail edge of her hijab aside moments before it dipped into the liquid. Taylor sat next to her, holding their baby on her lap, bouncing him gently.

Daniel was crying and screaming incoherently. Davy was frustrated. 'Come on, Daniel. Please, Yana's finished all her breakfast.'

Even though his noises made it hard for me to concentrate, I had to step in.

'It's okay,' I assured him. I took the polenta and mushroom scramble from him and put the plate on the ground for Seven. 'What do you want to eat?' Davy shook her head.

Daniel banged his head on the table repeatedly, his ginger hair waving. Figuring he'd be safer if I moved him, I picked him up. He thrashed, kicked, and wailed with each step. I set him down on the sofa's soft surface.

I sat down cross-legged on the floor, using my weight to

push the coffee table out of his way, and waited for him to calm down.

After a few moments, his convulsions slowed and soon he rocked, hugging himself.

'Hey, I get it, mate,' I said. He sniffed and wiped snotty tears on his sleeve as he looked up. 'No more mushrooms. Promise.' I offered him my pinky.

Snort. 'Promise?'

'I swear.'

He linked his pinky with mine, still sucking back air.

'What do you want for breakfast?'

He leaned towards me and whispered his request.

I nearly leapt out of my skin when Yana popped up behind the sofa – when she wanted to, she could be terrifyingly stealthy. 'Babies,' she shouted. 'Daniel says he wants to eat babies. You should hide Nadeem, Auntie.'

'Baked beans. He said baked beans, not babies.' I stood up and held out my hand to Daniel. 'Come on, let's see if we have any. If we don't, we'll get you some in time for lunch, okay?'

He accepted my hand, sniffing softly. Davy was already digging a pot of beans left from last night's dinner from the fridge. She popped it into the microwave.

Once we got settled at the table, Faz looked up, her eyes puffy and dull. 'Tell me they start sleeping soon,' she begged. Her son was twelve months old. She and Taylor had opted to remain celibate; they lived together as friends to raise their kids as co-parents. It was similar and yet completely different to my relationship with Davy. Except the baby ban meant Nadeem would be their only child.

Davy smiled and shook her head from her position in front of the microwave. She popped it open and stirred the beans. 'They are all as unique as we are – I can tell you that much,' she said as she pressed the button to start it up again.

Yana reached out to touch the baby on Taylor's lap. He responded by grabbing her arm and biting down on it. Before any of us could intervene, Yana screamed like a banshee and slapped the baby.

Everything happened at once. Nadeem wailed. Davy shouted, 'No, we do not hit. Not ever,' as she grabbed Yana and led her away from the table. Seven, who'd been snoozing next to the power-cycle, ran to the scene and barked. Yana broke free of Davy's grip and raced around the room howling. Faz pulled Nadeem to herself. The microwave pinged.

Davy ran after Yana as I placed the bowl of beans in front of Daniel. She caught the girl and gently lifted her arm to inspect the wound. 'Just a bit of redness. I'm so sorry about that, Faz.'

Faz nodded before peering into Nadeem's mouth as he flailed and cried. 'Aha, now I know why he didn't sleep. Another incisor popping through.'

Davy hoisted Yana into her arms and stroked her wavy brown hair. 'Come on, Yana. Today's a big day. You want everyone to see that you're a big girl, right?'

'I am not a girl.'

Davy flinched as Yana shouted in her face. 'You're not a girl?'

'No,' Yana yelled.

Davy held Yana firm. 'Okay. You don't have to be a girl if you don't want. Are you a boy?'

Yana shrieked again. 'No, I am not a boy. I am not a girl. I'm not an anything.'

Davy nodded her head. 'Okay. That's fine. What are you?'

Yana hurled herself out of Davy's arms and ran across the

room, roaring, 'I'm Yana. You can't make me be a girl or a boy or a person or anyone. Just Yana. That's all I am.'

'Okay, that's okay. I'm glad we've cleared that up.' Davy smiled at me.

The front door opened as another family entered for the next breakfast shift. 'Sorry, everything's taking a bit longer this morning,' I said. 'We'll be out of your way in a minute.' Turning to the kids I added, 'Hurry up and lick your plates. We'll go home and watch videos for a bit.'

This had been a long morning already and it was just gone half seven.

———

*SOUVESTRE DOME, DEVON ISLAND COLONY, MARS*

Just over an hour later, we walked to the school. Families from all over the colony were heading to the same place.

Daniel clung to my right leg. Seven trotted calmly by our side until she spotted Amos chasing something I couldn't see. Probably a bird or a bee or – I don't know. *Children are very strange.* She set off after Amos, barking at him. Daniel let go of my hand and followed her.

Davy took my hand as we watched the interaction from a distance. Amos stroked Seven's head and she wagged her tail. Amos was growing like a weed. At just over two and a half mears – sixty months – he already stood almost to Jupiter's shoulder. I'd been a tall kid too but gangly and awkward, whereas Amos had inherited Nora's graceful movements.

The other kids were all younger than Amos. In a literal sense, he was peerless. The twins were eleven months his junior and many were younger still. Daniel stood nearby, sucking his thumb and looking up at the dome.

'Only babies suck her thumb, Daniel,' Amos said. I'd noticed the kids didn't use masculine pronouns.

Yana ran to them, shouting, 'You're not allowed a talk to my sib.'

Daniel turned from them and ran back to me, grabbing my hand. Yana and Amos shouted at one another unintelligibly.

Tom rounded the corner, emerging into view along the path from Seacole dome. A host of children converged on him, vying for his attention. He hugged them all and then moved to continue on towards the new school, kids hanging from all of his limbs.

Seeing Tom had his hands full, Davy opened the door. Everyone followed her in.

I almost fell over as a small, black-haired whirlwind blew past me. 'Auntie Tom,' screamed Amos, as he grabbed his teacher for a hug.

Tom returned his embrace. 'Shhh, Amos. It's time for inside voices.'

When he released the child, he stood back up and turned to face Davy, me, and the other parents in the room. 'Shall we?' He led us to the inner door and opened it, revealing the new classroom. A bunch of us had worked all weekend getting it ready for today.

Tom raised his arms and spun around. 'Well, kids. What do you think? It's all shiny and brand new, just for you. The first ever class on Mars. You can still smell the paint on the walls.'

Yana shouted, 'What's paint?'

Amos put his hands on his hips. 'What's Mars?'

'Mars is where we are,' replied Tom with a grin.

'No, stupid. Devon Island is where we are. Ever-body knows that,' bellowed Yana. Not for the first time, I thought, *that child is loud.*

Davy was standing by the door. 'Devon Island is the name of our colony. Everything else afară is called Mars.'

Amos balled his fists and jabbed them into his sides. 'Well, duh. Then obvusly this isn't Mars. Mars is afară, but we're inside.'

Davy laughed as the outer door opened again. Korri walked in with his son plus Gurdeep and Georgie's two kids. Amos and Yana ran to greet them as Little Gabe showed off a rock he'd found.

Davy put a hand on Tom's arm and said, 'Look at Little Gabe. The bigger he gets, the more he looks like his mum.'

Tom exhaled noisily. 'I miss her.'

Amos turned around to Tom and replied, 'I seen his mums yesterday. You could probly see 'em at dinner if you want.'

Tom smiled. 'Come on, kids, into the classroom. It's time for school.'

THUNDERDOME, DEVON ISLAND COLONY, MARS

Perched on the balls of my feet, I pulled a bunch of potatoes up by their leaves and added them to the growing pile in my basket.

One row over, Cobb attempted the same manoeuvre – but only succeeded in tearing the leaves. 'Get up here, you jackasses,' she shouted at the innocent vegetables.

Jupiter chuckled. 'I'd be tempted to hide from you too if I knew you were going to shout at me.'

'All due respect, *Jupes*, go f—'

'Try grabbing a little further down, so you're pulling the stems rather than the leaves.' I cut the sergeant off. Once upon a time, I wouldn't have dared.

'Zip it, kid. I'm still your superior officer.'

That was true, technically. Yet every day that passed – every mear – made it harder to force myself to act like it. The Islanders had welcomed us into their community.

*For I was hungry and you gave me food; I was thirsty and you gave me drink; I was a stranger and you welcomed me.*

But we insisted on holding ourselves apart. Well, some more than others. The sergeant still made us wear our uniforms when working. Most of the team wore them all the time.

'I know what I'm doing, all right? My hand slipped,' Cobb barked before sitting down in the soil. 'Ugh. I am so sick of potatoes.' She slapped the broken leaves into her basket.

I bit my tongue to keep from laughing out loud as Jupiter quipped, 'You volunteering for toilet duty again?'

The sergeant glared at Jupiter with fire in her eyes. 'That is not what I'm saying and you know it.' She picked up a curved fork tool and stabbed at the stubborn tuber.

Jupiter said, 'I used to miss meat. When we first got here, I was constantly wishing for bacon to add to everything. Oh my days, I swear I'd have added bacon to a cake.' She stood up and brushed herself off, before bending to pick up her full basket. 'But now?' She shrugged. 'If I woke up tomorrow to find a pig standing outside my flat begging to be eaten, I don't think I could do it.' She carried the basket to the end of the row to empty it.

Cobb shook her head. 'You're English – ain't you people boil everything? You wouldn't know good food if it bit you,' she said when Jupiter returned.

It was the first time she'd shown any awareness of a culture beyond Florida. I sidled along the row to the next potato plant. As Jupiter squatted back down, she said, 'I've been rich. I've been poor. Lived in four countries and visited twenty-three more. Had week-old watered-down rice and seven-course meals. I've eaten at street food stands in Kolkata and Michelin-starred restaurants in Paris. Believe me, I know good food – I love food.'

Cobb brushed soil from the potatoes delicately, like she

thought they'd escape again if she wasn't nice to them. 'My granny made the best – you're going to be horrified by this – oxtail.'

'Oh my days! Yes, mine too,' Jupiter said.

The sergeant looked surprised. 'For real?'

Jupiter nodded. 'And curry goat, too. But anyway, do you know how much resource input meat requires? Heat and light and water that could be used to feed us would be used to grow crops for animals to eat so that we could eat them. Aside from being inhumane, it's also inefficient.'

I couldn't argue with that – but Sergeant Cobb could. I rolled my eyes and listened to her futile ramblings.

———

THE CRAFT DOME, DEVON ISLAND COLONY, MARS

That evening, I had a standing engagement. Every Saturday. It had started as a sort of penance – like community service I'd assigned myself for my sins. I'd done similar work in the past. Before the pandemic. Before the MENaCE. Before Mars.

But this … this was different. It had become something more. Almost – but not quite – friendship. My escort and I climbed the stairs. A few steps further and we arrived at the door.

As I buzzed, I mentally continued the Bible verses I'd recited to myself earlier. *I was naked and you clothed me; I was sick and you visited me; I was in prison and you came to me.*

'Come in,' called Katya over the intercom. Leah turned the key and swung the door inwards. Katya appeared, holding a dinner tray up. She smiled. 'Thank you, Leah. Dinner was delicious.'

Leah accepted the tray with a nod – which was more than most people granted Katya. Leah turned to me. 'I'll collect you in an hour, yeah?'

I nodded and pulled the door closed behind me. The bolts thunked home. When I'd first started visiting Katya a few months after we arrived, someone would stand guard just inside the door. At first, I struggled to understand this community – their belief in human rights wouldn't let them take Katya's life. They said they believed in justice and second chances and rehabilitation – and yet they were shocked that anyone would willingly spend time with Katya. The hurt was too deep, the wound too fresh. So, they shut her away in her apartment and pretended she didn't exist.

Katya smiled at me, as she always did. 'How are you?' I wondered… Did she always do her hair and makeup? Did she spend all her evenings dressed for going out while sitting at home alone?

'I'm well, thank you,' I replied. 'How are you?'

'I'm doing great. Yeah, I made a new lippy this week. A tiny sprinkle of carrot and beetroot powder to make it a sort of peachy colour. Would you like to try it?' She held a tiny container up for me. 'Go on, I want you to have it. The whole pot, I mean.'

'Thank you.' No one here wore much in the way of makeup, but Katya's lip glosses weren't uncommon. She'd given me a pot previously. To my surprise, I found I enjoyed the way it felt.

I allowed her fingers to brush mine as I accepted it from her outstretched hand. It was difficult to live without human touch.

After a second, I lifted the bag I carried and removed the contents. She watched as I set the box on her small table by the front window.

'A board game?' She looked sceptical.

'I was such a game geek in high school,' I said. 'DnD, Risk, Settlers of Catan, Pandemic – I suppose that one would be in poor taste, though. Exploding Kittens – which was always in poor taste. Good fun, though.'

'And you thought we could play … together?'

I lifted the lid off the box and began rifling through the contents. Looking back over my shoulder, I said, 'Yeah. Come on – give it a try at least.' Something occurred to me. I cursed myself for not thinking of this before. 'I mean, I'm sorry. Unless—'

'Unless a bit of competition makes me fly off the handle into a murderous rage?' She looked at the floor.

I flinched when she put a hand on my shoulder, muscles involuntarily clenching. 'Relax, I promise I'm okay. While I won't deny I have anger management issues, I take my meds and Faz is helping me work through things. I'm making progress.'

Taking a breath, I forced myself to relax.

'Besides, competition has never been a trigger for me. My issues are very much tied to sexuality – not board games. Let's do this.' She sat at the table and held a hand up, inviting me to sit opposite her. 'Please?' Her smile showed what appeared to be genuine warmth. 'Star Realms? Is this one of your favourites?'

I took my seat and unfolded the instruction sheet. 'Actually, I've never even heard of it. Found it in the library and thought it looked interesting. Let's see if we can figure it out.' I scanned the page quickly and began divvying up the cards. 'Okay, so, players begin with a small deck of low-value cards, each of which has either a spending power denoted by a gold coin or a damage value denoted by a red rifle sight.'

I dealt and then placed the rest of the cards to one side. 'This is the trade deck. So now we each shuffle our cards.'

Katya opened by buying a battle station. 'Were you working in the crèche today?'

I bought a blob fighter and a cutter, with which I did some damage to Katya. 'No, the garden – over in Thunder-dome. With Jupiter and Sergeant Cobb.' I repopulated the trade row and drew five cards, ending my turn.

'Ah.' We'd discussed my difficulties with the sergeant previously – Katya had a way of getting me to open up. 'And how'd it go?'

'It's funny – I find it increasingly difficult to bite my tongue around her. Today, she had to remind me that she was still my boss.'

Katya destroyed my target base. 'And is she?'

'What?' I was engrossed in planning my next move – buying a hive.

'Is she your boss in the garden? Does she know more about agriculture than you?'

That made me laugh. 'Cobb?'

Katya nodded earnestly. 'Does she?'

Instead of answering, I said, 'You Islanders have a very different approach.'

Katya put a battle station down as a base. 'You prefer working with babies, eh? If I've understood the game correctly, this will shield me from any attack worth less than five, yeah?'

'Yes to both.' I felt my shoulders slump. 'Another mear and I'm going to have to start thinking about a new job. With the baby ban, it's been thirteen months since the last baby was born. Little JJ's one of my favourites.'

'Who do you think you're kidding?'

I inhaled sharply – I couldn't tell anyone the truth but especially not Katya.

'They're all your favourites.'

*Oh.* A small smile crept across my face. 'Yeah, it's just the adults I have trouble with – or at least, one adult at any rate.'

Katya discarded her cards and drew five more. 'Jayne's not so bad.'

I arched an eyebrow. 'Jayne… You know that's not actually Sergeant Cobb's name, right?'

She looked up at me, puzzled. 'It's not? What is her name, then?'

I set the blob wheel base I'd been holding down on the table. 'You know … I have no idea. She refuses to tell anyone. Lo— Um, Lieutenant Pearce knows it.'

'Huh.' She rested her wrists on the table. 'If I understand the rules, scrapping cards removes the dross from my deck, giving me a better chance of drawing higher value cards. Is that right?'

'Yup.' I felt myself getting lost in the game, same as I did back on Earth.

Before long, Katya laid a card on the table, destroying my base. 'Twenty-three damage. Is that it? Have I won?'

I looked at my remaining cards and the board. 'Yep, looks that way. Well done – good game.'

She smiled.

I checked my phone. 'Our hour's pretty much up anyway. What do you think, Katya? Should we play again next week? A different board game, if you'd prefer. Or I can find something else – we could go back to knitting.'

For a split second, her features fell – but she was quick to cover it up with her friendly visage. I was the only person who visited her of my own volition. Her only other encounters were in the context of work or therapy or a meagre handful of seconds with people dropping off or collecting things. 'This is fine.'

I put my hand on hers. 'I'll be back again next Saturday.'

'Can't you stay a bit longer?'

She seemed so small and vulnerable as she spoke – it was hard to reconcile this woman I had grown to know with the murderer I reminded myself she was. But for all that, she was still one of God's children.

I touched her shoulder. 'I'm sorry, Katya. I'm meeting Devon at the pub.'

Was that a flash of annoyance in her eyes? From previous discussions, I'd gathered that she wasn't Devon's biggest fan. I wondered if I'd imagined it. She swallowed and looked down.

She lifted her hand to touch mine on her shoulder. 'Thank you for coming. I'm grateful for your company.'

I opened my mouth to reply just as the buzzer sounded. Leah was back to unlock the door.

'Try that lip gloss, eh? I think it'll be really pretty on you.' Her eyes glistened as she spoke. *How would it feel to be locked in your home for months and mears on end?*

Without thinking about it, I hugged her. I was a big hugger – never with Katya, though. But in that moment, she seemed to need it.

I stood back and squeezed her hand as the key turned in the lock. 'I'll see you next week.'

MEAR 4, DAY 4

SOUVESTRE DOME, DEVON ISLAND COLONY, MARS

'Good morning, class,' said Tom. He'd invited me to speak to the school. We stood side by side at the front of the classroom.

The children responded with an assortment of words all jumbled together, calling out greetings and variations on Tom's name. A few kids called him auntie; others just called him Tom. I assume it was Rafa who called him mum, but who could say with these kids? There didn't seem to be any rules.

Tom continued, 'Devon is here to talk to us about history. Say hello, class.' The kids were all sitting on the floor. Towering above them made me uncomfortable, so I settled myself with them. Seven, delighted I was now at her level, put her huge russet front paws into my lap and gave me a big kiss. *Ugh*, I wiped her slobber away. When I snapped my fingers, she lay down.

Tiny hands shot up all over the room. Kids called out greetings and questions and non sequiturs all at once, overwhelming me. Daniel crawled forwards and lay with his body curled around Seven.

A couple of kids went for the standard opening gambit. 'Hi, Devon.'

Not all. 'When did history start?'

'What if there was a bee but it was as big as me?'

'Why don't you got a baby?'

'What colour is the sun?'

'Was a crocodile actually a real thing?'

Trying to process everything that had just been said, I tapped my lip six times.

'Hold on, everybody,' Tom cut in. 'One at a time, please, and try to stick to questions about history.'

'It's okay,' I said. 'I'm happy to answer everybody's questions on pretty much any topic. Only I need you to ask them one at a time, okay?' Heads nodded. Good.

Tom leaned over and whispered, 'You may regret that.'

'Amos, I think I heard you ask when history began. Let's start with that. History basically means everything that happened before right now – so in a way it never began and it never ended. But usually when we talk about history, we mean the bits of it that have been documented. For instance, the earliest known use of written language was in Iraq.'

'What's an Iraq?' I wasn't sure who'd spoken.

'Iraq is a country on Earth,' I explained, trying not to let the overlapping questions get to me. 'A country is like a colony – if a colony was surrounded on all sides by other slightly different colonies. Actually, Gabe, some of your ancestors came from Iraq. Adina, I think you asked a question at the start. What did you want to know?'

Adina tilted her head down and mumbled. I was about to ask her to repeat it when Tom spoke. 'Kids, I really think we ought to stick to questions about history, please.' A melodramatic groan went up from the class.

'No, it's fine. What's your question, Adina?'

Adina had Brian's brown eyes behind thick glasses like Georgie's. She grinned coyly and turned to her brother, Little Gabe, whispering in his ear. Gabe giggled then said confidently, 'Adina wants to know why you don't got any babies.'

Tom cringed.

'That's an interesting question,' I replied. 'Well, when we came to Mars, we worked hard to maximise the genetic diversity of the next generation.' Blank faces stared up at me. The age range in the class was two to three mears old. 'Hmm… You're probably not interested in the reproductive laws governing the size of the colony, but the original plans called for every colonist to have at least one child – which would have taken us from one hundred and sixty to more than three hundred and twenty in the first generation. We had expected the colony to grow – slowly and steadily – from there.'

Tom cleared his throat. People usually did that when they wanted me to get to the point.

'Anyway, Daniel is biologically my son, but I was never pregnant because I don't like the idea of a living creature growing inside me. Babies are parasites. Gross, no thank you.'

Yana bellowed, 'YOU'RE MY MUM TOO!'

It was impossible to carry on, as Seven leapt up and barked at Yana to be quiet. I snapped my fingers for the dog to lie down. 'Yes, and Yana is my daughter too.' I looked at her and continued. 'Because you're part of my family, but you're not related to me biologically.'

Yana huffed and sat back down, arms crossed. Tom took the opportunity to try to get his class back on topic. 'Right, that's enough fun time. Devon is here to talk to us about Earth history.' This unleashed a whole new barrage. All the voices blended together in a cacophony of meaningless noise.

Tom gestured at the kids to be quiet. 'If you have questions about Earth, please raise your hand. Devon will call on you one at a time.'

I selected Rafa first. 'Did you have dinosaurs on Earth?'

'There were dinosaurs a long time ago. During the —'

'Jevver ride one?' Rafa shouted out.

But Yana interrupted, clamouring, 'How did they fit inside the domes?'

I tapped my lip. Just three times – I had this. 'The dinosaurs died out a long time before any of us were even born.'

'What about horses? Were they on Earth? Did you ever meet one?' I couldn't tell who was speaking. Was it one child or several?

'Yes, I have met horses. I mostly lived in big cities, though, and horses lived in rural areas.' This, to them, was every bit as fantastical as if I had met a dinosaur or a unicorn or a dragon.

'Where did they live?'

I said that during the day they walked around in fields called paddocks, but at night they slept in their own buildings.

'Horses built flats?' All around me little faces were aghast at this not-quite revelation.

'No,' I said. 'People built homes for horses to sleep in.'

This was met with sheer disbelief. Eyes widened and jaws fell slack. 'There were buildings just for horses?'

Ysabel was horrified. 'Why didn't horses just sleep in the flats with the people?'

I shook my head. 'Not practical. Horses are too big to fit

into a human-sized home.' I suspected they thought horses were similar in size to Seven. 'Besides, they poo everywhere and they stink.' This was met with raucous laughter.

Someone demanded I explain how horses smelled.

'Er, sorry. I don't know the chemical composition of the odours.' They found this hilarious for some reason.

Daniel sat up from where he was curled around Seven. 'You said the horse walked around in a field, but that's nonsense. She would trample all the crops and then the farmer would shout at her. It's not prackal.'

Fighting the urge to flap my hands, I told myself I would get through this. 'Ah, you see, on Earth, not all the ground had to be covered in plants. We didn't worry about making sure every square centimetre was used to maximum efficiency.' His brow furrowed in displeasure.

Another little voice piped up. 'How could you be sure there'd be enough oxygen in the domes for people to breathe?'

'There were no domes on Earth.'

This was met with wild disbelief. 'That's stupid. The air would escape.'

I tried my best to explain the concept of a planetary atmosphere, but they didn't buy it. After a while of this debate, Little Gabe raised his hand. Pleased by this unexpected turn to a more orderly state, I indicated he could speak.

His lips quivered slightly. 'What happens when we die?'

Tom stood up like he was going to say something, but I could handle this. 'Oh, that's a fantastic question. First, the body is stripped of its clothes. A surgeon removes any viable organs, blood, eggs, sperm, and inorganic implants. Then it's frozen using liquid nitrogen.'

The kids were silent for the first time since I'd arrived,

which pleased me. 'Then a machine shakes the frozen body so hard, it crumbles to dust. The remains move to another machine where all the water is sucked out. And then another machine takes out all the metals, including sodium. Whatever's left over is packed up in a box made from potato starch. We bury the box in the cemetery garden and within half a mear, it's completely absorbed into the soil. Often we plant a tree above the box, which serves as a reminder of that person.'

The silence held for a few peaceful, wonderful seconds. Before the kids launched a volley of queries about the process.

After an hour of being deluged with questions about everything and anything, I took my leave.

'Bye bye, stinky bum poo bottom,' called Anuj.

Tom escorted me out. 'Well, Devon. That may not have gone how I expected, but it was certainly entertaining to witness. Thanks for coming by.' He was chuckling to himself.

I had no idea what he meant by that.

*LOVELACE DOME, DEVON ISLAND COLONY, MARS*

I lay on my back on the mossy ground and stared up at the panels of the dome. Even now, part of my brain screamed at me to get out, to seek shelter, to retreat to one of the other domes – as if they were somehow safer just because it was Lovelace that had failed us before.

Failed Iulia. And Henri and Renaud.

Failed me.

But I lived – I was still here to tell my tale.

I shook my head to clear it before standing up. Lunch break was over. Brushing the detritus from my trousers, I headed back inside.

Mehmet was lying on the floor. His daughter and my son had him pinned down, sitting atop him. As soon as he spotted me, JJ leapt off Mehmet and ran squealing towards me, his bare feet slapping the floor as he ran.

The colony's two youngest children were already over a mear old – the terrible moos, I'd heard someone say. We had reluctantly agreed a one-in-one-out policy. No more babies allowed until someone kicked the proverbial bucket. *What a depressing thought.*

'You got them to stop crying.'

Mehmet flipped himself onto his front, dropping Darna onto her butt. He walked his feet forwards until he was in a downward dog pose. As he gradually pulled himself up, she tried to mirror his movements. To my shock, JJ ran back and did the same.

'Yoga? You got screaming toddlers to calm down by teaching them yoga?'

He pressed his palms together and bowed from the waist. 'Actually, I started doing some stretches because they were doing my head in.' He rolled his neck. 'But they copied me, so I went with it.'

I shook my head. 'Hey, man, whatever works for you.'

He bent down and picked both kids up, one in each arm. 'That's my motto.'

'Anyway, cheers for that. I needed a minute to get my head together. Got a meeting with Davy this afternoon.'

Mehmet nodded. 'Elevated solar panels?'

I blew out a breath. 'Yeah, but no.'

'Ah.'

'Ah, indeed,' I replied. Our most recent idea was to install solar panels atop towers – high enough to evade the dust that blew around the planet in its pathetic excuse for an atmosphere. Unfortunately, it wasn't feasible. The supports would need to be too deep, the structures too high.

And if we couldn't solve the problem, then our kids would find themselves plotting out further reductions in colony size.

'Well, on that happy note,' he said. 'I've got to drop Darna at the crèche. Want me to take JJ?'

'Oh, would you? Thanks, bud.' I bent and kissed my

son's brown locks. 'Hey, pickle. Mummy will see you in a few hours, yeah?' I braced myself for a screaming tantrum, but instead he nodded and ran after Darna. Turning back to Mehmet, I said, 'Thanks. I'll see you in an hour, yeah?'

He nodded then turned towards the two kids. He extended his arms and flapped them like bird wings as he chased after them.

———

*THE CRAFT DOME, DEVON ISLAND COLONY, MARS*

A few minutes later I walked into the civic office. Jupiter wasn't at her desk, so I went straight into the meeting room. The fact it was a clear summer day afară meant we could turn on the window walls. It was an extravagant use of precious electricity, but one we could easily afford when there was plenty of sunlight. If all our days were like this, we could turn on every window in the colony, bake cakes in every oven, and still let our population grow. The window wall was showing a moving image of Niagara Falls. Davy stared at her tablet, deep in thought.

I motioned at the display. 'You hate Niagara. What's your phrase? It's crass, commercial, and overcrowded.'

She leaned back in her chair. 'Why anyone would coat a natural wonder in a thick layer of garish plastic is beyond me.' I couldn't help but think about the fact it was home to two power stations that had a combined output of almost five thousand megawatts.

I filled her in on the findings of the study into erecting an elevated solar farm. With each sentence her shoulders fell. By the end, she was slumped over the table.

I waited for her to regain her composure. After a few

moments, she inhaled deeply. She sat up, squared her shoulders, and said, 'Back to the drawing board.'

Unsure what to say next, I nodded. This was my job, my problem to solve – before it became our children's problem.

The front door opened and shut. It was too early for the other cabinet ministers to be arriving. 'Must be Jup—' Davy's words were cut off when the meeting room door was flung open.

Lone Starr closed the door and leaned against it, his arms crossed. Sweat matted his fair hair and his Adam's apple bobbed up and down.

'Ma'am.' He turned to me and added a second *ma'am*.

When it became clear he wasn't ready to say anything else without prompting, Davy broke the silence. 'How can I help you, Lone Starr?'

He ran a hand through his short hair. 'I need to get this all out. It's probably not going to make a lot of sense but bear with me. Please.'

I'd never considered how young he was.

'Would you like me to make—'

Lone Starr cut Davy off for the second time in as many minutes. 'No, sorry, just let me—' He shook his head. 'We were chosen for this mission because we were young, healthy, strong – but mainly because no one would miss us. Have I ever told you that part? Not one of us has family, friends, wives... No one would notice our absence. That was another thing that surprised us about you – that so many of you still have people back home. I mean, literally everything about you guys surprised us, but that one... That one... It seems so little, right? You exchange emails with people on Earth.'

He wrung his hands. 'About a mear ago, Gurdeep put me

in touch with Asha Mifsud – former gunnery sergeant in the US marine corp.'

*Why did that name ring a bell? Oh!* My hand shot up to my mouth. Gabriel's mother. Georgie had mentioned they'd been exchanging messages. She'd been so pleased to see her grandson.

Lone Starr took a deep breath. 'As you know, I've been in regular contact with my commanding officers back in Washington. Until today, my crew have taken their orders from them.'

*Until today?*

'I had a message from base this morning.' His breath caught – I wasn't sure he was going to be able to carry on. 'I've been ordered to re-arm my troops and to storm your cabinet meeting today. I am to take command of the entire colony, giving you the option of serving under me or facing execution.'

While I had no idea what he was about to do, his facial expression and body language told me it didn't involve attacking either Davy or me.

*Was he here to arrest us, though? Maybe.*

'I've been advised that there will be a wave of "prioritised migration" to Mars in coming years and that it is my duty to prepare this operation to receive thousands of American citizens.'

A frigid chill ran down my spine as I considered who the current American government would give preference to. Besides, this colony couldn't support more than the 250 we already had. And Lone Starr didn't need me to tell him that. *Unless…*

'Thing is, ma'am, it's all a lie.'

He seemed to have got stuck there, so Davy prodded

him. 'What's a lie, Lieutenant?' She never called him by his rank; none of the Islanders did.

'All of it. My colony, my country, my orders.' He swallowed. 'My government.'

This was his first command – and he wasn't supposed to be in charge. His commanding officer had been killed in the same meteorite strike that had injured me.

Davy gestured across the table. 'Why don't you take a seat?' She looked at me then motioned towards the drinks table with her chin. I poured a cup of tea for Lone Starr and returned to my chair.

'Now, explain what you mean.'

Lone Starr picked up the tea then set it back down. He took a deep breath and held it for longer than I would have thought possible. 'The MENaCE. It's an acronym. The Mars Early Nuclear and Construction Expedition. We were the advance guard of what was meant to be a much larger mission.' He turned to me. 'Much like your own advance team, ma'am.'

His breathing was beginning to slow. 'Except our mission wasn't about agriculture or sustainability – it was about building a nuclear reactor.'

Davy and I silently mouthed the last three words to one another.

'We were to build the initial base and get everything up and running. Our mission was then to be followed by a much larger one. The next one was to bring families – farmers, livestock, crops, houses, all that jazz. Our job was to build. We were given materials to do our tasks and five years' worth of rations.'

He finally took a sip of the tea. 'But then three months before the Hohmann transfer window, they told us they weren't going to be ready in time. A slight delay, they said.

And meanwhile, we finished building the reactor. It was ready to churn out more electricity than we knew what to do with. The powers that be told us to sit tight and wait for the next window.'

Lone Starr picked up his mug and drained the contents in one go. I retrieved the insulated pot from the cabinet and set it in front of him in case he needed any more.

'Of course, as you know, we received information that they wouldn't be launching in the next window either. That's when we were first apprised of your colony and ordered to head out and join forces with you. We had no idea what to expect of you – they told us you were a military base from a European country.'

He ran a hand through his hair. 'With no personal contacts, we had no one to tell us what life was really like back home. Radio signals only travel by line of sight and so our connection to Earth was via videos sent to us by our higher ups. The trip here was nightmarish. The major, he was the one who knew what he was doing. He was supposed to lead the whole mission, but then it was just me.

'Anyway, after Gurdeep gave me Dr Mifsud's email, I started talking to her and, um… That woman set me straight. The America we've been serving – it doesn't exist anymore. There is no resupply mission coming. They haven't got the resources. So, ordering us to conquer Devon Island is just part of their fantasy. They want to cling to the idea that some part of the Grand Old US of A is still going strong.'

Lone Starr laid his hands down in front of himself. 'I have never disobeyed a direct order in my life. But today I was ordered to betray the colony which has become my home.'

I held my breath. Out the corner of my eye, I spied Davy

doing likewise. At length she said, 'Well, Lieutenant. What are you going to do?'

The silence hung in the air like a hummingbird hovering, wings flapping faster than the eye could see. 'I severed ties with Earth. Which is to say, I've done precisely nothing – except decide that I won't do as ordered. I don't believe they have the capacity or the resources to do anything about it. Oh, they'll bluster and bloviate and threaten me with a court martial, but they can't reach us. And from what Dr Mifsud tells me – the evidence she's shown me – they couldn't do anything to stop a militia in Wisconsin, never mind a rogue squad on Mars.'

The muscle in Davy's jaw that had been standing out since he'd first arrived receded a bit. 'So, what now?'

He ran a hand through his hair again. 'Now I tell my squad what happened. I expect they'll all agree with my decision. If any don't, we'll deal with that then. And I propose the next move would be to connect this place up to the reactor that's been sitting there just waiting.'

A muscle in my left eye began to twitch. Or had it been twitching for a while and I was only now noticing? 'How much electricity are we talking?'

Lone Starr's eyes darted towards me and then returned to Davy. 'It's running on minimum output now – but it's designed to crank out enough to power a colony more than double this size for multiple generations yet to come.' He raised a hand in metaphoric self-defence. 'I've been under strict orders not to let you know about it. I'm telling you now because – well, because I'm playing Benedict Arnold here. I'm switching sides. Now, I'm hoping you'll grant me and my company full citizenship in exchange for—'

I wondered briefly if he knew Canadians heralded Benedict Arnold a hero.

Davy was on her feet. She hugged Lone Starr where he sat. 'Of course we will. At least, that's what I'll recommend to the cabinet. I doubt anyone will disagree. Don't you see what this means? We can lift the baby ban! Lone Starr, you've saved our colony!'

MEAR 5, DAY 1

THE CRAFT DOME, DEVON ISLAND COLONY, MARS

'Good morning, Prime Minister.'

'That's the last time you'll ever get to call me that, Jupiter,' I replied.

'Yes, Prime Minister.'

I glared at her for a second before cracking a smile.

Today was election day – and the fifth anniversary of our life on Mars. At midnight tonight someone other than me would be announced as our second prime minister. It had been my job for four mears – two consecutive terms.

They'd been good mears – or at least, I mostly remembered the good in them. But I was ready to move on. From tomorrow, I'd do my hours as a farmer and a teacher, but I would let go of government responsibilities. The school was ramping up to add a second class – the kids who'd been too young to be part of the first cohort. And Gurdeep had asked me if I'd like to buy her out of the shop and cafe so she could open a bakery.

I sat down at my desk and ran a hand along its worn

surface. But then instead of packing up my office, I got lost in thought.

Twelve months had passed since Lone Starr offered up the nuclear reactor in exchange for full citizenship for himself and his team. They'd all chosen to opt in, thankfully. Lone Starr had become a full-fledged member of our government. Cobb managed the relocation of the reactor to a new site and Lisa had taken charge of hooking us up to it.

The reactor's new home was closer to us than the original, but it had to be near an ice sheet to serve as a water source. We'd built a series of small recharge stations at fifty kilometre intervals between here and there.

Most importantly, the reactor had allowed us to lift the baby ban. We'd started slow – only ten pregnancies so far. But the reactor was on track to be connected a few weeks from now. Once it was up and running, it would be a baby free-for-all in Devon Island. Well, not quite. A new population cap had been set at 500. Future governments could decide when that figure needed adjusting.

'Knock, knock.'

Startled, I looked up to see Lisa standing at my door – I hadn't heard it open.

'Hey, Lis. Come on in.' I waved a hand at the seat next to me.

She dropped into it like a dead weight.

'Late night?'

Letting her head fall onto her hands, she replied, 'Ugh. He's been getting so good at sleeping through – but last night he was up every hour. "Mummy, I'm thirsty. Mummy, I peed the bed. Mummy, I'm bored. Hungry. Wanna play a game. Read story."' She shook her head. Her smile was contented but exhausted.

I squeezed her shoulder. 'I don't understand why you

insist on doing this on your own. Surely if you shared parenting resp—'

'Stop. Staaaaahp. As exhausting as solo parenting is, sharing my space with someone? Nuh-uh. No way. Not happening.'

'Still a commitment phobe?'

She shrugged. 'Hey, you know me.'

'I do indeed,' I said. 'And look at us now – we've come full circle.'

She chuckled. 'Oh man, your horrible little campaign office in Toronto?'

'Wedged in between that restaurant and the, um, what was it?'

'A real estate agent,' we said in unison. Lisa had wandered into that cramped, smelly office and asked to be put to work, supporting my election campaign.

'Can you imagine if anyone had said to you then that you were going to turn your back on politics and move to Mars?'

A thought occurred to me and I burst out laughing. 'Do you know the first thing I ever said to Gurdeep?'

Lisa cocked her head to the side.

'I put on my toughest face and said – are you ready for it? – I said, "There is nothing on Earth that could persuade me to leave my position as an MP."' I sank back into my chair, laughing at the memory. 'The debate last night went well.'

'I thought so,' Lisa said. 'But then I'm hardly unbiased.'

Resting my elbows on the table, I said, 'I might even vote for you.'

She shrugged. 'Hey, if I can't convince my campaign manager to vote for me, I probably don't deserve to win.'

I heard the outer door open and then Jupiter's voice. 'Well, hello there. Not that it's not lovely to see you, Daniel, but shouldn't you be at school?'

'Ahem,' I said in my stern-parent voice as I walked out to the building's small front office. My son looked up at me, his face a picture of innocence.

'I wanted to see how the election was going,' he replied matter-of-factly, putting one hand on his hip. 'Hi, Lisa,' he added.

'Mmm hmm. Well, for one thing, there's no election going on here. Everyone votes on their phones.' I had placed my vote for Lisa this morning at breakfast, explaining to the kids what I was doing and why it was important. 'And for another thing, you're supp—'

Devon stepped into the room with Seven hot on her heels. 'Hey you, I thought I might find you here.' Devon greeted me with a quick squeeze of the hand and a peck on the cheek. 'Tom messaged me.' She nodded greetings to both Lisa and Jupiter.

She turned back to Daniel. 'I think Tom might be getting a bit jaded, young sir.' Careful to ensure Daniel didn't see, she looked at me and stifled a laugh. 'Apparently, "Daniel has a habit of thinking rules don't apply to him,"' she said. Her impression of Tom was on the nose – mannerisms, inflections. She even plucked at her sleeve as she spoke. 'I got a whole lecture on how swiftly and efficiently Mars can kill people. "The rules need to be taken seriously. It's how we keep ourselves alive." As if I didn't know that. But you, Daniel. We've spoken about this. You know better.'

Daniel looked at his feet. 'Yes, Devon.' He refused to call us anything but our names. Having more than one name was dishonest, according to Daniel – a great sin in his mind. Lisa excused herself and left.

Devon cocked an eyebrow at our wilful son. 'And what do you have to say for yourself?'

'I'm sorry.' He wouldn't look at any of us.

Devon crossed her arms over her chest. 'And?'

Daniel blew air out his nose. 'I won't do it again.'

'Thank you,' Devon said. Looking at me, she added, 'Told Tom I'd bring him back.'

I smiled at my wife. 'I could have done it, you know.'

'I know,' she replied. 'But I figured you had enough on your plate this morning. I don't mind. Besides, I've got a maintenance program running on my printer. Not much to do for the next half-hour anyway.'

'Thank you,' I said. She always tried to anticipate my needs. Who could ask for more in a relationship?

Tugging on my sleeve, Daniel demanded, 'Aren't you going to tell me how the election is going? Who's winning? Is it Auntie Lisa or Desmond? Who will be the next honcho?'

I bit my lip to keep from laughing. 'Honcho?' *Where on Mars had he learned that word?*

'It means person who is in charge – doesn't it? The prime minister is the honcho for the whole of Devon Island colony,' he replied in all seriousness.

Devon and I exchanged a discreet glance. 'Honcho is a loan word from Japanese meaning squad leader,' I explained. 'It's usually "head honcho", but yes, technically it's appropriate.' It was important to take his queries literally – he didn't like indirect answers and he did *not* tolerate being brushed off.

'Come on, you,' Devon said. 'Let's get you back to school.'

Devon made to take his hand but, at that moment, Jupiter's baby reached out towards him. Daniel looked at Jupiter. 'May I please hold Orien?'

Jupiter and I shared an unspoken exchange. 'Oh, go on,' I said once she'd nodded.

Jupiter stood up and began untying the wrap holding the six-week-old infant to herself. 'You be careful,' she said, patting the sofa to encourage him to sit. Once he was settled, she set the baby in his lap.

I knew he'd be careful – Daniel had a gentle manner. And in spite of his disregard of rules, he was a cautious child.

She winked at him. 'I wouldn't let just anyone hold Orien, but since you're such a responsible young person who's just about to return to class…'

'I'll walk with them,' I told Jupiter. 'I should be back in about twenty minutes. Do you want me to pick you up a drink or anything?'

'You stopping for coffee?' she asked.

'Honestly, I think if I have any more caffeine, I'll burst a blood vessel,' I said.

Daniel looked up at us. 'I don't believe that's possible.'

'No, probably not,' I said. Jupiter picked her baby back up, so the rest of us could leave. Devon and I each held one of Daniel's hands and Seven trotted along at Devon's other side.

There were competing campaign screens right outside the door. On the left, Lisa's face – with her eyes so serious. It faded to her campaign slogan: 'Vote Lisa for Experienced Leadership.' On the right was Lisa's competition. Above his handsome black face in big letters it read 'Vote Desmond'. At the bottom, 'A Fresh Voice for Devon Island.'

His big campaign promise was two weeks' annual leave for everyone of working age. It definitely had its appeal, I had to give it that. It had been way too many mears since any of us had a proper holiday. But then, where would you go? What would you do with yourself?

Would people be lured by the promise of a vacation? I

didn't think so, but I wouldn't be putting any money on it. I hoped people would opt for Lisa's leadership, but I'd have to wait and see just like everybody else.

Either way, the future looked bright.

*Afară*: Outside-outside, beyond the dome. Differentiated from *outside*, which refers to the space under a dome, but not in a building. Loan word from Romanian.

*Anyways*: Canadian colloquial variant on anyway.

*Day*: A Martian day. Equivalent to one Earth day plus approximately thirty-seven minutes.

*DownBelow*: Utility area beneath the colony. Full of pipes, cables, large equipment, and disused vehicles.

*Food-ag*: Food and agriculture. The team responsible for the colony's plants and wildlife.

*Garburator*: Canadian colloquialism. A garbage disposal unit installed under a kitchen sink that shreds food waste into small pieces.

*Hour*: One twenty-fourth of a Martian day. Equivalent to one Earth hour plus approximately ninety-nine seconds.

*Inside*: The space within a building. Differentiated from *afară* (outside-outside, beyond the dome) and outside (space under a dome but not in a building).

*Mear*: Martian year. Approximately 669 Martian days. Equivalent to 1.88 Earth years. So far as I know, the term was coined by science fiction author Robert J. Sawyer in his novel, *Red Planet Blues*[1].

*Minute*: One sixtieth of a Martian hour. Equivalent to one Earth minute plus approximately 1.6 seconds.

*Outside*: The space under a dome but not in a building. Differentiated from *afară*, which refers to outside-outside, beyond the dome.

*Scud*: Dr Ida Scudder Memorial Hospital.

*She/her/hers*: Particularly amongst the children, these are treated as gender-neutral pronouns.

*Yous*: Colloquial plural of 'you' employed in certain parts of Canada, the UK, and Ireland.

---

1.  https://www.goodreads.com/book/show/32737298-red-planet-blues

## WHAT'S REAL?

Some of my beta readers have questioned which bits of the book are based in reality and which ones are purely from my own imagination.

## DEVON (ISLAND) IS A PLACE ON EARTH

Devon Island is situated in Canada's far north and it is the largest uninhabited island on Earth. It is notable for two reasons: the Haughton impact crater and the Flashline Mars Arctic Research Station project. The Haughton impact crater is considered one of Earth's best Mars analogue sites. It has been home to a series of Mars simulations.

- https://en.wikipedia.org/wiki/Devon_Island
- https://www.marsinstitute.no/hmp
- http://fmars.marssociety.org/about-the-fmars/

*SHIP NAMES*

All seven of the colony's ships are named for female astro-nauts, space scientists, and engineers.

- Mary Jackson: https://en.wikipedia.org/wiki/Mary_Jackson_(engineer)
- Katherine Goble-Johnson: I took a bit of liberty with this name. This was partially to differentiate the ship from the *Jackson*, but also because in the film *Hidden Figures* she was known by her previous name, Katherine Goble. Ms Johnson died in 2020 at the age of 101. https://en.wikipedia.org/wiki/Katherine_Johnson
- Dorothy Vaughan: https://en.wikipedia.org/wiki/Dorothy_Vaughan
- Maggie Aderin-Pocock: https://en.wikipedia.org/wiki/Maggie_Aderin-Pocock
- Kalpana Chawla: https://en.wikipedia.org/wiki/Kalpana_Chawla
- Samantha Cristoforetti: https://en.wikipedia.org/wiki/Samantha_Cristoforetti
- Roberta Bondar: https://en.wikipedia.org/wiki/Roberta_Bondar

*GETTING BIBLICAL*

Jamie – who you may have gathered is somewhat gender non-conforming – recites Bible verses to themself. I've taken a small liberty with these, in that the various verses are drawn from different translations.

- Romans 15

- Psalm 23
- 1 John 1:9
- Matthew 5:4
- Psalm 9
- Romans 12:2
- Isaiah 25:6
- Matthew 25:35–36

## POOPING ON MARS

Believe it or not, I agonised for ages trying to figure out how to deal with human waste on Mars. That is, I did so until I discovered someone got there before me. Because, of course they did.

A company called Sun-Mar in Canada has developed composting toilets for the Hawaii Space Exploration Analog and Simulation ('HI-SEAS'), a NASA-funded Mars mission simulation.

- https://sun-mar.com
- https://en.wikipedia.org/wiki/Composting_toilet

## HOHMANN TRANSFER WINDOWS

Space missions using a Hohmann transfer must wait for the required planetary alignment to occur, which opens a so-called launch window. For a voyage from Earth to Mars these launch windows occur every twenty-six months. A Hohmann transfer orbit also determines a fixed time required to travel between the starting and destination points; for an Earth-Mars journey this travel time is 259 days.

- https://en.wikipedia.org/
  wiki/Hohmann_transfer_orbit

## *BALLISTIC CAPTURE*

Unlike Hohmann transfer window missions, ballistic capture flights can be undertaken at any time. Additionally, they don't necessitate the dangerous and expensive braking manoeuvres that Hohmann transfer journeys do. As stated in the story, the disadvantage is the longer duration.

- https://www.scientificamerican.com/article/a-new-way-to-reach-mars-safely-anytime-and-on-the-cheap/
- https://en.wikipedia.org/wiki/Ballistic_capture

## *ECTOGENESIS*

Ectogenesis is gestation outside of a biological womb. It sounds like science fiction and really it still is. But in 2017 a team of scientists made history by developing an artificial womb – for lamb foetuses in later stages of gestation. And as far back as 2002/3, a fertility and reproductive health researcher named Dr Helen Liu (for whom Helen Souza in the book is named) grew mouse embryos almost to full term in a womb she grew in her lab.

- http://www.slate.com/articles/health_and_science/
  human_nature/features/2005/
  the_organ_factory/the_mouse_and_the_rat.html
- https://www.scientificamerican.com/article/could-artificial-wombs-be-a-reality/
- https://en.wikipedia.org/wiki/Ectogenesis

*WATER*

Human life requires a lot of water. A lot of it. But the good news is, it's reusable. Water can be re-treated and reused, over and over again. But where to get the water in the first place?

I've assumed they brought a fair amount with them. But also, much of their needs will be supplied by Mars. There is water on Mars – it's just too salty to use. So I've assumed they bring in Martian water from the surface and use a technique called freeze water desalination to purify it.

- http://cryodesalination.com/
- https://www.bbc.co.uk/news/science-environment-44952710

*VAT-GROWN DAIRY PRODUCTS*

Many people may have heard of vat-grown meat products but not many are familiar with the idea of vat-grown dairy products. But they're real.

- http://www.perfectdayfoods.com/faq/
- https://www.wired.com/2015/04/diy-biotech-vegan-cheese/

*COMBATTING LOW-GRAVITY BONE LOSS*

One problem real astronauts face that our colonists would need to deal with is bone loss due to being in low- or no-gravity settings. I have assumed muscle wastage can be dealt with by simply exercising with heavier weights than one would on Earth; however, this wouldn't do anything for the loss of bone density the colonists would be faced with. That's where TGS-6 comes in.

- https://www.ncbi.nlm.nih.gov/pmc/articles/PMC2533787/

## 3D PRINTED DISHES

These are literally and actually made of Mars. For real.

- https://www.cnet.com/news/3d-printing-for-the-moon-and-mars/

## WHAT HAPPENS WHEN WE DIE?

Devon's response to Little Gabe's question is based on a process called promession. It was developed by a Swedish company, Promessa. They even adapted it for NASA to allow them to bring remains of astronauts killed off-world back to Earth. Of course, that's not practical for the colonists of Devon Island, so they're using the process as originally developed.

- http://www.promessa.se/
- https://www.vice.com/en_uk/article/4wmg7p/what-would-a-space-funeral-look-like

ACKNOWLEDGEMENTS

Where do I even start?

Decades ago, I read a story – not because I wanted to, you understand, but because I had to for school. I can't recall the writer's name. The story may (or may not) be called 'The Five and Twenty'. Whatever it was called and whoever wrote it, it planted a seed.

That seed grew into the first draft of *Devon's Island* – which at the time included this novel as well. My alpha readers, my first beta readers, and my first editor all told me the same thing: *Holy crap! What is this mess? It's way too complicated. What's even happening?*

Together, they persuaded me that what I had written was two different books. Focusing on the earlier timeline, I set to work building the story back up again. More beta readers, more edits, and a whole lot more work later, *Devon's Island* was published in January 2020.

And I say, if you published a novel in 2020 and it didn't end in a surprise deadly pandemic, were you even trying?

Anyways… Once I handed *Devon's Island* over to my copy-editor, I returned to working on what had originally been the later timeline in the original draft, turning it into the book you hold in your hands now.

Over the past year, a whole army of people have helped shape this story. I learned so much from my beta readers, editors, and diversity readers. And then, in the spring of 2020, as I was reading the brilliant *Embers of War*, I saw Gareth Powell re-tweeting something about an online science fiction convention. I signed up to attend. One thing led to another – I'm still not sure exactly what happened – and somehow I ended up in a writers' group.

The WiFi Sci-Fi writers' group has been the most amazing gift. Anne Corlett made it all happen and taught me about psychic distance. Katrina Middelburg introduced me to THAD[1]. Céline Badaroux and Jeff Parke are enthusiastic cheerleaders on everything I write. The whole group has been such a fantastic accident; I'm so grateful to everyone in it. And I have to single out Dan Smith for his extraordinary generosity in applying his expertise to the MENaCE story line.

I'd also like to thank Genevieve Zander, Shannon Massey, Max Watson, John Farrell, and Eva Monteiro for their brilliant beta reader services.

My first stop in editing this book was Michelle Meade, who looked at the big-picture elements. Her feedback was fantastic – some of it was hard to hear and a lot of my work ended up in the deleted scenes folder. But I know this book is all the better for her interventions.

After that came the sensitivity readers, whose job it is to tell me when I'm being accidentally insensitive to groups I'm representing. And then, at long last, I passed it over for copy-editing. I'm so appreciative of Lucy Rose York's services on this front. She dug into the meat of this vegetarian story to make it the best version of itself it could be. I'm phenomenally grateful to have her on my team.

Hannah McCall of Black Cat Editorial Services provided expert proofreading services. Any mistakes you find now are because I forgot to incorporate her corrections. And Rejenne designed the beautiful cover you see on this book.

For two plus years, my friends and colleagues who asked me to socialise with them received the same reply: I'm sorry I can't come to your party; I need to stay home and play with my imaginary friends. And then Covid hit – suddenly we were all staying home. But at least I had my imaginary friends to keep me company.

I still owe an unspeakable debt to Anna, who was gracious enough to allow me to borrow not only the story of Nora's conception but her name, as well. And for Jupiter's name, too.

Lastly, not only did my legally contracted life mate, Dave, serve as science consultant for this book, he also put up with more than any human being should ever have to. He's listened to me talk about this story every single day for three years. He's awesome.

---

1. talking-head avoidance device: https://dawinsor.com/2020/05/11/how-not-to-write-talking-heads/

Photo © Lex Fleming

SI CLARKE is a misanthrope who lives in Deptford, *sarf ees* London. She shares her home with her partner and an assortment of waifs and strays. When not writing convoluted, inefficient stories, she spends her time telling financial services firms to behave more efficiently. When not doing either of those things, she can be found in the pub or shouting at people online – occasionally practising efficiency by doing both at once.

As someone who's neurodivergent, an immigrant, and the proud owner of an invisible disability, she strives to present a realistically diverse array of characters in her stories.

 twitter.com/clacksee

## ALSO BY SI CLARKE

*Devon's Island*

*Past Imperfect* (short story) – get it now for free at https://storyoriginapp.com/giveaways/ea99ab98-c8eb-11ea-82db-5b412cb075c5

---

## REVIEWS

If you enjoyed this story, please consider leaving a review on:

- Goodreads
- StoryGraph
- your preferred ebook retailer